For the hopeless romantics.

The Friendship Contract
Copyright © 2022 by Mia Heintzelman
All rights reserved. No part of this book may be reproduced or utilized in any form or by any electronic or mechanical means, now known or hereafter invented, including photocopying and recording, xerography, or in any information storage and retrieval systems, without written permission from the author, except for the use of brief quotations in a book review.

First Levi Lynn Books edition February 2022.

Levi Lynn Books can bring authors to your live event. For more information or to book an event, visit our website at https://www.miaheintzelman.com.
Editing by Danielle Acee and Danylle Salinas
Cover design and Formatting by Dot Covers
Manufactured in the United States of America

Cataloguing-in-Publication Data

Name: Heintzelman, Mia, author.
Title: The Friendship Contract / Mia Heintzelman
Description: Mia Heintzelman | Las Vegas: Mia Heintzelman, 2022.
Subjects: Romance | Humorous fiction| African American romance.

This is a work of fiction. Names, characters, places and incidents are either the product of the author's imagination or are used fictitiously, and any resemblance to actual persons, living or dead, business establishments, events or locales is entirely coincidental.

Author's Note

Please note that this book contains sensitive topics such as foster care, homelessness, and abandonment. Includes profanity and sex.

This book can be read as a standalone.

The Friendship Contract

A Novel

MIA HEINTZELMAN

LeviLynn
BOOKS

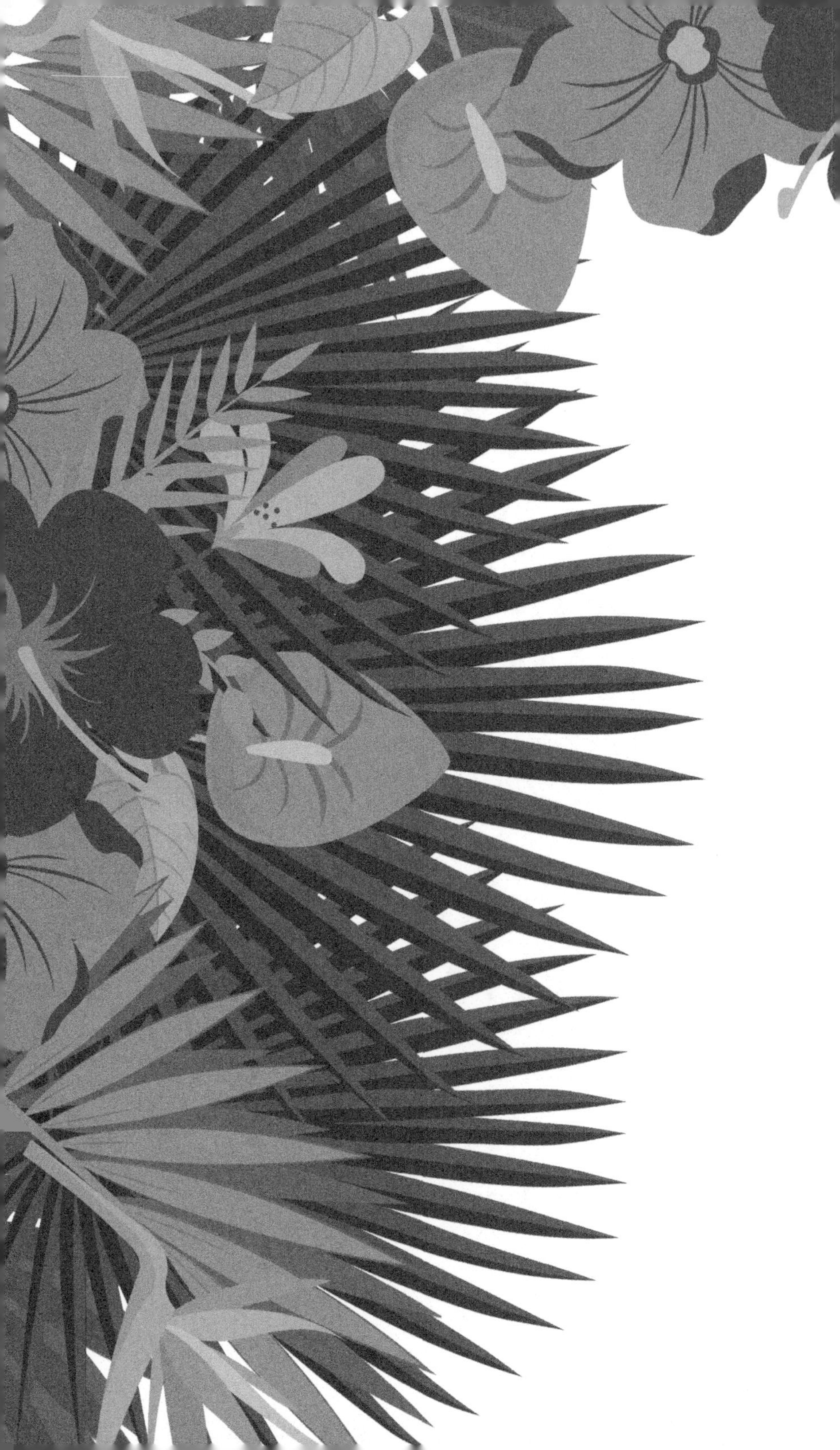

CHAPTER 1
Allegra

A Tuesday date night should not wind me up. It's not like Kyle and I are a brand-new couple still so hot for each other we barely make it through appetizers before we claw off each other's clothes in a questionable-looking bathroom stall. Though, with his new ViddyChat marketing campaign, our schedules have been off. We're lucky if we see each other in passing let alone make time for romance (don't even get me started on sex). But somehow, the fancy French restaurant invitation with its thick, expensive navy cardstock and wispy gold lettering... Tonight feels like an occasion.

You don't ask your live-in girlfriend of almost two years to a place like Mots Doux—on a *weeknight*—for a casual dinner.

My brain autofills: *Kyle Andrews and Allegra Malone cordially invite you to...*

"Stop it, Allegra," I chastise myself as I stare at the sad-looking heels section of my closet shoe rack.

I left the office half an hour early, weaved through traffic, and stabbed the elevator button for Kyle's high-rise condominium like I was being chased, all to raid my closet for the perfect outfit that somehow yells, "Pop the question so we can feast on ridiculously overpriced fine dining and have celebratory sex!"

In spite of what my best friends and law firm partners, Damon and Lea think, and the faulty instincts I inherited from Mom to me it matters what I wear to take my first steps into our betrothed future.

So, it's the red suede heel versus the black patent leather slingbacks.

"Ugh," I groan. They're the sexiest pairs I own, though neither are giving me "marriage material" vibes.

With a sweep of my fingers through my razor-cut hair, I suck up my pride and whip out my laptop to send a ViddyChat invite. After a few minutes, Damon and Lea pop into their tiny squares on the screen. They're still in the office. Their twitching lips and rapid blinking tell me they're ready to be entertained.

With a skyward flick of my eyes, I heave a sigh.

"I'm only calling you to help me figure out what to wear."

"Good because we only answered to talk some sense into you," Lea quips as she bats her fringe of mink eyelashes.

Let's just say, a marriage with Kyle isn't something Lea's dying to see on my menu, even if it is at a fancy French restaurant. She's an endgame person who reads self-help books and listens to "Best Practices of Successful People" podcasts on her daily drive. She's all about tough love. She focuses only on the things we *can* control…even if they're the hardest.

On the "loyalty principle," she loathes Kyle, and thinks I can do better than a materialistic man who works late (because he's building a telecommunications empire), breaks dates (Rome was not built between nine to five), and detests "backyard barbecues." Which, that last one concerns me but I'm not in love with his family functions either. Well, function. I've only been to the one. Though, I'll take loud music, dominoes and Spades, and dancing in the delicious-smelling smoky air over his parents quiet—I'm talking pin-drop quiet—dinner with his mom politely smiling at me between bites.

Yeah, sue me. Hello? It's called compromise.

So what if I've only met his parents once in two years, how is that a red flag?

A placating smile stretches Lea's full, wine-stained lips. I sense she's ready to call me on my shit. But I'm not wrong about tonight.

I slip on one heel from each pair and twist, giving the camera my best angles.

"Red or black?" I ask, ignoring Lea's unsolicited commentary, for which I neither have the time nor the patience. It's 5:40. Kyle will be back and ready to leave by 6:20 for our seven o'clock reservation. I still haven't picked an outfit or even thought about which of my gazillion lipsticks to wear.

I clear my throat and arch an eyebrow expectantly at the screen.

"Any thoughts, D?" Not that Damon ever comments on my outfits. I'm only asking to take some of the steam out of the argument I sense brewing inside Lea.

In true diva form, Lea tosses me a blank stare. Then she tucks a blown-out, ebony strand of hair behind her diamond-studded ear before she deems to lower her chin to survey my heels.

Now, this is my fault. For a nanosecond, I think she's going to bite her tongue and help her best friend.

But she promptly reminds me she is Lea Cook "Always be Closing," attorney at law. Her truth will be heard.

This is the triple-edged sword of our friendship. Whether it's brutal honesty or simply being present while one of us licks our wounds, The Trio always comes first. It's the unwritten, binding consideration always at stake. Just like Lea and I pretend Damon's old hip-hop dance crew moves are still funky fresh. Unless she's way off base with a case, Damon and I let Lea take the lead. *For our own sanity.* And when necessary, they're always ready to tell me when I'm confusing "fun for now" with forever.

In law school, we forged an unbreakable bond then promptly applied the contracts, compliance, and legal issues terminology we learned to ourselves. Our friendship was binding— enforceable via tough love, on an as needed basis— and irrevocable.

It stuck.

Now, we're Allegra Malone, Damon Dawson, and Lea Cook, esteemed partners at Malone, Dawson, & Cook, LLP, an intellectual property and technology law firm. The business was both conceived and masterminded in the library stacks during our days at William S. Boyd School of Law, where we first became The Trio. We're a badass legal team, weeding out the copy-pasters of the world who consider it business as usual to profit off stolen ideas. Patent, trademark, copyright, trade secret infringements, we do it all. Which means our needle-sharp minds pierce straight through bullshit to determine what's real.

And Lea's about to use hers to talk some tough love.

"Al, you and Kyle are about to fly to Hawaii on Thursday for your brother's wedding. Aaron doesn't need his mopey big sister looking butthurt during the ceremony because you thought Kyle was going to propose. I don't want to hurt your feelings, but he won't."

Lea closes her eyes like continuously stressing *her opinion* that my spastic nerves are "merely the foolishness of a hopeless romantic," is exhausting for her.

Because, of course, she will.

I love *hearing how my relationship instincts are shit.*

This is the "as needed" part I mentioned. Have I had a string of bad relationships? Yes. Am I in love with love? Yes, but name a woman who grew up watching Disney movies who doesn't want her happily ever after.

"This is not a *me* thing, Le," I say defensively when Damon snickers. This undoubtedly means he agrees with Lea, but he's attempting to appear neutral. I'm about to tell him to pick a side when I realize, to them, my reasoning is circumstantial. Unless I can help them see things from my perspective...

Shit. Where did Kyle put the invitation?

"What's different about tonight?" Lea, prepared to die on this hill, doesn't miss a beat. I let her continue with her rant as I walk over to Kyle's nightstand. Seeing nothing on top, I pull out the drawer, searching for a glimpse of the blue cardstock. Underneath a stack of papers, I find the remote control that's been "lost" for the past two days, EarPods, lube, and...extra-large condoms "for big guys"?

I spit out a laugh because...*yeah, no.* I know first-hand what the man isn't working with in the family jewels department.

Kyle is tall, lanky, thin, and blond with a clean-shaven, store-bought-tan baby face. He wears slim-cut suits I can't even get my thigh into, and size nine shoes, so...just...no.

"What?" Damon asks, a smile quirking his full lips.

Now, Damon could probably fill... Wait, what? Uh, no. He's family, Allegra.

Lea and I have been down this route about my ancient college crush on Damon. You don't risk throwing your best friend into your messy dating life, no matter how attracted you are to him.

"This is..." I shake my head, shoving the crazy, awkward thought aside. "Nothing, I was looking for the invitation... nothing." I laugh it off.

Pushing the drawer closed, I remember Kyle bringing up

his gym bag, along with a few more donation boxes, from his trunk yesterday. Some people do spring cleaning, Kyle does summer purging.

"That's what you're looking for? I don't need to see the invitation." Lea laughs. "He's just taking you out to grab a quick bite to eat. You're acting like this is the Met Gala and he's got Tiffany's on standby."

I dip out as she's talking to check the living room, then kitchen. As I turn back to the bedroom to check the closet that's when I overhear Lea drilling in on her "quick bite" angle.

"At Mots Doux?" I shoot her a pointed stare. "First, it's a new French restaurant in Southern Highlands. Second, it's formal wear, invitation-only, and upward of 1,000 dollars a plate—"

Damon blows out his cheeks. He releases an impressed whistle. "*Fuck*. A 1,000-dollar bite, Al?"

"Relax, I'm sure he got the invitation as a kickback from a client," Lea says, undeterred. "Even if he didn't, the man invented ViddyChat, for Christ's sake. Look at his condo." She holds out her palm, glossing over the fact I call this place home, too. "A couple grand isn't a big deal for him. Trust me, this is just dinner."

Her certainty—based on my dating history, there's a fifty-fifty chance she's probably right—grates on my nerves as I duck into the closet.

It's the principle.

Is it so farfetched that a man would want to propose to me?

"Al, I know I'm being hard on you, but it's *because* I love you," Lea says. "If you can give me three reasons why you're *in love* with him, I'll rest my case."

I open my mouth to argue that Kyle is...well, he's...and I...but we...

"All I'm saying is, don't settle unless you love him." Lea's voice is soft and sympathetic. "I'm begging you, as your friend who loves you and the legal counsel representing your heart. Marriage shouldn't be worth settling for. Don't make tonight about anything other than a meal with your bougie boyfriend."

Damon smiles.

I bite the inside of my cheek to stifle a laugh because she's not wrong. Not that I'll let her know as much.

If there's one thing Kyle loves, it's flaunting his money. Everything is always, "Drinks all around!" and slipping the black card to the server before anyone else gets out their wallets with him.

"Whatever, Le," I say, spotting Kyle's duffel peeking out from underneath a pile of discarded clothes on the floor in the back of the closet—*next* to his laundry basket and still-unpacked suitcase. I tug the bag free and plop down on the floor.

"Al, you lead with your heart when...maybe you should shield it," Damon says, jolting me from my stupor. But I stop to listen, anyway. A person as quiet as Damon Dawson makes you listen when he finally talks. I know it's going to be something worth hearing.

"What are you saying, D?" I swallow. "You think I shouldn't be with Kyle?"

My heart revs with anticipation, jackhammering against my chest. It's one thing, having Lea make a case in her no-nonsense, face-the-facts manner. But this is Damon, who stays out of anything dating related—my rumpled, sweet best friend who guards my drinks in clubs, the guy who keeps an extra bottle of Louisiana hot sauce in his fridge in case I stop by, a man who schedules his entire calendar around our Trio Wednesday dinners.

"He's cool enough, I guess." Damon shrugs. There's no conviction in his tone until he asks, "Is Kyle who you really want to be with? I know you've been together for a while. I can't speak for Le, but I'm going to be real with you. I didn't see this being a 'forever' thing." He presses his enormous fist to his lips, the muscles at his jaw taut with concern.

"Yeah," I say.

It's so strange. Thirty minutes ago, I'd been 1,000 percent sure about my future with Kyle. I know we've had issues I chose to ignore, but why does Damon's opinion of him bother me so much? Why am I now looking at Kyle—at any future we'd have together—with fresh eyes? *Have I been leading with my heart?*

I'm a thirty-six-year-old hopeless romantic. Of course, I want love and marriage. Not so much the white picket fence or the kids just yet, but I want my "happily ever after" all the same. I want to travel. I want to explore with my other half. I want to dance like we're drunk. I want us to laugh at corny "Am I the Asshole" tweets. *Ninety percent of the time, if you need to ask, the answer is yes.* I want to watch old movies together and experience them anew because I'm watching them with him. Otherwise, what have I been doing? Why even date?

Lea's expression softens. "We don't want to see you hurt again, Al."

"I know."

I turn back to Kyle's duffel. The air feels charged when I tug open the zipper. My breath hitches. My heart slows to a thud. I physically cannot close my mouth. The expensive-looking navy cardstock isn't there, but inside his tennis shoe is a small teal box—the perfect size to fit an engagement ring.

Maybe it hasn't all been lip service and empty promises. Maybe my instincts are just fine.

Anxiety swirls in my gut.

Before I officially freak the heck out, I pry open the lid, needing to confirm it's not another pair of stud earrings.

A sparkly two-carat solitaire on a white gold band blinds me. The diamond is bigger than I would've ever needed. The setting is simple and delicate, yet majestic somehow. It makes me excited in a way I'd hoped I'd feel whenever—*if* ever—I were to get engaged, no matter how farfetched it seemed.

"Al?" Damon calls my name.

It might be the reality of holding a gorgeous engagement ring in my hand and knowing it's for me, but butterflies soar in my stomach. My heart cartwheels in my chest like it's a summer day in a field of swaying heather.

I slowly slide the ring onto my finger. A seed of hope burrows into my mind and heart, taking root.

"So, if Kyle were to propose, you think I should say no?" I ask before lifting my gaze. My voice is as stilted, as unsure as I feel.

Damon scrubs a hand over his face, the muscles at his jaw tightening. "Only you can decide, Al. Do you really think he's going to ask?"

I suck in a lungful of air, hold out my left hand to the camera, and listen as my two best friends gasp in disbelief.

"Oh my goodness," Lea breathes the words.

But Damon says nothing. And this is the moment I need him to voice his opinion most and be *real* with me, not tell me he doesn't think what Kyle and I share isn't a "forever thing." I need him to explain in vivid detail why. *Or why not.*

What does he know or see that I don't? If Kyle isn't for me, then who is? And what the heck is taking him so long?

Lea cuts straight to the chase. "What are you going to do?"

I'm still, my nerves on edge, waiting for my brain to autofill a response. But the only thing that comes to me is, "I don't know."

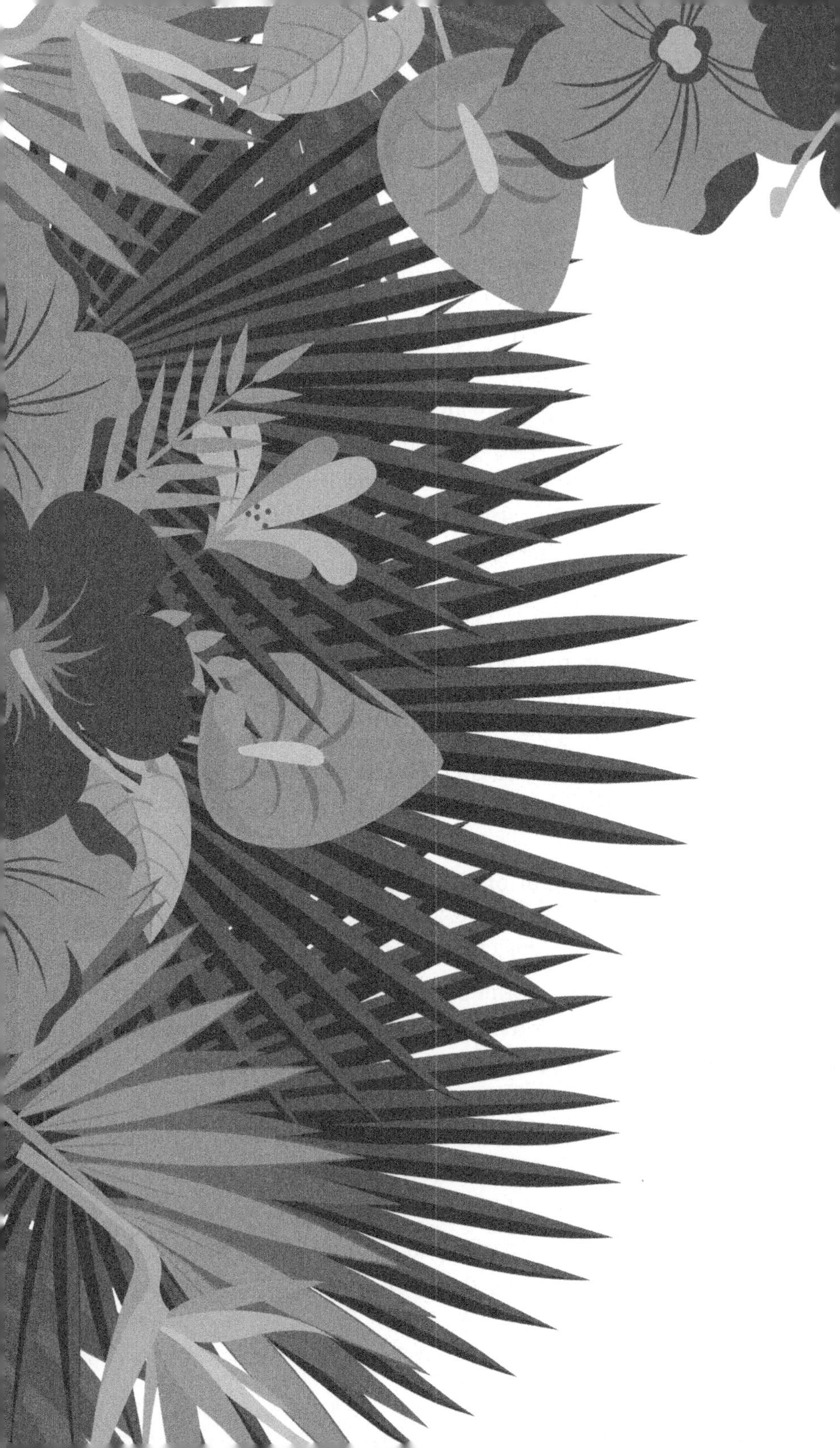

CHAPTER 2
Allegra

Kyle and I listened to music for almost the entire forty-five-minute drive to Southern Highlands, and I still don't know what I'm going to do when he proposes. I steal glances and smile shakily at him in the darkness of his car, hoping to glean some new sense of understanding about my feelings for him and the choice I've got to make. When it comes down to it, what scares me the most is my indecision.

Shouldn't I be certain about the guy I'm going to marry? Shouldn't I know I want to spend forever with him and have some semblance of what our life together would be like beyond awkward family dinners? Also, do I want a life of scheduled sex nights, picking up his dirty laundry from the floor, and more time alone in his gorgeous condo than with him?

"You're awfully quiet," Kyle says. He doesn't even take his eyes off the road. Between the two of us, I don't know who is more nervous.

He thinks I don't see the sweat glistening on his forehead or the way he keeps tugging at his shirt collar like the ring is burning a hole in his jacket pocket. Had I not found the ring or talked with Damon and Lea tonight, I'd have wanted to say something reassuring to let him know he didn't need to be nervous with me. After tonight, we'd be a family. I'd finally be someone's fiancé. Eventually, someone's wife.

But I found the ring.

And Damon's words won't stop replaying in my head making me second-guess everything.

"Yeah, I just...had a long day at work. I've been chipping away at my caseload, you know? I don't want to leave Damon and Lea with all my pending cases."

He flips on his blinker and veers into the right lane to exit the freeway. I figure that's my cue to ease the mood a little and see where his head is. *Where is mine?*

"Mom called earlier," I say. "They've already checked into the hotel."

Kyle nods. He scrapes a hand through his freshly cut hair and tosses me a quick smile. "Yeah? They're already in Hawaii, huh?" he swallows again.

"Oh, my gosh, yeah. Mom, Aaron and Piper, Aunt G, even Julie and Nico." A laugh bubbles up from my throat as I list my family members—all of whom Kyle can't stand because they're "too loud and overbearing." And it occurs to me, even if the feelings are mutual, that I could be marrying a man who doesn't like my family. I imagined my husband seamlessly blending in at family cookouts. Dancing to Frankie Beverly and Maze, playing Spades or dominoes with my cousins, or barbecuing while shooting the shit about his favorite sports team.

Kyle doesn't even like sports.

He doesn't dance or play games—video or board games. He'd *never* man the grill, lest he soil his dry clean-only clothes or get smoke in his perfectly tousled blond hair. The image of Kyle in a tailored suit wearing a "king of the grill" apron is a hot mess.

I know we're different people with different upbringings, and we're compromising, but now they all feel like giant red flags. Should they be? Am I just overthinking everything now because I can't stop thinking about what Damon didn't say?

"That's good," he says.

"Yeah, give them sun, a beach, alcohol...you know the wedding weekend is already underway..." I trail off.

Our flight is early on Thursday, and Kyle hasn't packed yet. He's usually packed weeks ahead. I guess our future really is riding on tonight. My answer to his proposal will decide everything—whether he's my wedding date, my roommate, my fiancé... Why even pack until he knows where we stand, right?

I get that.

Ugh, but no. This is Kyle. We bought tickets and he's got a ring, and he hasn't packed. Does he think I'll say no?

Should I?

He turns down the music and slows to turn onto a long, sweeping, tree-lined lane. I don't pick up the conversation because at the end, in all its incandescent, Parisian glory is Mots Doux.

It sparkles in the night sky like a firefly.

"Wow." I blow out an impressed breath.

We're met at the end of the winding drive by an impeccably dressed server who exchanges Kyle's invitation for two glasses of La Côtes du Rhône wine. We traipse—because walking wouldn't be fancy enough for the elegance of this place—up a grand staircase into what I can only describe as fine dining fantasy.

It's a fresh, fashionable take on a French bistro with ornate fireplaces. Antique mirrors catch the light of crystal orbs strung from the ceiling. The mainstay white tablecloths are surrounded by rich blue chairs and settees, and there are bursting pops of fuchsia orchids centered on the table.

Vibrant, modern art decorates the textured walls. Somehow, even tucked away on the outskirts of a Las Vegas mountainside, Mots Doux echoes the pomp and ceremony of Manhattan's cosmopolitan food scene.

My nerves ramp up.

A marriage proposal in a place like this is a fairytale dream.

"Kyle, this place…" My mouth falls open. I don't have the words to express how special I feel tonight. He's gone through so much trouble. Sure, he admitted during the drive, the invitation was indeed a gift from the marketing firm his company is using to promote ViddyChat's new personalized cell phone features, but I don't care.

"Yeah, it is a great place," he parrots, as the hostess guides us between a long row of fully dressed tables to seat us.

She tells us our server and sommelier will be with us shortly. Then she leaves us alone once again.

I scan the room, taking in a secret glimpse of an elite society in their fine clothes enjoying their lavish lifestyles. *Just a regular old Tuesday, for them.* Now, it will be for me, too. All I need to do is say yes.

This will be my life.

The thought weighs heavily on my chest as I think about Damon and Lea and our nights grabbing drinks at Shane's and our weekly Trio dinners. They reel across my mind like a feel-good movie montage.

A pang of sadness flares in my gut.

Kyle's career is just getting started. His marketing campaign is going to take the video communication world by storm. And as the face of the company spearheading this new venture, he'll take off too. He'd need me, his fiancée, more than ever to support him and be with him. Which means The Trio will take a backseat.

I squeeze his hand on the table and flash him a smile I hope he reads as reassuring. "Thank you for tonight."

"*Puis-je prendre votre commande?*" A slender, pursed-lipped man in a starched black tuxedo asks with his pen ready. I'm assuming that's to jot down our order.

I haven't even seen the menu, but for two to three minutes, Kyle spouts off perfect French, smiling, carrying on, and completely in his element. I'm impressed, and even a little turned on. We usually grab takeout or eat at local family restaurants. Tonight, I get to try on this life for size. It's not a backyard cookout, but it could be a wonderful life if I let it be, right?

When the man walks away, Kyle briefly lowers his head to his phone, then centers his attention on me.

I sit up straighter, mentally preparing myself. *This is it.*

"So..." he says.

"So." I smile back.

And that's it.

Kyle doesn't say more. He doesn't reach inside his jacket or butter me up with idle chitchat. He doesn't bring up Hawaii or my brother's wedding or the fact he's yet to pack a single article of clothing when we're supposed to leave in two days. *Supposed to.*

For three full courses of the longest dinner ever, he chews his steak frites, making chalkboard-scratching level noises, smiling in between bites like he's enjoying torturing me. While I pick at my steamed mussels, he washes his food down with overpriced—like, obscenely ridiculous at 3,500 dollars a bottle —wine.

If I need to take the bottle home, I'm going to get every drip from it, I think. But then it hits me.

Why didn't I think about it before?

Of course, Kyle won't propose tonight. He said it himself;

the invitation was a last-minute gift from a supplier. He didn't have time to plan. Plus, why do it in a restaurant, anyway, when he can get down onto one knee to the backdrop of a breathtaking tropical island paradise with all my family around to celebrate?

My heart squeezes at the thought he'd do that for me because he knows how much I love family. It's the sweetest thing.

Relief washes over me as Kyle asks the server for the check. I tip my glass to my mouth, swallowing my second full glass of wine, then refill it. We'll go home, I'll help him pack for Hawaii, we'll end the night drunkenly happy with him inside me, *hopefully*. We don't need to decide anything right now.

Yes, good sleep is what I need. I'll wake up refreshed with a clear head and warm feet, naked as the day I was born.

I always think better without clothes.

Kyle checks his phone again. I toss him a soft smile. But then he shoves it back in his pocket, meeting my gaze with the same devastatingly gorgeous grin that got my attention the night we met.

"Allegra..." He swallows. For a split second, I wonder if he is going to go through with the proposal tonight after all. I suck in a breath and hold it. "I've been wanting to talk to you about our future."

I squeeze his hand, slowly releasing my breath.

Just say it, and I'll know.

Kyle scrubs his free hand over his face. When he settles his attention on me again, his shoulders slump at his sides.

"Allegra, I think we should break up," he says at the same time as I think, *no*.

It's so low, I almost convince myself I didn't hear it over the raucous pounding of my heart in my ears as I acknowledge what would've been my answer. But then he flashes a sheepish smile to the couple at the table beside us before dragging his attention back to me.

Confusion, shame, anger, and relief swirl around in my body.

My pulse slams into my neck as I withdraw my hand from his to polish off my wine.

Neither of us wants to get married, but he wants nothing *with* me.

I shake my head, close my eyes, scrounging for scraps of the past two years and trying to piece together the big picture. What was it all for? Have we just been passing the time? If so, why even ask me to move in if he didn't see any sort of future for us? Why have I been wasting my time? Anger swells in my chest, overtaking every other emotion. What the hell have I been doing? Cooking and cleaning *his* condo. Picking up his fucking laundry off the floor like he isn't a grown-ass man who can do it his goddamn self. All to start from square one again at thirty-six.

Breathe. Do not be the angry woman.

And the ring…

"Why?" I fidget with my cuticles because I can't look at him yet.

The room blurs.

There could be a totally reasonable explanation. He might've had the ring for a while then changed his mind. Maybe he forgot it was there, or he's holding it for a friend. *Or maybe I'm not marriage material.*

"I think you're an amazing woman—"

"Don't do that," I cut him off. "After all this time together, I think I deserve a straight answer. Is there," I flick my gaze up at him, "someone else?"

He has the nerve to look offended when he let me get dressed up for a celebratory occasion all the while, he was planning to end our relationship. *Who breaks up with their girlfriend at Mots Doux over almost 4,000-dollar wine?* It's unfathomable. And yes, it's hypocritical of me, considering I wasn't sure I didn't want to marry him until five seconds ago, but what happened to communicating and being up front with each other?

His hesitation as he deflates against the back of his chair, like he's weighing how much he wants to say, tells the entire story. He is certainly the asshole here.

But I still need to hear it from him.

"Yes," he says simply, staring past me toward the door.

I nod, anger stirring in my chest.

"The ring is for her," I mutter. It's not a question, it's another log on the fire. I'm not only pissed at him, but I'm also incensed with myself for being so desperate to be what he needed, I lost sight of my own needs. Laughing, playing, dancing, talking, friendship, love. And for all that's good and holy, sex.

Once again, I've proved my instincts aren't trustworthy.

At one point or another, every one of my family and friends who've met Kyle hinted he wasn't right for me. Did I listen? They said that Kyle and I didn't fit together. Smug and pretentious, a snake in a snazzy suit, Lea said, specifically. And I ignored them. Because of my personal insecurities, I wasted two years on a man who has not only cheated on me, but who was too much of a coward to end the relationship before he secured my replacement.

"You know about the ring?" he asks.

The thought of Kyle proposing to another woman smears across my tongue like bile, and a tiny burp barges past my lips. "Excuse me," I say right before I start laughing uncontrollably. That's what he's concerned about? Not my feelings or my heart, not that my whole life is about to change, but that I know about the ring before *she* does?

"You're such a coward and an asshole," I say with a smile. For the first time, I truly see him for what he is: a pretender. All he cares about is himself. No, scratch that. He also cares about money and pretenses, what others say about him, how things will make him look, and what his dad thinks of him.

I'm outright roaring with laughter now.

"Who is she? I'm dying to know who this dynamic woman is who'll plug right into your world," I say through giggles.

"Lower your voice." His tone is sharp and curt.

I'm rightly out of fucks to give, though.

"Oh, *right*," I whisper loudly. "I forgot we're not supposed to let others know we're human." I turn to the raven-haired woman at my right, who is pretending she isn't listening to us and failing horribly. "What do you think? Should my boyfriend of two years—who I live with, mind you—end our relationship before picking out a stunning two-carat rock for his side piece?"

The pot-bellied man with the comb-over sitting across from her fixes her with a warning stare. So, I turn to my left.

"That's enough," Kyle all but growls, coaxing another hysterical giggle from me.

Delirious, heartbroken drunk black woman has got to be better than an angry black woman.

"You, sir? Do you have a mistress on the side, too?" I ask, sweetly.

At that, Kyle fumes like he'll spontaneously combust from embarrassment. His face is fire-engine red, and his jaw is tighter than an Instagram influencer's ass.

"If I tell you, will you please stop this?" he bites out. "Allegra, you're embarrassing yourself."

I blow out a chest full of air.

"I don't know. This is so much fun, and I feel all warm and fuzzy inside. My entire universe is turning on its axis. Literally." I giggle, swaying as I lean back on the hind legs of my chair. "What isn't funny about this to you? I've got no place to live, no plus-one for my baby brother's wedding, no boyfriend or fucking fiancé—"

He cuts me off and that's when it hits me. I don't love Kyle. I don't think I ever did. He's been my roommate, plus one, date, boyfriend—*if* we can call him that. It doesn't hurt any less to be tossed aside, but he's not the love of my life.

And I'm not his.

"Allegra don't act like this surprises you." Kyle leans in, his blue eyes wild and stormy. "You'll bounce back the way you always do. We haven't been happy for a while, and my company—"

"There it is!" I all but shout. "Exactly what I was waiting for. This isn't about you and me, Kyle. It's never been about us. This is about your daddy's money. You're hoping Viddy-Chat will finally make him proud of you. With all its success, you need someone by your side who'll fit into..." My head swims. I sway to my right. "...the pretty picture in your head."

I tip back into my chair and lose my balance. Flailing my arms, I feel myself falling when the pot-bellied man to my left steadies the chair, righting me.

But then he pins Kyle with a reprimanding stare.

Echoes of intolerance reverberate between them. I realize I am embarrassing Kyle and myself. After tonight, Kyle will recover. I'll be left homeless and alone. He's right, too. At some point, I will bounce back. But getting dumped and sitting helpless while my world flips upside down doesn't hurt any less.

Deep down, I think I knew. My life is about to take a hard turn, but I'm relieved to find out about Kyle now instead of years down a road paved with regrets. I'm angry, sad, numb. But I'm certain tonight happened the way it was supposed to.

Damon was right.

I may not know what love is—what it looks like or feels like—but I know what love isn't. Kyle and me...it was never a "forever" thing.

"It didn't have to be this way, Allegra," Kyle bites out.

I fish my phone out from my purse, open the Rideo app, and discover the wait time is over an hour before a car can pick me up. Desperate to get out of here, I send a 911 text to The Trio group chat along with the address, then push myself to my feet.

One by one, I remove the diamond earrings he gave me. I set them on the tablecloth next to him. Before I leave, I center my blurry gaze on Kyle and leave him with one last parting note. "Fuck you, Kyle. Have a nice life. Oh, and for the record, you are not a big guy, and you have *never* required extra-large condoms." With that, I grab the wine bottle from the ice bucket and walk away.

Behind me, the raven-haired woman spits out her drink.

I am now absolutely certain. He was always a "fun for now" I'd somehow confused with a "forever."

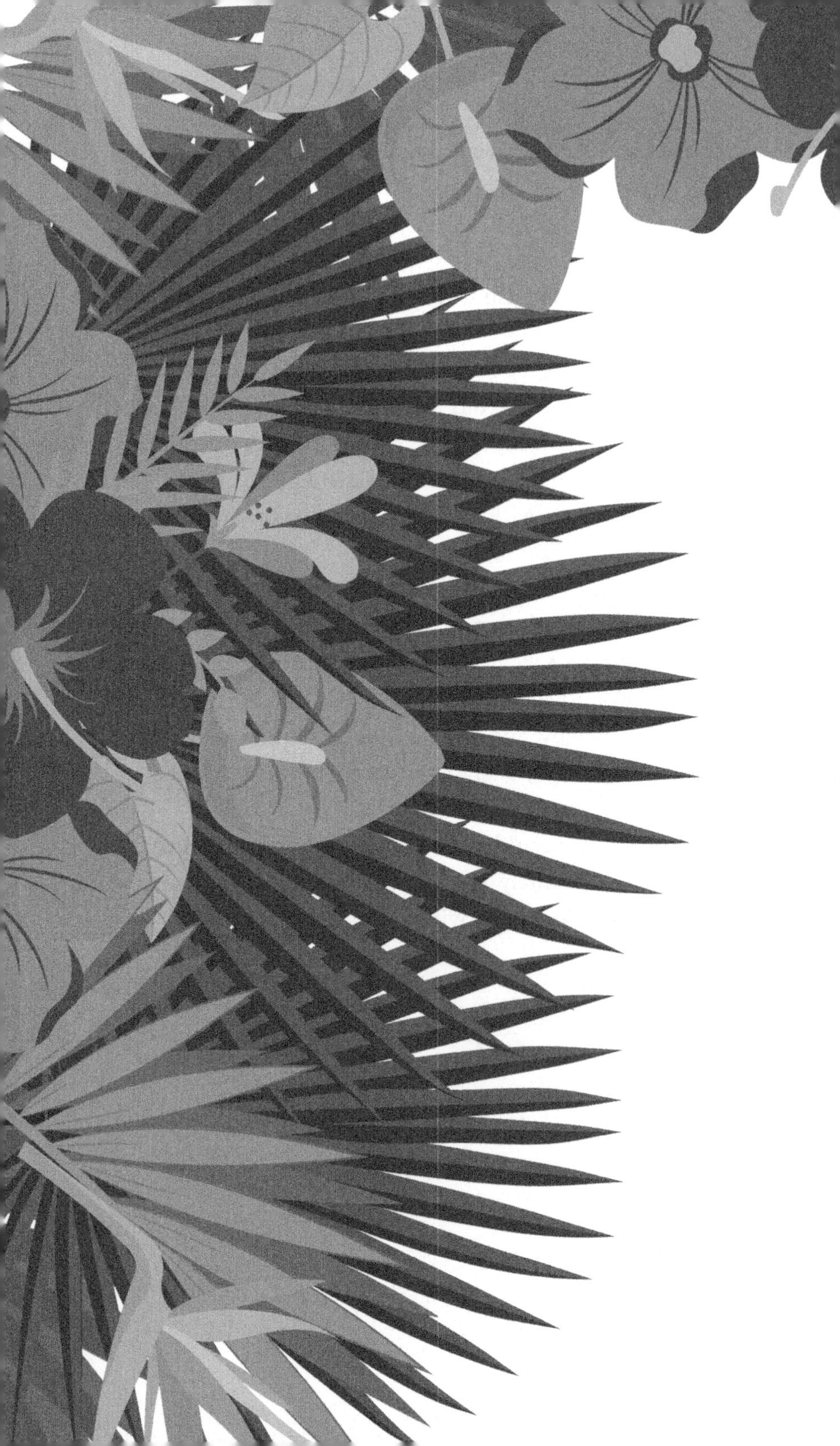

CHAPTER 3
Damon

"In 200 feet, turn right onto Mots Doux Lane," my GPS taunts me as I pull to the stop sign.

I'm restless, my heart is pounding in my ears, and I'm nauseous as I lower the music volume and round the corner onto the private lane. As the glittery bright lights of Mots Doux come into view, I'm tempted to turn back around. *Let Lea be the one to console Allegra tonight.*

"Why did I have to open my mouth?" I drag my hand over my head, gripping the base of my neck. The one time I speak up, the night ends with an emergency text. The killer part is, deep down, I'm relieved. If I'm picking up Al, Kyle's proposal couldn't have landed well...which means she's single.

For the first time in a while, we both are.

I'm going to be real with you. I didn't see this being a forever thing.

"Seriously with the 'concerned friend' route, Damon?" I huff out an annoyed laugh. How many times have Allegra and Lea both dated wannabe players and fuckboys who didn't deserve them? How many times have I bitten my tongue and let them figure it out on their own because I knew it wouldn't last?

I knew it wouldn't last.

On the dash, my phone pings on Bluetooth with a text notification from Lea. I press the push-to-talk icon to have the message read aloud.

"A text message from Lea Cook." My car's robotic female voice filters through my speakers. "Stop being a punk. Tell her, D. This is your chance." I shake my head, reaching to close the app, but another notification pings. "A text message from Lea Cook. I'm serious. I don't want to hear about you missing your shot for the next decade."

I huff out an exasperated laugh from my gut.

"Nothing's changed," I yell back at the dash. "She needs an ear to listen, a shoulder to cry on. That's it. I'm not trying to be her rebound!"

The words echo in my head, and I know it's the crux of my frustration. No matter what happened in that restaurant tonight, she left her home with a man with whom she's been in a serious, cohabitating relationship for years. So, it's not a question of whether I want to be with Allegra. Under different circumstances, I'd jump at the chance. But this is marriage. If it's over with Kyle, anyone who follows will be a stand-in.

I slowly press down on the gas, then something appears in my peripheral vision. I slam on the brakes, whipping the door open as I push to my feet.

"Allegra?" I call out.

She's on the side of the road, slumped at the base of a weeping willow tree with a champagne bottle in hand.

"Damon?" she croaks.

"What are you doing out here?" I round the hood and rush to her side. "What if I hadn't seen you?" Unfiltered concern bleeds into my tone.

"*Ugh.* Why'd didn't Lea come?" She groans.

"Glad to see you too, big head." I chuckle, crouching down to slip her red heels onto her feet then gathering her purse. "*Thank you, Damon, for helping me.*" I tease her good-naturedly. "*You're such an amazing friend for getting out of bed to drive all the way to Southern Highlands to rescue me.*" Her face is inches from mine as I tug her to her feet and wrap her arm around my shoulder to help her to the car. "Any of the above will do, but I'll settle for a 'thanks.'"

Her half-lidded green eyes drift to me. She sighs.

"Look at me. I'm a mess," she whines. Her head bobs as we walk. "I've got raccoon eyes. My face is probably all puffy and splotchy. I drank half a bottle of stupid, expensive champagne. It wasn't even any good, I just didn't want to waste it."

That's when I notice the earrings Kyle gave. The ones she wears all the time. They're gone.

"Waste not, want not," I say, remembering the lesson I learned from one of my longest foster homes. They'd meant essentials like food, clothing, toys, but that stuck with me for very different reasons. At eleven years old, learning the dangers of high hopes was a valuable lesson. Never wish for things that don't come with guarantees. Certainly, never expect things from loved ones that they can't give you.

"Anyway, I didn't think you'd *want* to come after what you said..."

Propping her against the car, I open the passenger door and settle her into the seat.

"How long have we known each other, Al? I've held your hair back while you threw up." I wince, struggling to find the slot to strap her into the seatbelt. "I've shielded your face from touching a public toilet seat, wiped up your tears repeatedly. So, what did I say that was so wrong?"

Why did I say anything at all?

When I hear the seatbelt click, I pull back to meet her gaze. She stares at me for a second too long to be insignificant, and I know she's the reason I couldn't *not* say anything.

"You, um..." Allegra swallows, and I'm probably reading way too much into it, but there's heat in her sweetly intense eyes. Or maybe it's just the champagne talking. The air zips with an electricity that leaves me buzzing with anticipation.

When she doesn't finish her sentence, I shut her door. I walk around to the driver's side, start the ignition, and make a U-turn to get back to the freeway. We drive for maybe ten minutes before we pass The Strip, then she turns to me.

"Before I showed you and Lea the ring." She twists in her seat to square her shoulders to me. "You said you didn't think Kyle and I were a 'forever thing.'"

"Yeah."

"Why? Who should I spend forever with?"

My mouth goes dry, the word "me" is lodged in my throat.

In my periphery, I notice her shaking her head as she fidgets with the hem of her red dress. "Listen, it's no secret that no one wants me to be with Kyle, and you stay out of my relationship stuff, so I don't know why, it bothers me so much. It's just that I figured when I needed you, you'd speak up. It felt like you knew why Kyle and I weren't right for each other. Like you had insight or intuition I could've used. I wanted to know more, see what you saw, *hear* you explain in the most layman terms what I was missing. But as usual, you clammed up."

My eyes are trained on the road ahead as I nod.

I don't want to do this here—not tonight—while she's tipsy. Not when she probably won't remember anything she says. If we're going to lay everything out on the table, I want it to be when we're both aware of what it all means. *If* it means anything at all.

"What happened with Kyle?" I ask.

Allegra rests the side of her head on the window. Behind her, the neon landscape blends into a colorful blur. That's how it always is for me with Allegra—she's always in the forefront while the world moves at lightning speed in the background.

It's all I can do not to rip my eyes from the road to watch her. After twelve years of friendship, I don't need to look directly at her to see her. I've taken extensive notes on the soft curve of her cheek, the golden highlights of her brown complexion, and studied the long, delicate slope of her neck crawling up to her sheared dark hair. I'm an expert on the fireworks show the streetlights cast in her watery green eyes.

"The ring wasn't for me," she says.

Her voice is a faraway murmur, her tone weighed down. I'm sure she's lost in her thoughts, thinking about what the end of her relationship with Kyle means, where she'll live, what her family will say when she arrives in Hawaii without him—single again.

As her best friend, I should be pissed on principle. I share Allegra's anger that not only was the asshole unworthy of her, but he had the audacity to cheat on her to the point he's proposing to someone else. I should reassure her through it all and tell her Lea and I will be here to support her and that she can have my bed and I'll take the couch for as long as she needs. I should do what we always do: find the bright side.

But I still can't get past her words.

She said the ring wasn't for her. Would she have turned down his proposal if he'd asked? If I had said nothing?

The rest of the drive to my loft, we sit in stifling silence, and the weight of those questions crushes down on me.

After I park and help her inside, I set up the pull-out couch with clean pillows, sheets, and blankets while Allegra browses through my fridge. I take a couple of minutes to gather a few necessities for her. Then I find her toeing off her heels in the bathroom and looking like those questions are weighing on her heart, too.

With a small knock on the door, I announce my presence.

"Hey, this should tide you over until tomorrow." I set a towel, washcloth, and one of my T-shirts on the counter. "In the morning, I'll go grab some of your things from the condo. There's face soap and body wash in the shower—spring fresh scent." I chuckle, awkwardly. "Anyway, the lotion and cotton swabs are under the sink."

She nods, and I edge my body toward the living room, but I feel tethered to this spot—to Allegra.

I hover just outside the bathroom door, hating the tension between us. I feel like I need to say something to make things right.

"Thanks," she says softly before I get the words out. "Listen, D—"

"You don't have to say anything. I'm sorry I made you feel like I didn't support you. You know I'd do anything for you. Just say the word."

She pulls me into a hug, and I lean into her familiar warmth, her soft summery scent, and let the unease drain from my chest and limbs. But no matter how much I love the feel of us together, she doesn't belong to me.

"We good?" I ask, pulling away.

She gives me another small nod. I'll take it.

Later, I hear the bathroom door open from my position beneath the covers on the couch. After all she's been through, the least I can do is let her sleep off the day in a proper bed.

"Um…" Allegra comes to a full stop at the edge of the couch. She scans the room, eyeing the blazing fireplace, the dim lighting, the television turned down low on the music channel. "What are you doing?"

Fuck. What am I doing?

"Uh..." I can't even hide the desperation in my tone.

She's wearing the T-shirt I lent her. Seeing how it barely covers her ass, I'm lamenting my oversight of giving her a pair of sweats or pajama bottoms to go with it. In the dark, she won't notice, though it's a physical struggle not to stare at her smooth, toned, golden-brown thighs.

"You can have the bed," I say.

"Uh, you don't have a TV in your room. I need noise to sleep," she says. "Before you tell me about your sleep sound machine with its calming white noise or ocean waves, they don't work on me, so scoot over." I don't have time to protest. She slips under the covers, easing in beside me. "What are we watching?"

She gets comfortable and commandeers the remote control, scouring the guide channel for "something happy and sweet," which I translate to mean a romance movie. Sure enough, she finds *The Best Man,* right at the scene where Taye Diggs and Nia Long dance to a soulful classic Stevie Wonder song to fight the urge to do more.

As Allegra shifts closer with every inch, I move away. I can't help feeling like we're watching movies to fight the urge to do more.

I could leave right now and sleep in my bed. But I hear Lea in the back of my mind telling me this is my chance and that she doesn't want to hear about missing my shot for the next decade. Strangely, for once, as I lie here next to my best friend, Lea and I are on the same page.

I don't want to lose this moment. I don't want to wonder what might've been. So, for the second time tonight, I let the need to be real with Allegra push to the surface.

"Want to talk about it?" I'm facing the television, though my focus is centered on the woman who's always been by my side... *and never within reach.*

"Not really." She laughs.

I lean over to nudge her shoulder with mine. "Is it your heart or your ego? Based on that empty champagne bottle, it could be your head, too."

"I don't know. All the above?" Allegra shrugs, releasing a resigned laugh.

Then she quiets for a few seconds, staring blankly at the screen like she's wading through memories.

"Mostly, ego, I think. It's exhausting starting all over again, but what Kyle and I shared...it was more like 'fun for a while.' We were more roommates than soulmates if you know what I mean."

"Yeah," I say. "As long as your heart is okay..."

"Hmm, mostly, it is."

My heart rate kicks up as I segue into the question that's been weighing on me all night. "What would you have said if the ring was for you?" My heart stutters and my breath lodges in my throat. "If Kyle had proposed?" It feels like any future we could have together is hinged upon her answer.

"No."

My pulse races. "No?"

Her body sags as she rests her head on my shoulder.

"I would've said no," she says matter of factly. "The ring was beautiful. I want my happily ever after more than anything. But it was weird. When he said he wanted to end things, all I felt was relief. All I could think about was how much I hated that he and my family never really meshed—"

"Ooh." I cringe. "Mama Malone detests that man with every bone in her body."

"Right? And she likes everyone, so that should've told me something right off the bat. Red flags all over the place..." I feel the tension in her arm and hand loosening, softening. "You and Lea are the people who know me best, so when you all didn't take to him, either... Like, what was I even doing?"

"Being you," I say too quickly. "Leading with your heart."

"Being stubborn to a fault, as usual." She groans. "You would think all these years advising people about the law, I'd have honed my instincts into something useful for relationship red flags."

"Al, the law is logic, reason, and proof. Love is something you'll know when you know."

My words land loud and hard. They feel heady somehow.

After a few seconds, I ask, "Bright side?"

"Is there a bright side?" She laughs.

With a kiss on her hair, I say, "You get to be here with me tonight."

"That is the brightest part of this wretched night." She giggles. "But, you know, there was a moment—before all the wine—I got this sense of overwhelming clarity. Kyle and I were never the right fit. Which...hindsight, right? But how can I get some foresight? Shit!" Her giggle blossoms into a burst of a full belly laugh.

There're mountains of truth in her statement.

"Anyway, at that point, my mind started doomscrolling through all the signs I ignored. The man hates sports—"

"Even basketball?"

"I know. *All* sports." She throws up her free hand, blowing out a laugh. "This is going to sound so dumb. It irritated me to no end that he always had an excuse or a work emergency to avoid a family cookout. Or dancing or watching old movies like this."

Like us.

That's all I hear—how well *we* fit together.

And for the rest of the night, we do. Our bodies meld to one another. The outline of her soft curves press against the hard lines of my chest. With every hour, with every touch, every shallow breath piercing the air, slow heat creeps over my aching flesh. I'm dizzy with need and desperate as she inhales softly, arching her back.

"What are we doing?" I whisper as I thrust my hips forward, trembling, edging closer still.

In answer, she reaches back, sliding her hand between us. She wraps her hand around my dick, working me within in an inch of my sanity.

I've wanted this so long it hardly seems real. Every sensation is heightened with Allegra because I know this woman. I know her mind and her heart. I know she gives with every inkling of her being. Now, I know how it feels to have her body needy and grinding against mine.

I'm exposed, flipped inside out.

Everything I am is at her mercy.

"Al, I'm serious," I say again, my voice gruff and strained, almost unrecognizable to my own ears. "We've been friends for too—"

"I need you..." She shoves the covers back then she drags her panties over her hip. I steady her hand, gritting my teeth as she grinds herself over my achingly hard erection. "You said you'd do anything for me—"

"Not like this."

Allegra twists and her tear-strewn gaze lands on me. "It wasn't supposed to be like this," she sobs, and I don't know if she's talking about Kyle or us, but I don't care.

"Don't cry. I'm right here," I whisper, rolling her body over until she's flush against me. As she trembles, I squeeze her close to my chest and rub soothing circles on her back. "I'm always going to be right here, Al."

Like she understands every implication of my promise, she tips up her chin to look at me.

For the tiniest moment the same sweet intensity from earlier in the car... it lingers in her unsettlingly soft, green gaze. Just like it did then, the air buzzes with electricity, sending my pulse thundering before she leans in.

Our lips are a breath apart. Though she won't remember any of this in the morning, when she leans in, I take my chance. Cupping the curve of her cheek, I drag my lips over hers. Just long enough to quiet her sobs, I savor the warm sweetness. The kiss is tender and soft, just how I imagined our first kiss would feel.

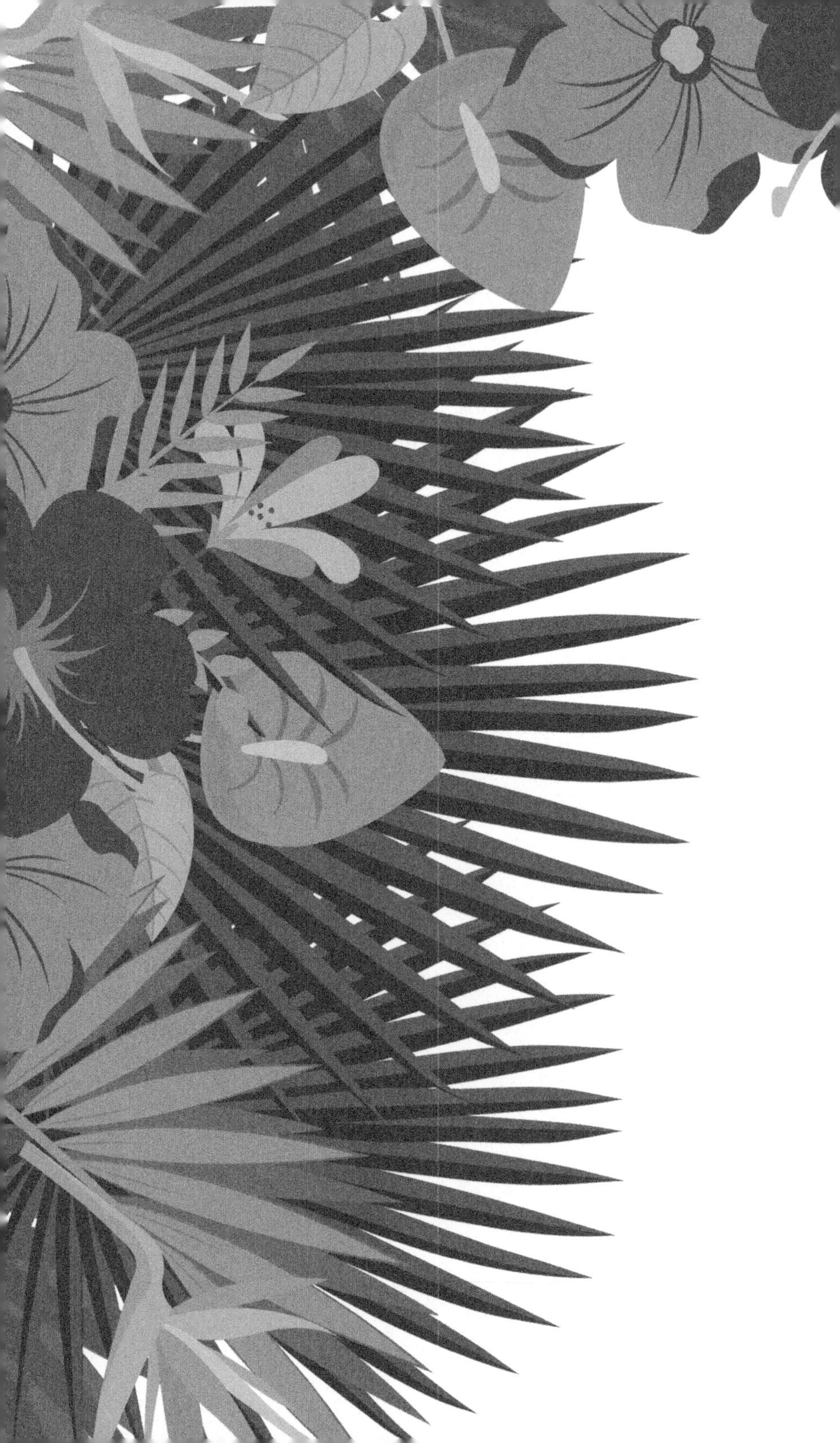

CHAPTER 4
Allegra

I can't stop staring at Damon. He's still asleep. But I'm awake, and all I can focus on is the way his thick, dark eyelashes sweep up in a perfect curl, the smooth texture of his cinnamon brown skin, the tiny heart-shaped mole under his right eye, his clean-cut beard, tightly shorn waves, the slight pout of his full lips and how good it felt to finally have them on mine.

My stomach churns.

I'm restless thinking about what I want to do. *What I always do.*

It starts with a kiss. The tenderness of holding hands. Immediately, I turn a flickering spark into an all-consuming flame, taking down everything in its path—no logic, reason, or proof. My universe becomes about the man of the moment. I change my hair, my clothes, my plans—my freaking address if need be—all in the name of love.

I know law, but what do I really know about love?

Maybe I should be listening to Lea's self-help books.

Yesterday, one question stood between me marrying Kyle. We were in a fancy restaurant surrounded by expensive art and crystal chandeliers eating overpriced food with a bunch of bougie people. If I'd been ready to say yes, I could've changed the entire trajectory of my life because of a snazzy invitation and the prospect of a proposal. Because I found a ring...one that wasn't even meant for me.

Hours later, I'm lying here on an oversized convertible sleeper sofa next to my best friend, my fingers pressed to my lips, retracing every fiery brush of that kiss. I'm looking at him like all these years, he's been hiding right in front of my eyes.

To my aching heart, it makes so much sense: why relationships haven't worked out with other guys, why I've turned every rolling stone, only to end up homeless and hopeless.

Deep down, I think I've always known Damon is who I'm supposed to be with—and the man I can't risk losing.

He means too much to me.

I feel the familiar pull in my gut. I'm reverting to hopeless romantic mode.

No. Not this time.

Tender kiss or not, my heart and my body can't be trusted.

Determined not to ruin my friendship, I allow myself one last longing stare then ease backward on the plush mattress. One leg, then the other, slips out of the cool sheets, and I step down. As I tiptoe over the hardwood floors of Damon's living room, I scan every surface searching for my phone before I duck into the safety of his enormous bathroom. If there's one person I trust to set me straight, it's Lea.

Once I'm inside, I swipe over to favorites and press her name before I step into the tub and slide the door closed.

"Le!" I whisper-yell when she answers. "Oh my gosh, I'm so glad you picked up. Holy shit, so much happened, and I don't know what to do. Like, is this real or is it a me thing? I thought I knew what I wanted but then he looked at me like...

and then I was in his shirt... but then I told him I needed him—"

"Stop." Lea blows out a breath. "Why are you whispering and what is that a weird echo?"

A fresh wave of nerves washes over me as I crack the shower door to peek out, praying I didn't wake Damon.

"I'm in the tub hiding," I say, my attention laser focused on the space beneath the door. Hearing no footsteps or movement, I continue. "Le, I'm freaking out and I need your brain to reason with mine."

"I'm not even going to ask why you're hiding in a tub and whispering. Just slow down and start from the beginning."

My heart beats a million miles a minute as I let the words rush out of me. "It's over with Kyle and I kissed Damon."

A few seconds tick by and I wonder if Lea heard me. But then she sighs, and I sense she's turning over everything I've said in her head, trying to connect the pieces. "Al, you just went from point A to Z. I need to know what happened in between. Last night you were trying on shoes and rings talking about marriage before we get a message to pick you up from the restaurant. How did we get from a proposal to kissing our best friend?"

I gulp. "Short version? After we left for Mots Doux, I couldn't stop thinking about what Damon said about Kyle and me not being a 'forever thing.' The entire drive red flags kept popping up. I was going to say no. Then Kyle said he wanted to end things which pissed me off because I kept thinking about the ring and how he'd lined up a replacement, you know?" I shake my head, anxiety swirling inside me all over again. "Purely on principle, I needed the story, so I drank like a fish, pried it out of him, then texted you all to pick me up—"

"Then Damon showed up and..." Lea says, moving me along.

"He put my shoes on and helped me to the car, and... He looked at me like the world faded away and all he saw was me. For like two seconds, I let myself remember how I felt about him back at Boyd. God, I had it so bad for him. But then he started dating Shawna Jenkins, so I said yes to Eric Reid. Then our timing was—"

Lea cuts me off. "Stay focused. So, you all stared at each other with hearts in your eyes and he kissed you right there in the car, or you kissed him?"

I give Lea the rundown, catching her up on everything—including the sex close call— that happened up until I climbed in Damon's tub to pour out my heart.

"Well, is this a me thing? I don't trust myself. I need you to tell me because I can't risk ruining my friendship with Damon. I can't risk messing up The Trio, Le."

I imagine Lea nodding along, her fingers pressed to her lips carefully weighing how honest she wants to be.

"Yes, based on your dating history, this is an Allegra thing. But..." she adds quickly. "In this case, this thing with you and Damon has been simmering beneath the surface for a while, so I don't think we can dismiss it as a crush."

"What I do?"

She blows out a breath. "Is Kyle's plane ticket transferrable?" she asks. *Shit. I completely forgot about Hawaii, and the fact that I'm now going to my brother's wedding solo.* "When you get here, we'll look at the caseload, and see if I can swing an impromptu vacation."

"Oh my God, Le. You are a lifesaver."

"Yeah, this is what you need," she says, like she's reassuring herself. "A long weekend to step back, slow down, be around family and friends, and when you get back, you'll be able to see things between you two with a fresh set of eyes. For now, do nothing."

"Okay, got it."

I swallow, evening my breathing when a knock sounds on the door startling me.

Lord have mercy, Allegra. Relax.

"Gotta go. I'll see you in a few. But thanks for letting me unload on you. Love you." She tells me she loves me too, then I disconnect the call, ease open the shower door, and climb out before I reply to Damon, "Yeah?"

"Everything okay, Al?" Damon's voice is still thick with sleep, though hints of concern bleed into his tone. Then there's faint pressure on the paneled wooden door. I imagine him leaning his weight against it.

Be strong.

No matter how sweet that kiss was, if last night proved anything, it's that I need to work on me. I can't shove Damon into my happily ever after. I can't lead with my heart this time. *Not without gathering all the facts for a solid case to prove we're worth the risk. I owe it to both of us not to do what I've always done.*

"Listen," Damon says, "I'm sorry about—"

On a deep breath, I swing the door open, unwilling to let this go any further. I shove aside the reminder of how good it felt to be held by him last night, reminding myself that I can't do things how I've done before.

He stiffens like he's waiting for me to lay in on him.

"Please don't apologize. Let's just try to be rational about this. We're both adults. Like you said, we've been through hell and high water together so let's not allow a kiss," I tilt my head to either side, both considering the facts of my case and downplaying what almost happened. "a kiss, and a little excitement make this awkward between us. Thankfully, one of us had more restraint than the other."

We both laugh because if it were up to me, things could've gone far beyond our lips.

Damon nods, the tightness in his shoulders draining.

"This feels like a rerun of yesterday...standing in a bathroom doorway like this again," Damon says. "Uh, I just wanted to make sure we were good and that I didn't go too far last night when you were vulnerable..."

Does he think he took advantage of me? I'm the one who made the first move.

"Yeah, about that...I vaguely recall arching my back." I try to put his nerves at ease. *The lies.* "There also might've been some tugging at my underwear. So, no we didn't go too far. It was all me crossing lines that I have no business crossing." I couple my raised eyebrows with a shaky smile.

Damon sucks in a soft gasp and traces his teeth over his lower lip like he's reliving the mental image I've not so subtly brought up. And I'm watching—more like gawking at—him with every inch of my flesh tingling in awareness. Good God, it's going to take every ounce of my willpower.

Long game, Allegra. We've got to build the case.

Then my phone pings.

"One sec," I say, checking the screen.

It's a text from Trish, the temporary paralegal we contracted for the Bliss & Makeup Co. trademark infringement case. Mostly, she does data entry, interviews, drafts, and distributes documents for us—administrative stuff. Since her desk is closest to my office, we've gotten close, grabbed wine a few times, and talked about our relationships and work. I've found we have a ton in common. Plus, she's great at her job, and I enjoy having her around.

If we can swing it financially, I'm considering suggesting to Damon and Lea that we hire her on full time.

When I unlock the screen, her message populates.

Trish Santos 7:13 am
Hey, heard about you and Kyle. Where are you? Damon's or Lea's?

Why is everyone at work so early?

Allegra Malone 7:13 am
Girrrrrllll, so much tea to spill. I'll tell you everything when I get there.

Trish Santos 7:14 am
...

"So..." I clear my throat, hiking up a shoulder as I smile at Damon. "I have nothing to wear to work, and we can't both show up late, so I'll let you have the bathroom." I ease past his broad frame, not exactly avoiding rubbing up against him. I'm human and pseudo-sad about my almost-engagement/breakup. *So sue me for copping feels where I can.* "Do you mind if I borrow a pair of your sweats to head over to the condo? I figure it's after seven, and Kyle should be gone by now."

Also, the sooner I get out of here, the better.

Damon is already near the shower, tugging his shirt over his head when he turns around to face me. Not an ounce of logic or reason, just physical proof. Right here before the judge and jury (my brain and dusty lady parts), my loudmouth, showboating libido takes over in a ruthless cross-examination.

There's undeniable physical attraction and a heart-clenching desire to drag the rest of his clothes off with my teeth and mount him.

Exhibit A: passion. Check.

Oblivious to my current struggle, he says offhandedly,

"Yeah. Whatever you need," like he isn't standing there shirtless in only loose-fitting black cotton pajama bottoms with the chiseled, hard ridges of his chest exposed.

I swallow and nod. "Okay, thanks."

We both know I'm lingering...staring again. But, *come on*. I'm going to need a much stronger defense. The friendship manual did not prepare me for this level of middle-melting attraction over a single sweet kiss from my best friend.

Back at Boyd, Damon was always more brain than brawn, erring on the side of nerdy-cute. He was in a dance crew styled as a cross between Soulja Boy and Lil' Jon. He was never really what anyone would call a "heartthrob." Most girls have never fallen all over themselves for him.

If only I was like most girls...

"Need anything else?" he asks, ruthless in his torture.

There's absolutely nothing sexual about the way he says it, but my overactive brain is in hopeless romantic, teenage girl mode. So, everything he says sounds like a sexual drawl, and I mentally add "in bed."

Why, yes, I need something else...in bed.

Because I'm not a teenage girl, and obviously, I need to get my shit together, I avert my gaze with a snap of my fingers, and say, "Oh, yeah," like we're mid-conversation. "Also, if you let me stay another night, can we switch up the sleeping arrangements? I just—"

"I completely agree," Damon says matter of factly. "It's probably better to ensure there isn't a rerun of last night. Or bring up the lines crossed..." He trails off, but I fill in the blank. *Or the fact I almost had drunk sex with my best friend and am currently fact-gathering to prove we're soulmates.*

I nod way too many times.

"Okay, cool." I'm breathless, completely affected as I pull

the door closed. "Holy shit, what am I going to do?" I whisper-yell to myself.

* * *

I make my way into Damon's bedroom where the bed is neatly made, and the curtains are drawn letting light flood in. I take my time, dragging my fingertips over his comforter and dresser, the framed pictures of The Trio, all smiling and laughing. I sniff his clean, spicy cologne on his nightstand, allowing myself to get lost in him, in this intimate glimpse of his space, and imagining me in it when I hear the shower turn off.

"What are you doing, Allegra?" I scrub a hand over my face.

No sooner do I rush into Damon's closet and find his sweatpants folded neatly in a storage cube marked "sweatpants" does the doorbell ring.

And then my phone pings.

"What is happening?" I groan, grabbing a navy pair of sweats off the top of the stack and yanking them on as I check my texts. A Trio group chat text.

No.

Lea Cook 7:52 am
911! Get here!

"Shit," I hear Damon say in the hallway before he calls out, "Coming!"

When I round the corner out of the bedroom, the two of us beeline for the door. I don't even live here, so I don't know why I'm going. I'm praying it isn't Lea, even though she's clearly in the office. I'd have a hard time explaining my version of "do nothing" with Damon, doused in water droplets, in a towel molded to his cute butt... Or why I'm one good wardrobe malfunction from licking him from head to toe.

He tosses me a chuckle over his shoulder.

"What?" I ask.

I promise I'm trying not to imagine us on a furry rug in front his sleek fireplace getting busy.

"Making yourself right at home, huh?" Damon chuckles. "Wearing my clothes, answering the door, taking in an eyeful..." The last part, he murmurs under his breath, but I hear, and own it with a guilty-as-charged shrug as he turns his attention to the door. "Who is it?" he asks, leaning to look through the peephole.

"A to B Couriers for Allegra Malone," a husky male voice answers.

Damon's eyebrows pinch together in a curious expression as he unlocks the door and twists the handle. When he opens it, his shoulders slump at his sides and he tilts his head in a "you can't be serious" gesture.

Neither one of us says anything as we step aside.

A crew of movers unloads Kyle's donation boxes full of my belongings along with my suitcase, packed and ready for a tropical destination wedding vacation.

I guess he took his pick of my friends, knowing I'd only feel comfortable staying with Damon or Lea.

When the movers are all done, we stand in stunned silence until I address the fact things in the complicated department seem to have escalated overnight.

"Shit, I'm sorry, D." I wince. "Look, I know when you picked me up, you were thinking you'd only have to console me for the night, tops. But if you store my stuff until I get back from Hawaii, I promise—"

"It's fine." He scratches his temple. "Stay as long as you need."

I hike up a bluff-calling eyebrow at his tightened jaw muscles.

He flexes his fingers. Slowly, his conflicted gaze drifts from the mountain of boxes lining the exposed cement walls of his gorgeous loft before he pins me with a resolved stare.

"D, you and I both know after last night it's probably *not* the best idea for us to be roommates." I fan my hand over the length of Damon's appetizing body gift wrapped in a towel like a billboard for Exhibit A.

Because this is my best friend who knows the dirty depths of my mind, he counters my raised eyebrow with his own, fanning out his hand to me.

"Seriously?" I purse my lips. "I'm wearing your old Boyd T-shirt with a pair of sweats I had to roll three times to fit."

"Al, I know we've been friends forever, but I'm still a man. Seeing you in my clothes, knowing your bare skin is beneath them, that my scent is all over you..." He throws his hands up. "Need I say more?"

Well, damn.

All this time, I thought I was the horny one, objectifying him for a happily ever after. This whole time, he's been getting off on it.

I scrape my hands through my hair with an ear-to-ear grin plastered on my face. "Okay, so um..." I tuck my lip between my teeth. "In that case, you need to go. Now!" I laugh. "We'll figure out sleeping arrangements later."

When he still doesn't move, I snap my fingers playfully.

"This isn't funny, D. I'm serious."

He finally stops torturing me long enough to get dressed and set a spare key on the kitchen island, and he leaves the loft. I wait ten requisite minutes to ensure he's long gone from the building before I pull the collar of his T-shirt over my mouth and release a loud, sexually frustrated scream.

"Holy shit!" I heave an excited sigh, pressing the soft fabric to my nose. I inhale the clean mix of spring fresh soap and Damon.

It turns out, the courier service did an excellent job of packing my things. I find my suits in a tall box marked "business attire," and pull out a black pantsuit. Then, I immediately swap it for my red draped-neck sheath dress.

Just because I'm totally not making a big deal—certainly not risking our friendship—doesn't mean I don't want to make Damon's jaw drop.

With Damon gone, I take full advantage of the high pressured, handheld shower head, and step out feeling like a new woman. I'm already late but I spend a few extra minutes putting on full contoured makeup, small gold hoops, and a few spritzes of my favorite Light Blue perfume before slipping into the sexy red heels from last night. Satisfied, I pull up the Rideo app then head downstairs.

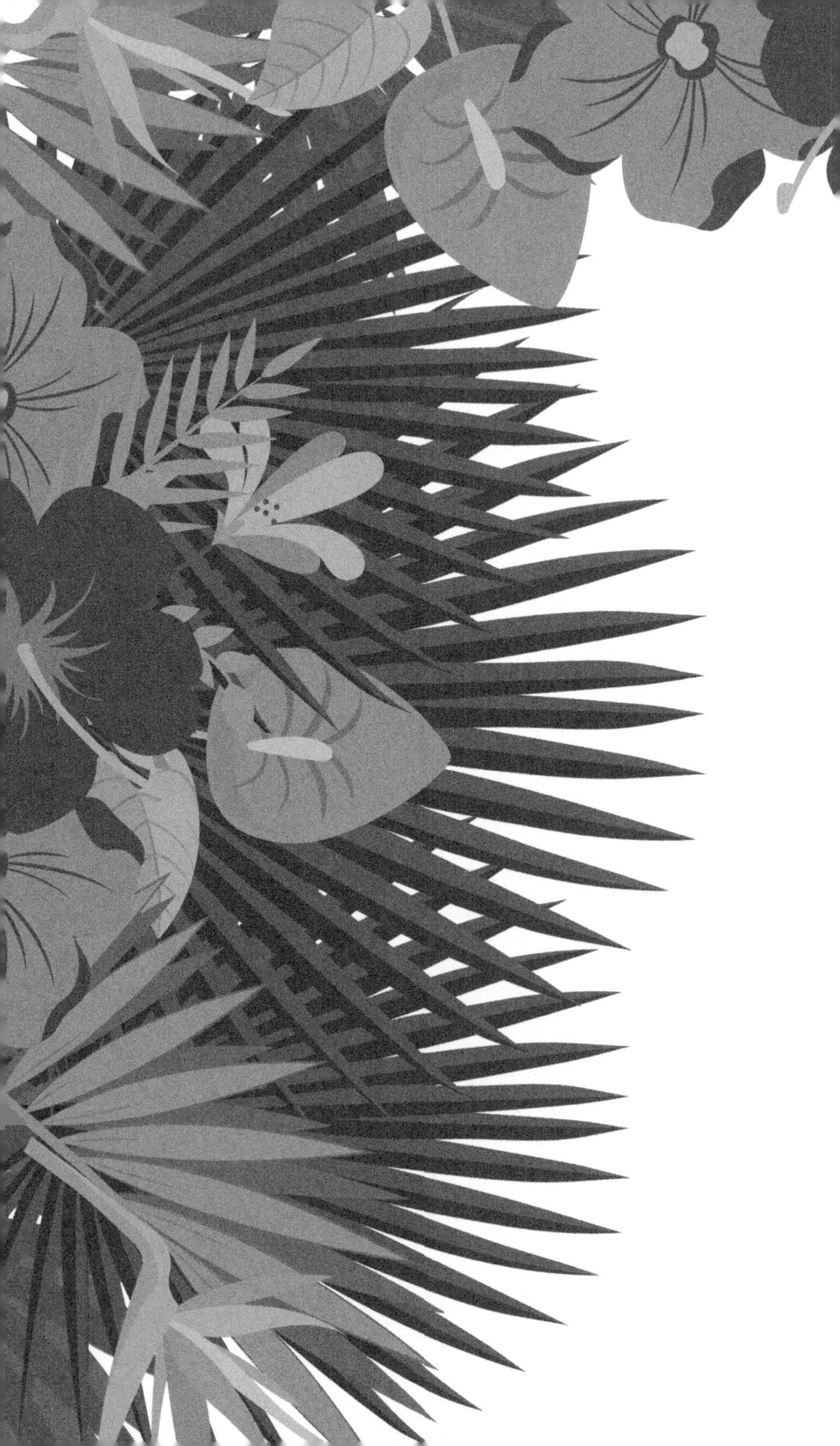

CHAPTER 5
Damon

Malone, Dawson, & Cook LLP isn't one of those traditional brick-and-mortar firms with the wood-grained walls, stately desks, and the name scrawled in gold across a formidable wall. We're a small outfit in a revitalized downtown high-rise. Like the up-and-coming wedding planning company that we share the sixth floor with to cut costs, our offices are bright, relaxed, and furnished with solid, yet not-too-heavy, modern furniture in pops of red, and enclosed in glass walls. Which is why I see Lea the second I step off the elevator.

Here goes nothing.

She's just outside her office, waiting with one hand on the door to close it behind me and the other dug into her scalp with a handful of hair like her nerves are shot.

I take a deep breath, flash Alyssa, the receptionist at Fallon Events, a quick smile, then turn to enter Lea's office.

I hope to hell this isn't about Allegra.

"First things, first. What happened with Allegra?" Lea asks as soon as I settle onto a chair facing her desk.

The snick of the door closing—and locking—sends panic

washing over me. Every muscle in my body tightens as I hedge my body to her.

"How's she doing after the Kyle catastrophe?" Lea asks. "Also, did you listen to me and tell her how you feel about her, or are we sticking with the two-decade plan?"

She scoots her chair closer to look at me. Right off the bat, I get the sense she knows more than she's letting on.

"So, you haven't talked to her?" I fish out my vibrating phone from my pants pocket.

Another message from Sheraton Private Investigators, the company my foster family hired to reach out to me.

I send it to voicemail like I always do, lifting my chin to meet Lea's intense gaze.

She flattens her palms together and presses them to her lips, still considering my answer. Or rather, my question. *Damn it.*

"No," she tilts her head with interest. "I figured, I'd let you take the lead on this one, but since you answered my question with a question..." She purses her lips and cocks her head, giving me an expression that says, my resistance would be less futile if I didn't fall into old avoidance habits.

With a small, guilty chuckle, I release a heavy exhale.

"Kyle admitted he was seeing someone else. Al gave him a piece of her mind, drank an entire bottle of wine, then came onto me—"

"Hold it. Define 'came onto' you," Lea says, fact-gathering. She's reading—more accurately, misinterpreting—my body language.

I slouch into the chair, running both hands along the cool metal arms, unwilling to meet Lea's assessing gaze. "She said she needed me while pulling close to me underneath the sheets. But I stopped her—"

"Uh, huh. Nope! Y'all totally hooked up—"

"No." It comes out sharp, defensive. "What the hell do I

look like trying to fuck my best friend while she's drunk and vulnerable?" I scrub my hand over my head, releasing a frustrated sigh. "Damn, Le. I care about her. I'm not trying to be some other dude's stand-in... You all are the only family I have. I'm not willing to lose her over a quick fuck. If we ever get the chance to be more, I want us to be for the long haul."

"I know," she nods, sighing softly. Her attention drifts to her computer screen for a second, but then she looks at me again. "So, nothing happened? Like, you didn't tell her you've been in love with her forever?"

The temptation to answer her question with a question claws its way from my chest, clogging my throat. But I think about Allegra and how we agreed not to make a big deal about the kiss. I think about how it took every ounce of my restraint not to let her drag down her panties and give her everything she wanted. How I almost did tell her how I feel outside the bathroom door earlier.

I bite the inside of my cheek and force myself to meet Lea's stare. "No, I didn't say anything," I grind out, letting the truth dissolve on my tongue.

Her gaze snaps to mine, the corners of her mouth twitching.

"Okay, I won't press you, but I don't know why you think you can lie to me. I'll be able to tell immediately when Allegra gets here, so..."

This time, I laugh outright.

"Was there a real 911 or did you just want to get me here to dig for lowdown, dirty details about your best friends?"

The switch from playful mode to business is visible in Lea's entire demeanor. Her posture goes ramrod straight—shoulders back, head up, dilated eyes glued to her computer screen as her fingers tap dance across the keys.

"Oh, it's real. Three-fold now," she says, angling the

monitor to face me across her desk. "While you and Allegra were playing footsies beneath the sheets, your girl was being shady as hell. She quit this morning in an email."

I scoot to the edge of my chair, confusion creasing my brow as I zero in on the sender. "Trish quit?"

"Read all three lines she probably threw together on her phone while taking her morning shit—like we didn't give her an opportunity when no one else did or help build up her resumé. Like Allegra wasn't about to suggest we take her on full time." Lea fumes, but I know it's just the hurt talking.

Trish was her first hire, and Lea had gone to bat for her during the interviews, despite her unprofessional clothes and gum-popping. Lea recognized her drive when Allegra and I were still on the fence.

Searching the body of the email for an explanation, I find none. It's the standard, thanks for the opportunity template. The "effective immediately" part throws me for a loop, though.

When I'm finished, I sit back, considering what this means for our caseload when we'll already be short-handed while Allegra's in Hawaii. I rub my hand over the scruff of my jaw. "Do you have an idea where she's going? Has she mentioned any headhunters reaching out to her?"

"Nope." Lea lowers her head, scratching her scalp. Then it occurs to me she said the 911 was real.

"Wait. You said the problem was three-fold..."

"I did indeed." Lea swivels her chair to the other side of her U-shaped glass desk, where she grabs a stack of files. "These are the ones Trish was working on, including a claim from Chat-Video owned by a woman named..." She flips the file open, staring at its contents. "Laura Hammond."

My throat tightens as my mind reels through all the calls I've ignored from the P.I. with whom I said I didn't want any contact. *Would the Hammonds take it this far? Would they hire my firm to file a bogus claim against ViddyChat just to open the lines of communication again?*

Lea continues, oblivious to anxiety snaking through me. "The woman's claiming trademark infringement against Viddychat, so now I have to wonder if there's a conflict of interest. We haven't taken the case yet, but did ViddyChat plant Trish here as a paralegal to shut down ChatVideo's claim against them?"

My head throbs as I try to focus on what Lea's saying. Before I ask what she means by conflict of interest, she groans aloud, clicking a tiny thumbnail at the bottom of her screen.

"Behold, problem number three. She posted this five minutes ago."

At first, I'm confused about why Lea's showing me her Instagram. But then I realize it's Trish's post. She's at a fancy restaurant in a short, tight purple dress. Her long, wild, honey-brown hair is down, and her dark doe eyes glitter with excitement. But then I look closer at the caption.

ABOUT LAST NIGHT...HE PUT A RING ON IT!

Fuck. Give me a break.

"Is she wearing—?"

"Yup," Lea answers my unfinished question by swiping to the next picture of...newly engaged Kyle and Trish. At Mots Doux. "That's the same two-carat monstrosity Allegra tried on last night in her closet while that dickweed was preparing to discard and replace her with a two-faced b—" Lea's attention flies over my head for a second before she yanks her screen around and clicks a few times. "Shit, Al's here," she whispers.

I shove aside all thoughts of Kyle, Trish, and the PI. I need to focus on the people who matter to me.

Turning, I catch sight of Allegra chitchatting with Alyssa,

and my entire body comes to attention. A caffeine buzz washes over me, remembering the thrilling torture of the fit and feel of her body pressed to mine last night. She isn't wearing my T-shirt and sweats, but she looks amazing in a professional yet sexy red dress and heels. She's beaming. Her entire face is lit up with a smile I hope I had a hand in putting there.

"Mm-hmm," Lea mutters knowingly. *"Something happened."*

Since I'm closest to the door, I stand and unlock it quickly before her suspicions arise. I have no clue how Lea's going to play this, but I'm happy to take a backseat.

Allegra shuffles inside Lea's office and plops down onto the chair next to me, facing Lea.

"What'd I miss? What's the 911?" she asks, her gaze darting between Lea and me as we share a look. "Shit. It's bad, isn't it? The last time you two looked at each other like that, Kosher Crew was breaking up." She blows out a quick breath that blends into a shaky laugh. "Lay it on me. Leave nothing out."

"It's about Trish..."

Al laughs it off, holding her chest.

"Dang, you all scared me. She texted me like an hour ago. Where is she?" When Lea pins me with a wide-eyed stare, Allegra stops in her tracks. "Okay, now you all really are making me nervous. What happened?"

Then, to my surprise, Lea tells her.

For the next ten minutes, she goes over the details of the three-fold shitshow. The resignation letter, the case files, Trish's Viddychat review—which Lea assures her she'll review while Allegra is in Hawaii—and finally the Instagram pictures Trish posted.

The entire time, Allegra's reactions escalate from hair touching to chest rubbing, to full flush creeping across her cheeks in embarrassment. Then she glances at me and excuses herself to the restroom.

Lea taps the table to get my attention.

"You know how she is when she's like this." Her tone is hushed, and her gaze darts over my shoulder. "There's no way in hell we can leave her alone at a wedding. You need to go with her to Hawaii tomorrow."

"Me?" *No.*

"Yes, you," she says, focusing on Allegra and me when we've had Trish here doing lord knows what. She could've been compiling confidential information. "We need to worry about what Trish shared with ViddyChat."

Lea slices her hands through the air. "It'll be fine. We haven't even taken on the claim, yet. The most she got was ChatVideo's address and some allegations, but I'll review everything again and follow up with the company to see if there's any validity to the claim."

I nod, relaxing a bit.

I can't go to Hawaii with Allegra.

It's bad enough that I got caught up in the moment kissing her. I can't be at a destination wedding surrounded by a blissfully happy wedding party with Allegra. And now with her stuff at my place...I don't want to confuse things any more than they already are. I can't lose this family.

Fuck.

"What about the rest of the caseload?" I'm grasping at straws. *Why don't we leave the ChatVideo case to another firm?* That's what I'm really asking. "I can stay behind, take care of Trish's files. You go with Al. It'll give you all chance to have some girl time without me."

"Uh, nice try. It's a long weekend. You'll be back by Tuesday. We can tackle everything on Trio Wednesday." She shrugs, but I sense this is all part of her anti-two-decade grand plan.

She'll work overtime if it means she doesn't have to listen to me pining for Allegra. "And for the record, I'm going to need you to take her down from the pedestal you put her on. Allegra is human—a fragile one, at the moment—but you all belong together."

I scrub a hand over my face, frustrated about the timing of this case, and considering Lea's word choice.

"Yes, I said, 'belong.'" She challenges me with a stare, adding a smug half-grin to drill in her point.

Lea and Allegra don't know the names of my foster family because those people never earned the title. But Lea knows it's the word my foster mom, Jan, used.

For a year, I wasn't the quiet kid sitting on the bed in the corner waiting to be noticed. I didn't look like them with my brown skin and dark hair, but I *belonged* to the Hammond family. I was just as much Jan's and Gary's kid as blonde and blue-eyed Laura, she'd said. She was going to make it official, too, which I was hard-pressed to believe. How many kids headed for adoption had I crossed paths with over the years while wishing for a forever home and a real human connection? It didn't seem likely. Then Jan filed the legal intent to adopt petition, and reluctantly, I let my hopes rise.

I was finally going to belong to a family. I'd get to call a house my home, and I'd share it with a doting mother, father, and a sister, who was cool for a girl.

One minute they're starting the adoption process, and the next Child and Family Services is taking me away.

The Hammonds gave me back.

I spent the rest of my youth getting passed from home to group home until I aged out of the system in extended foster care. I learned that pipe dreams are just that, dreams with no take-backs, not even if that family has continued trying to connect through a P.I. for the past twenty-five years.

I focus on reality, and beyond The Trio, I never get too comfortable trying to belong.

With The Trio, majority rules. I'm hoping that suing her ex is an instant no for Allegra. Maybe while we're in Hawaii, I can convince her to vote against taking the ChatVideo case, too.

"All right, I'll go." I flash Lea a grateful smile, then give it a few more seconds of lead time before I go after Allegra.

* * *

After a minute waiting outside the women's restroom, it's quiet. I rap the back of my knuckles against the door.

"Al, it's me," I say. "Is this going to be a thing with us, talking through bathroom doors? If so, should I bring the mints and cheap cologne?"

A small, emotion-choked laugh rumbles through the door before the light pad of her footsteps grows closer. Her head is hung low, and her golden-brown cheeks smeared a bright pink as she opens the door just enough to let me inside.

"Is there any chance you won't," a tiny hiccup spills into her words, "be here every time my life takes a sharp, downward dive into hell?"

"Not one," I reassure her, tipping up her chin and pulling her into a hug. She lets the full weight of her leaden body lean into me. I feel a twinge of guilt, loving the chance to be her support system on this level.

After every breakup, heartbreak, knockdown, Lea and I've been around to clean up—tears, discarded clothes, wine bottles and pizza boxes strewn across the "adorable" rental home of moment. I've dropped by with ice cream or chicken wings with ranch dressing and Louisiana hot sauce, depending on her mope craving. But Lea always got to hug her tightly, hear the first laugh through tears or to dance to happy music, and to talk about what comes next...

"I'm glad it was you who came," Allegra says.

Her warm breaths ease, evening out against my neck as I rub circles on her back. "Me, too."

"Trish texted earlier. She wanted to know where I was. I thought she was already here. Just 'checking in, being a friend' after what happened last night. You know?" She huffs out a mirthless laugh. "Then I, stupidly, texted her back, telling her I'd bring her up to speed on everything that's happened—"

"Everything?" I hike up an eyebrow.

She winces. "Um, no. Please don't make me regret telling you this."

I chuckle.

Allegra pushes out of my arms, swatting my shoulder playfully. She scrubs her hand over her face, shaking her head.

"See..." She laughs through her tears. "I'm trying to have a heart to heart, and you're over here stroking your giant ego." Her expression is a mix of humor and humiliation, and I'm here for every second.

"All right, I'm sorry." I hold my hands up. "Finish what you were saying." I don't expect it, but Allegra walks back into my open arms, wrapping hers tightly around my waist and resting her head on my shoulder.

Her perfume bands around me—a clean citrus and cedar scent that makes me want to cling to her.

"Anyway, it makes sense now," she says, all the laughter dissolving as she relaxes against me. "Kyle was gathering boxes the past few days for donations. Not once did I see him put any of his stuff in them. All this time, he was planning my exit. Which means, last night, in between dumping me at Mots Doux and proposing to Trish, when the coast was clear, his courier service was packing my things."

"Damn, Al. I'm sorry."

"When I texted her where I was this morning, all he needed was the delivery address—she helped him erase the last of me." She sucks in a lungful of air. "Obviously, it's a good thing I'll be in a whole other state tomorrow, so I won't be tempted to hunt her down...but it's the betrayal from two people I trusted that hurts the most."

For a few moments, I let the quiet soothe her, softening the sharp edges of the truth.

"Bright side?"

Allegra releases a small laugh. "Is there a bright side?"

"You got an awesome new roommate," I say.

"There is that." She squeezes me tighter, her shoulders shaking. "If only I didn't grind myself against him in a horny, alcohol-fueled moment of shame."

"Hmm. Maybe you can make it up to him in Hawaii..." At this, Allegra gasps, looking up at me. "We thought you might need a plus-one upgrade."

Allegra eyes me sheepishly. "And you don't mind? You sure you're ready to Electric Slide and Cupid Shuffle with my family? Because they will expect a lot from a former Kosher Crew front man. I'm just saying..."

I flash her my most stern, screwed mouth, "What you talkin' 'bout, Willis" expression from our days bingeing the television show *Diff'rent Strokes*. But it lands about as hard as a feather.

"For the last time, I don't do empty promises, Allegra Marie Malone. Don't tell Aaron, but Mama Malone told me I'm like the sweet, level-headed son she never had. I can't wait to cut a rug with her." I kiss her forehead. "Anyway, I said I'd do anything for you, and I meant it."

From the bottom of my traitorous heart.

Allegra's phone pings.

Then pings again.

And again, and again.

She slips it from her pocket, then takes one look at the screen before letting her shoulders sag at her sides with a groan. "And so it begins," she says. Flipping it to me, there are five messages and counting, from family and friends who she says follow Kyle on social media, wanting to know if Allegra needs them to put a contract out on Kyle or buy him a new pair of cement shoes.

So, yeah. A vulnerable Allegra and me in Hawaii.

Should be fun.

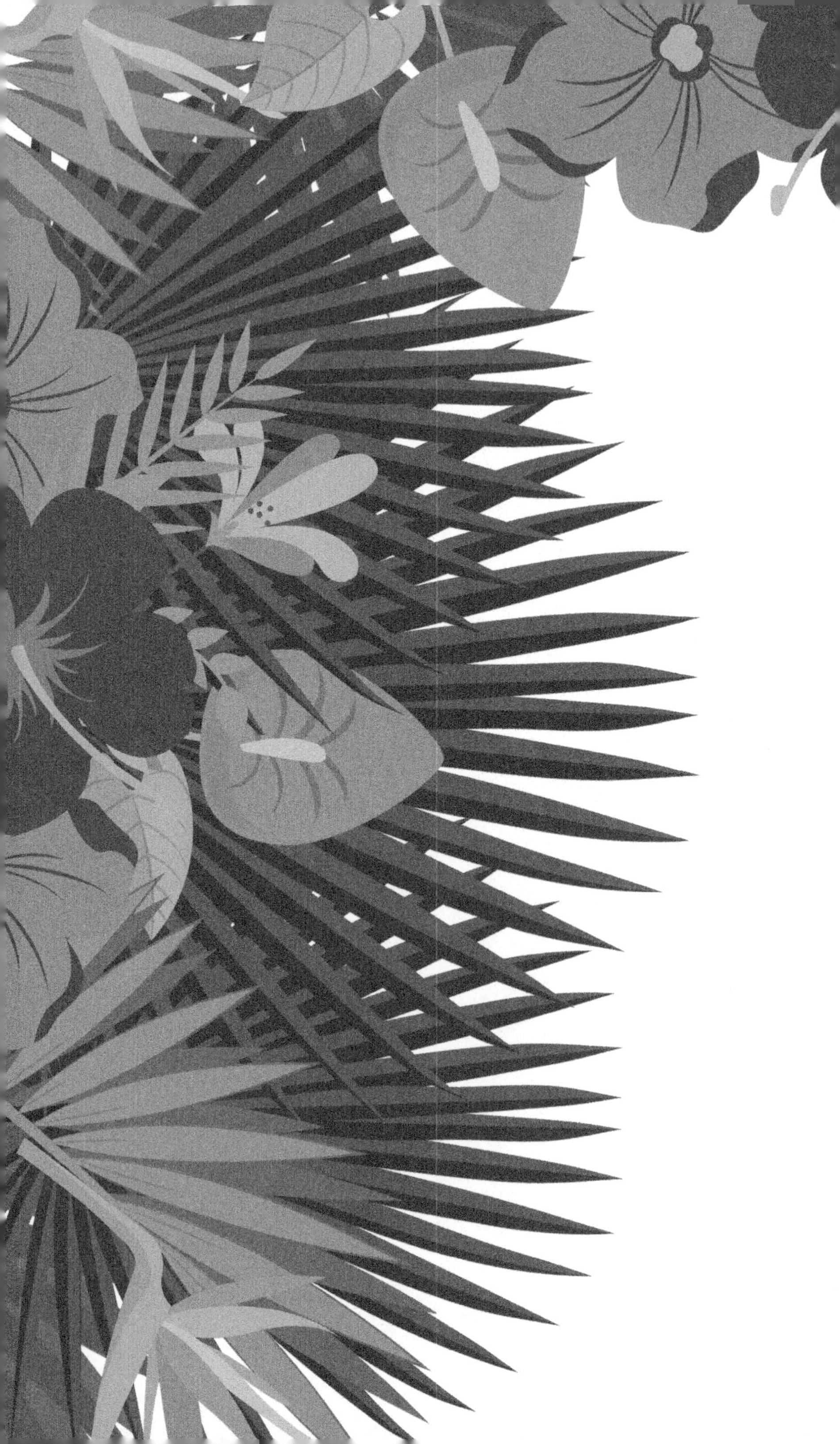

CHAPTER 6
Allegra

We made it through the night without any incidents. After shelling out a ton of miles and haggling with the airline, we were not only able to book Damon on the flight, but we got business class seats together. All of which, zapped our energy, leaving us to watch a full *Godfather* trilogy marathon—seated on opposite ends of the couch—to recover.

I'm counting it as a win.

But this morning we're at McCarran Airport, boarding a seven o'clock flight bound for five days in a tropical paradise to celebrate love while my libido is still pissed at me.

I slept on the couch.

Alone.

I toss a glance a few steps ahead at Damon's cute butt in his "comfy travel sweats" and bite down hard on my lip.

"Physical appreciation cannot be the only key point," I remind myself. *Though his presence on this trip is powerful evidence of thoughtfulness and affection.*

I roll my suitcase forward, then come to a stop next to him. I'm still tucking my ID back into its wallet slot when, for the umpteenth time, my phone vibrates. For my sanity, I finally turned off the volume. It's yet another concerned message from a family member who has neither met nor heard of Kyle. This time, it's my twice-removed cousin, Terry, the nosy pot-stirrer. So, for the umpteenth time plus one, I ignore the phone.

I'll see most of them in six hours. At which point, I'll effectively defer all Q&A for Aaron and Piper's sake...or until I think of a more permanent solution.

I text Mom that we're boarding so she doesn't worry, then pull down the widgets at the top of the screen. "Airplane mode is a magical invention," I say, tossing Damon an energetic smile as he inches forward in the line again.

"They'll all be waiting when we land," he reassures me, blowing out a breath as he seems to realize the truth in his statement. "I'm wondering if this was a good idea—"

"It's too late now." I shrug. "They've already closed the sky bridge doors, so you're stuck."

He snaps his fingers, feigning disappointment. "Dang it."

After a few minutes, we're making our way to our economy seats. We have the row to ourselves, so I take the window and he takes the aisle to put off any seat hoppers until takeoff. After he's stowed our suitcases in the overhead bin above us and I've tucked my purse and his backpack beneath the seats in front of us, we settle in for the flight.

"So, what's your plan?" Damon asks, shifting to face me once the plane's leveled off at cruising altitude.

"The plan?"

He reclines his seat and slips his neck pillow in place, getting comfortable.

"About the Kyle situation?"

"The thing is, I don't want to focus on me or Kyle or Trish or the fact that you're stuck with me as a roommate. This is Aaron's wedding. My brother and his blushing bride deserve to have a drama-free weekend. And Piper is so freaking quiet. She won't say anything, but she'll shoot me one of her wide-eyed, quiet stares like she's berating me on the inside." I huff out a laugh. "Believe me, that kind of spotlight is never welcome."

A flight attendant stops by our row to take our complimentary drink order and offer us an array of sandwiches and snacks for purchase. We both opt for sodas and the cheese and cracker platter. We'll eat a proper meal when we get to Kauai.

My mind keeps reeling over what to say to my family. How can I explain that my life just got turned upside down? Talking about it will only make me want to break down.

"What's going on in that head of yours?" Damon asks, jolting me from my thoughts.

"How I really, *really* wish we could just stay in the air." I laugh. "Like, if that was an option...I don't know. Can we talk about something else? Something happy, preferably."

Damon closes his eyes, probably still tired from waking up so early.

"Tell me about where we're staying. The hotel, the grounds and ocean views, the beds..." He trails off, so I'm halfway certain he doesn't notice me panicking about our accommodations.

"Okay, Piper picked it, so you know it's a five-star location." I laugh more to myself than about my bridezilla sister-in-law to be. "Let's see, the website said it's a luxury resort and spa. The pictures online show absolutely gorgeous white sand beaches, tropical gardens, like a dozen pools to choose from..."

"What about the room and the beds?"

"Well...about that."

His heavy-lidded brown eyes flutter open. "What's wrong with the beds?"

"Nothing is *wrong* with the *bed*." I enunciate the word, cringing. When Damon says nothing, I continue, needing to explain. "Look, I know this is going to be weird after the other night, but I tried to change to a double. They're all sold out, but..." I dig in my purse for a pen and my journal, skimming for a blank page. "I have an idea..." *That just might give my case some legs.*

At this, Damon presses the button to put his seat back in the upright position.

"By all means, I'm on pins and needles," he says.

"Seriously, D. I've been thinking about it a lot—this, us, all that's happened, *happening* with us." I click my pen and crease the page, scrawling in bold blue caps across the top and underlining it. "If we think about this from a purely logical perspective, we're two people under extenuating circumstances, right?"

"Sure."

"We're close. Some would say we're more family than friends, and one of us, me, is receiving support from the other: you. It makes sense that a kiss would complicate matters between two single adults who care tremendously for one another. Except..." I'm on a roll, rambling, but based on Damon's deadpan face, the jury seems to be still out. "Now, we're friends, roommates, wedding dates, and in a handful of hours, hotel bed buddies."

Even I wince at what sounds like fresh hell coming from my mouth.

Damon's lips twitch, but he fans his hand out for me to continue.

I hold up my palms against the air. "Fine, that sounds bad, but you get the point. Our friendship just got put to the test in multiple ways. So, my proposal is—" I stop myself, shaking my head, feeling a brand-new aversion to that word, then start again. "My *solution* is—"

"A friendship contract?" Damon's attention shifts to my journal, reading the title I've jotted down.

"Yes," I say, lowering my chin and squaring my shoulders to him before I look up. "A real one. It won't be like a business deal or anything. But you must admit, we know contracts and compliance. We abide by them, we enforce. It only makes sense to draw up rules to keep us focused on what matters..." But even as I say it, an idea springs to mind that could rightly solve everything.

"Whatever you're thinking, it's scaring me," D mutters.

I press my fingers to my lips, focusing on the vision forming in my head.

At first, I thought we'd put together some rules about creating a pillow barrier between us in the hotel bed. He'd agree not to share longing stares or check out my ass when he thinks I'm not looking, and I'd avoid rubbing it on his morning wood. *And checking out his ass.* But this...it would accomplish all of that while keeping Aaron and Piper in the spotlight.

And build my case.

"Before you say anything, hear me out." I take a deep breath. "My whole family knows things just ended with Kyle, right? They wouldn't think twice about me bringing you as a new plus one. But that's not going to stop them from talking about what Kyle did. Or asking where I'm living and every other question under that sun that's not about Aaron and Piper on their wedding weekend."

"So..."

"What if we pretend we just started a new relationship?" I blurt out.

For a second, it's not clear whether Damon hears me because he stares at me blankly again. But then his brow creases like he's just realized that's the whole idea and I'm not playing a horrible prank on him.

"What..." He stops himself, screwing his lips to the side, I'm guessing considering his next line of questioning. "I get how that'll distract from the Kyle and Trish situation. I'm just failing to understand how it's a solution for our friends and roommates complication."

Complication?

In my mind, it couldn't be clearer. But how do I explain this to him in a way that doesn't make him feel like he's being used? *Even more.*

I tilt my head to either side, acknowledging his perspective.

"If the other night proved anything, it's that we have chemistry, right?" I ask, marking a series of bullet points beneath the title. "So, finally getting together is completely believable. My family already loves you. They'd be ecstatic for us, which means they wouldn't give a second thought to the Kyle mess, and they'll know I'm safe living with you."

Plus, I get to build an unobstructed case for love on a trial basis.

"You really think this is a good idea?" Damon asks.

"Yes. I know it sounds like my head is all over the place, but we tell them that Kyle and I broke up, that you and I realized how good we were together, so I moved in with you. Simple." *And not an outright lie.* "Beyond that, we dance, eat cake, and celebrate all the wedding festivities."

All humor fades from his expression.

"Simple as that, huh? Open-and-shut case." He stares at me with that far-off look he sometimes gives me, like he's subliminally telling me the simplest decisions are the ones that always end with the most at stake.

The earnest, pleading look in his eyes melts me, and I know rules aren't optional.

I feel too much for Damon.

"We don't have to get wild with it." I shrug, releasing a

shaky laugh. It seems too simple, like the solution's been here all along. "When we're out of eyesight, we abide by a distinct set of rules..."

Damon tilts his head to read the first bullet point. "Tell no one." Except Lea, I mentally add. That's followed up with "No sex." *Because, duh. What's the point of faking it if we're getting really* real?

I turn to him, feeling encouraged. Our plan is taking shape. "So far, so good. What else?"

He unfastens his seatbelt and scoots into the middle seat. If he's doing anything, he's doing it with intention. "No holding hands," he says completely serious.

"Um...handholding?"

"It's too intimate," he explains. "Something about the gentle touch feels close and sexy, almost like foreplay. It means something deeper."

I swallow and nod. I'm blindsided by a rush of hot fire radiating between us. The air feels like it's charged with electricity. How does he make something I'd do with my grandmother or one of my young cousins sound like it needs an adult-only rating?

Shit.

I turn and jot down, "no handholding" next to the third bullet point.

Over the next hour, we hammer out a few more, including "no catching feelings," "The Trio comes first," and "daily check-ins" to see how we're feeling about the contract on the friendship meter. Finally, we hash out the details of how we're going to act at the wedding.

Newly, desperately in love, obviously.

It'll be a performance, but I don't doubt we'll have a problem pulling off when we both sign and date the bottom of the page to make it binding and official, or when Damon doesn't return to the aisle seat, or when we share his blanket and EarPods in the darkened cabin during the inflight movie, or as we doze off with my head resting on his shoulder and his head on mine, and certainly not when he kisses me on the forehead before he falls into a restful sleep.

Nope, not one piece of admissible evidence in the lot.

* * *

When we land in Honolulu, we have an hour before we need to be at the gate for our connection to Lihue Airport. With no plane change, we're luggage-free as we walk in serene silence to the food court, skipping the burger, fries, and pizza for The Honolulu Cookie Company because our priorities and endorphins are obviously in the right place. But then we remember we only had cheese and crackers during the flight and make a pit-stop at Chow Mein Express, which turns out to be a lucky decision.

We're helped by a super-cute cashier with the bright smile and flowing sheets of black hair who looks at us like we're bonafide celebrities after we tell her we're from Vegas. She asks about the resort where we're staying on Kauai, raves about the gardens I read about online, and encourages us to check out the ones here.

I had no clue that by "here" she meant inside the airport.

She draws a map of the terminal on a napkin, leading us to gorgeous cultural gardens on the grounds.

To our sheer amazement, it's not a tourist trap.

The second we step outdoors, we're hit with warm, fragrant breezes as we approach a red pavilion just like the ones in Hong Kong. It's surrounded by pine and bamboo trees with vibrant orange koi fish swimming in picturesque ponds.

"How did we not hear about this?" I ask, beaming up at

Damon.

"I don't know, but I feel like I'm already on vacation. I want to eat my Chinese food in this amazing Asian garden." He chuckles, lost in our surroundings. "How is this still part of the airport?"

We plop down on a bench and slurp lo mein noodles while we listen to birds chirping, and we soak up all the colorful, tropical foliage. I veto all attempts from Damon to bring up the ChatVideo/ViddyChat claim. If Lea finds any merit to it—Kyle or not—I'm in for the fight. For now, we wait for Lea's word, and let this garden officially set the tone for vacation.

When we're good and stuffed, we toss our containers in a trashcan and set a timer, intent on making it through the Japanese and Hawaiian gardens before we need to haul ass back to the gate.

It's quiet and empty, and it feels like we have the entire garden to ourselves.

Damon chases me across the zigzag bridge, tucked between more pine and swaying willow trees, teasing me the whole way.

"What kind of nerd makes up a friendship contract?" He touches his curled fingers to his head and does the "mind blown" gesture.

A man on a bench looks up from his book to laugh.

I'm quick to point out how *we* both signed it, so Damon's complicit in said act of shameless nerdery.

"You snore!" he calls from up ahead, laughing a full body laugh, rumbling over his shoulders. "Also, I hate to tell you this," he stops, holding his stomach as I slow to winded stroll, "the corners of your mouth were glistening back there on the plane, so you're a drooler nerd."

"I don't drool!" I yell back, gaining on him as we zip over waterways full of carp and past stone lanterns that I'd die to witness at dusk. "Whatever, D. At least I don't chew with my mouth open..." *Like you've got no home training,* I almost say. I bite my tongue like I always do when I remember, growing up, he didn't have one.

He spent eighteen years house-hopping in the foster care system. After that, time was up. He was on his own, living in group homes, working two full-time jobs to put himself through online college before he applied to Boyd. Then Lea and I and our families became his family.

When I reach the entrance to the Hawaiian garden, Damon is staring straight ahead, waiting for me at the end of the bridge. "About time you showed up." He nudges my shoulder, smiling the adorable half-grin that makes my stomach flip.

The garden is more than pathways, bridges, and stepping-stones connecting to other gardens. It's a lagoon with waterfalls cascading over lava walls, more koi fish, banana and coconut palms, exotic ferns, ginger, and monstera. The birds of paradise are so bright and beautiful, I'd lose my words trying to describe them.

"I wish we could see this place at night," he says, the wistful tone of his voice drawing my attention to him.

I catch myself watching Damon, replaying the fun easiness we shared today, his lighthearted expressions, and his low, rumbly laugh. In the light, his eyes aren't just brown. Up close, they're an unsettling deep amber hue. Against his warm cinnamon complexion, they seem to have fiery flares in their depths. Then there's the perfect outline of his lips I've *got* to kiss.

Presenting Exhibits B through at least H, all in one package, my heart contends.

"Me, too," I say, finally. "Do you think the friendship contract is stupid?" I ask after a beat.

"Nah, but the fake relationship feels forced," he says. His voice is low and easy. "Do you think Mama Malone is going to buy a fake relationship? You think Aaron won't see right through it?"

I let my arms sag at my sides with a sigh, sensing he's right. "Okay, let's scrap it."

"Good choice." He chuckles, flipping his wrist to check the time, and reminding me about Mom's text from before I turned my phone on airplane mode. She'd asked me to let her know we'd landed in Honolulu safely.

I look down and change the setting back, and my phone immediately vibrates like crazy with missed calls and texts... Instagram notifications.

"Brave, turning it back on." He dips his chin to look at my phone before turning back to the water.

"For like two seconds. Promised Mom I'd check in with her between flights."

He nods.

After I send the message, temptation gets the better of me. I can't help myself. I open Instagram, and I'm inundated with a flood of images and comments.

My throat closes.

I'm not sure how long I stare at the photo of Kyle and Trish, thinking about how they betrayed me, and the hurt I feel. *I need to unfollow them.* Seeing them also makes me think about the great time I've had with Damon these past couple days. Today has been a glimpse of light in the darkness. The instincts I inherited may not be that faulty after all if I've somehow ended up right where I'm supposed to be.

I get lost in my thoughts, and it's long enough for Damon to notice the photo on my phone.

He tosses me a quick glance, darting his gaze between me and the screen. His expression pinches. Something passes over his face I can't quite place. Hurt? Disappointment? I can't be sure.

My cheeks heat. "Hey."

He gives me a slow, disbelieving head shake.

I could analyze the strengths and weaknesses of us being together, but the hurt on Damon's face is the critical weakness undermining my case. You don't hurt the ones you love. It's the only objection that matters.

"The timer went off," he says, his tone clipped. "We need to get back to the gate." Then he turns away, walking toward the airport entrance.

"D." My voice cracks as I call after him.

My mouth goes dry, watching his weighted silhouette grow smaller as the distance between us widens. More than anything, I hate the idea I could hurt Damon. It's Thursday, and I've felt like I've been spinning in circles with my feet never quite reaching the ground since Tuesday. Nothing comes into clear focus.

But he's been here—the friend who genuinely wants the best for me.

How many times has Mom warned me I can't want something for another person more than they want it themselves? I've got to be better for him...for me.

For once, I need to focus on the most important key point. Damon has always been right by my side.

If today proved anything, we could work. *If I let us,* my heart objects.

I dig my nails into the palm of my hand, staring down at my feet before I work up the nerve to look back at my phone.

"Fuck it."

First, I unfollow and block Kyle on Instagram. Then I do the same with Trish. For good measure, I swipe to contacts, deleting them both as callers too. If I'm really gathering the facts to make a case for Damon and me, it's going to take more than a half-assed effort hidden behind the guise of a contract.

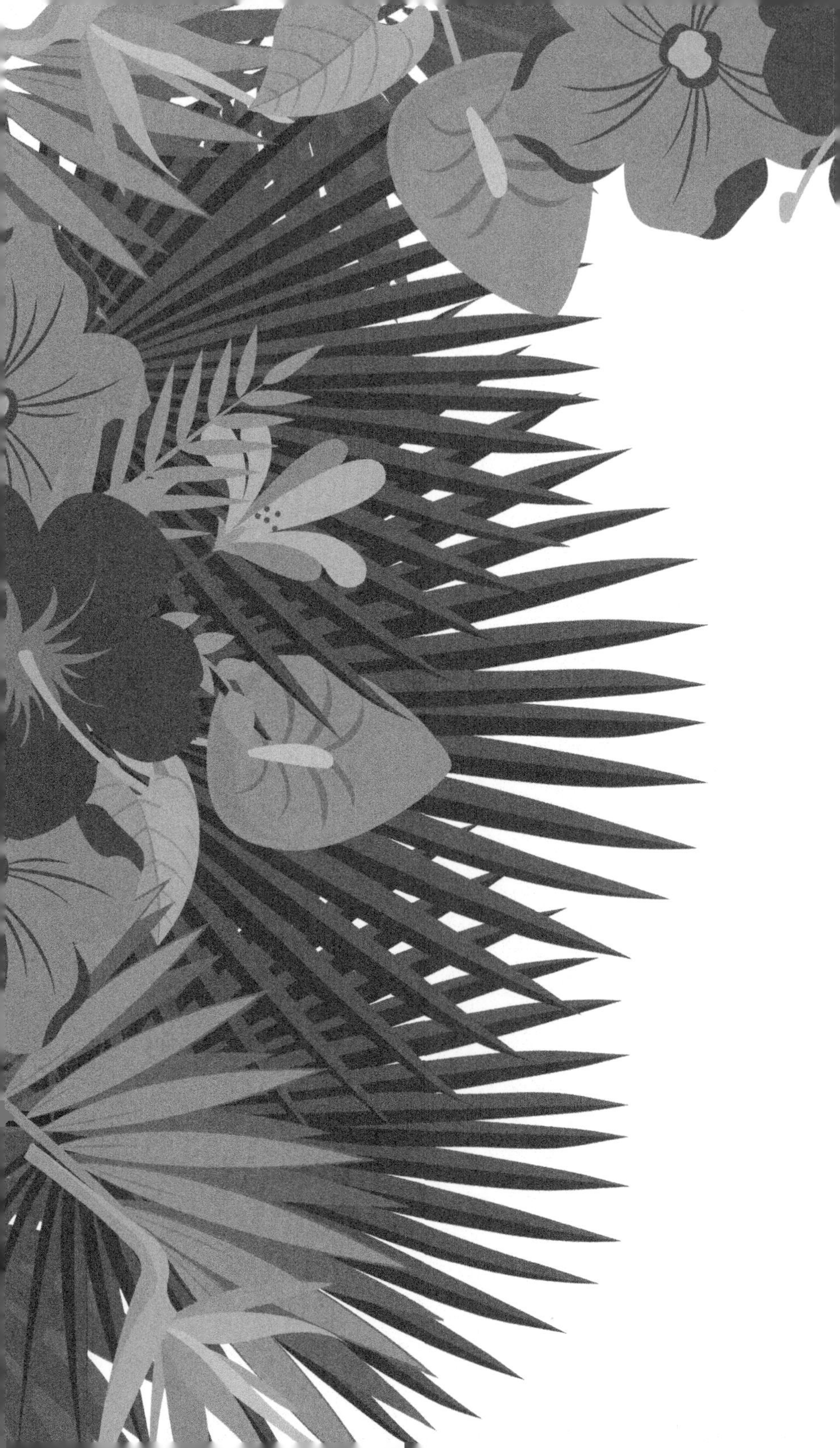

CHAPTER 7
Allegra

At the gate, I pour through my phone, through the texts and emails between Damon and me. It's all there. The language we use with each other—the familiar greetings and nicknames, the LOLs, all the happy emojis, the "just checking ins" and "is it cool if I drop bys." The times he'd brought food or talked about how much fun we'd had at this hole-in-the-wall bar or that wild party. The times we talked about absolutely nothing for hours and hours just because.

Then there's the invisible fine print—the argument no one can counter.

The time gaps when we had no digital correspondence because there was no need. After each of my failed relationships, Damon didn't need to text or email. He was physically with me—on my couch, in my kitchen, sitting on Mom's porch right next to me, laughing, listening, making sure I bounced back.

A weight settles behind my ribs, my heart determined to slip through the bars. How can this not be love?

"D, I don't know what happened back there, but I want to clear the air," I say after we board and settle in our seats.

I stare straight ahead because if I look at him, I'll lose my nerve.

Deep down, I feel like I need to say something to get us back on track before we're surrounded by my family and the moment is lost. But as much as I want to brush off those few minutes before we left the airport gardens, I know what Damon read into me looking at the photo of Kyle and Trish.

I want to blurt out that I unfollowed them because I want to explore these new feelings between us without the weight of my past crushing down on me and that all the facts are leaning toward an inarguable conclusion that Damon and I should be together.

"Please stop making a big deal. We're good," he says, turning to stare out the small window.

Wow, this flight really is short.

Outside, picturesque mountain ridges draped in tropical rainforests dip into the turquoise blue waters. Everything around us invites me to get into a vacation state of mind. But my head is still reeling from the disappointed expression on Damon's face as he'd walked out of the airport garden.

"Seriously? We've barely exchange two sentences since we left the garden."

My pulse quickens as he turns around to face me, looking exhausted by my attempts to talk about us.

Am I reading way too much into him walking away? Maybe it wasn't hurt or disappointment.

"So then...is something else bothering you?" I chew the inside of my cheek, searching his smooth expression.

"Al—"

The flight attendant cheerily makes her way back down the

aisle. With a sweet "*Mahalo*," she instructs us to prepare for landing.

We both smile as she flits a glance to seatbelts to ensure they're buckled, but when she leaves, the moment feels lost, and I feel like asking again will create a problem more than solve one. So, I shove aside the uneasy feeling in my stomach.

As the plane descends, I clutch the armrests wishing it was Damon's hand.

I don't press the issue as we land, deplane, and gather our luggage. On the hotel shuttle, we continue our stilted silence until we arrive at a luxurious resort that pictures could never do justice. Set along a white sand beach on the South shore, it looms through the palms with bustling greenery on a grand scale.

Waiting for me at the entrance is Mom, Piper, and a line of dark-haired clones that are all Skipper-doll-height and stature with perky ponytails. They're wearing painted-on smiles and tasteful pale pink bridesmaid sashes.

Behind them, Aaron is with his guys, and they're all dressed for sun and fun.

"Last chance. If you want to talk about anything..." I say to Damon as I stand and loop my purse strap over my shoulder. I dart my gaze outside the shuttle window. "We probably won't see each other for a bit. Mom said Piper's wedding weekend itinerary is *serious*." A shaky laugh spills from me.

"I'll bet it is," he says.

I hate how self-conscious I feel when I've never let anything come between us before.

"Anyway, there's a bridesmaid luncheon and shopping scheduled before we return. Then it's time to change for the bachelorette party tonight. I'm sure Aaron's lined up a bunch of excursions and beach activities for the guys, too, so..."

"Al, I promise. *We're* good," Damon says, but there's no conviction in his tone.

I nod, biting back the emotion clogging my throat.

Disappointment settles in my stomach as I toss him one last pleading stare before I exit the shuttle.

Immediately, I'm hugged and kissed as introductions and pleasantries are exchanged with the few women I don't already know. Most of them are Piper's sorority sisters or coworkers. Since we have a few more hours before check-in, Mom arranges for the bell person to stow Damon's and my luggage in her room so we're free to jump right in.

Because we're on a schedule (which I hear with a British accent despite the fact that Piper is from Orange County), I'm handed an honorary sash with the words "Sister of the Groom" embroidered on it. *And* a folder.

It's an actual three-ring binder with hole-punched pages of color-coded and tabbed "essentials." It includes a by-the-half-hour "Malone/Yates Wedding Weekend" itinerary, nearby restaurants, a resort map complete with event key, and the reception music playlist...just in case Damon and I want to choreograph an extravagant duet dance-off in the middle of the cake-cutting.

You never know.

Except, now, I do.

As we weave through the resort's acres of picturesque gardens and inviting pools toward what I'm told is a secluded stretch of grass overlooking a sunny beach, I think about Damon... It's strange, but I miss him already. *I've been missing him since we left Honolulu...*

A warm gust of air swarms over my skin as I fall in step with Mom.

"So, how was your flight?" Mom asks sweetly as we lag behind the group. I sense the urgency in her tone. We've got maybe a couple more minutes before we're stuck at a table eating teensy cucumber sandwiches with the crust cut off and petit fours to accompany Earl Grey tea, knowing Piper's pride and sensibility.

"It was nice. Quiet." *Too quiet.*

Mom tosses me a sidelong glance. "Did you forget your earrings today?"

I reach up to my bare lobe, tracing my finger over the spot where the earrings Kyle gave me used to be. I never took them off when we were together.

"I forgot to put some on," I say.

"Mmm... And how are things?"

I bite back a laugh, turning to my adorable little mommy.

Pamela Malone—or Mama Malone to the masses—is beautiful and brilliant. Unlike me, she's a "hope-full romantic," as she likes to call it. She asked for, believed in, and received a lot of "almosts," though none of them, including my father, ever stuck. So, the two of us became the "pair of happy shoes." We aren't the same, but we're certainly each other's mirror image —complementary counterparts. Later, we became the tripod when Aaron came along, but he still likes to joke about how much he hates being the third shoe.

His dad didn't stick, either.

"*Things,*" I mock Mom's syrupy sweet voice, "are as they should be. I'm here with my family at a stunning luxury resort ready to celebrate my brother's nuptials to a woman he loves."

Her big brown eyes crinkle around the edges of her fair, brown cheeks. "Mmm hmm... You know, it would be nice to hear about my daughter's life from her instead of the twitters and posts," she mumbles.

I sense we're at an impasse. Either I tell her what's going on in my life, or she'll fill in the blanks—correctly or not.

"Look, I know everyone's seen Instagram, but it's really no

big deal," I say, hating that I've resorted to Damon's failsafe response. But the fewer lies I tell Mom, the fewer regrets I'll have to add to my mounting list. "Kyle and I are over, and he's moved on. The end."

Please, just leave it there.

Because she's my mother, who follows her gut, she keeps pressing.

"Are you and my Damon going through something?" *My Damon?* "I noticed you two weren't as friendly as you usually are when you're together." She releases a sigh as she tosses me a sidelong glance. "Are you two...an item?" The inflection in her voice rising hopefully as she grazes her fingertips over her chest.

Now, Mom is a less credible witness than, say, a friend or a brother who has seen Damon and me together and sensed something more between us. But she's here, and I need every testimony I can get at this point.

"No, Mom," I say. "We're friends."

I like to say I got faulty instincts from Mom, but they're more like scenic-route instincts—they take the long way around, eventually making it to the destination. From her stuffy strawberry-wallpapered kitchen, this woman—who barely comes up to my shoulder and still prefers a flip phone—created an all-natural haircare line of moisturizing shampoos and conditioners, scalp oils, and curl enhancers. She did it based on a gut feeling long before natural hair products were moved from the dusty back-corner convenience store shelves to the main aisle. *And before someone recognized the growth potential of her business and copied and pasted on a new label to undercut her burgeoning success.*

When your mother is wronged, it stays with you. Sometimes, it even builds legal careers.

All's well now.

She flashes me a curious expression.

"He's my best friend." I'm clinging to the edges of the truth about Damon and me. I'm not all the way clear on the truth myself given how things were on the connecting flight, but she doesn't need to know the lines between Damon and me are blurring.

"Okay." She barely contains her smile.

"But Mom, this is Aaron and Piper's wedding weekend," I rush to add. "Damon and I really don't want to take the spotlight off them—"

"Sure thing." She waves me off, but her entire demeanor lifts. She's all fluttery lashes, sky-high cheekbones, and tugged up corners of her mouth as she practically floats to the long, fully dressed table set for ten.

As expected, there's a signature cocktail to go along with a champagne-colored theme— The Peach Beach Bellini—plus fancy finger food to nibble on before we get started with a series of printable games.

"Chels..." Piper flashes her already-tipsy best friend and maid of honor a pearly white smile. She nods, signaling for her to distribute the first set of cards for the feature game of all baby showers and wedding-related get-togethers, What's in My Purse?

From the start, everyone at the table except for Mom gets one point for a smart phone. I and Piper's three bridesmaids Gemma, Serena, and Tiffany—who are outfitted in the season's brightest and most stylish cruise wear—all sip our Bellinis and rack up more points for pens, makeup, and credit cards. We think we're really doing something when we get five points for chewing gum and receipts, high-fiving with team spirit.

In an unexpected twist, though, it's Mom who pulls out the win with ten points each for nail polish, a fifty-dollar bill, a brush, and a freaking selfie stick. The thing looks like a light saber on steroids when she extends it for the server to capture a snapshot of the group.

It might be the excitement of the wedding combined with sickeningly sweet alcohol, but when the games move into trivia territory with, He Said, She Said, the entire table loosens up.

"Who initiated the first kiss?" Serena reads from the card.

Not one person suspected soft-spoken Piper.

"What?" She holds up her palms, unsure why we're shocked. "Seriously, if I would've waited for Aaron to kiss me, I doubt we'd be here today, so you're welcome for the getaway." She cheeses, taking an uncharacteristically long pull from her champagne flute before dabbing the corners of her mouth.

"Well, now we need to know who is more romantic." Gemma hikes up an eyebrow as she unravels the hairband from her ponytail, gathering it to make a fresh one. "I don't know, now...maybe you're not so innocent."

There's collective murmuring and teasing about Piper being a freak in the sheets, not in the streets, before she admits Aaron is the mushy one in the relationship. She presses a delicate hand to her chest, her shoulders curving inward as she tilts her head.

I want that intimacy so badly.

"Guys, he's so perfect. Like, I don't even know how I got so lucky. He brings me flowers and surprises me with jewelry. On Valentine's Day, I got this completely embarrassing display of roses, chocolate, a stuffed bear I can physically lay on because it's so huge," she gushes.

None of that does it for me. Ultimately, I want the love of my life to propose with an understated ring. But that's as far as it goes for me and jewelry. I care much more about the time we spend together watching movies, talking, making each other laugh, and being there when I need him and vice versa.

A warm, salty breeze dances over my cheek. I listen to the

waves crashing in the distance, pressing my hand over my heart as I think about Damon and how he didn't give it a second thought when I needed him to pick me up from Mots Doux on Tuesday. He took me away from it all and gave me the comforts of home in his space. There's a shifting sensation beneath my ribs at the memory of our kiss.

By the time I look up, they've apparently changed the game to Would She Rather, and every pair of eyes is on me.

"Sorry, I was just... What was the question?" I ask.

It's Chelsea who centers her attention on me. She's tall with rich brown complexion, a brick-house build, and a cornucopia of springy curls bustling from her ponytail. She's got sex appeal coming out of her invisible pores.

"Right, so the question was *Love & Basketball* or *Brown Sugar?* Pipe chose *Love & Basketball* because Omar trumps Taye. But then we sort of veered off course talking about movies with best friends falling in love..." she trails off, and it's clear that it's for effect as she tosses an open mouth smile around the table before she continues. "I'm wondering about yours..."

"My what?" My cheeks heat, and I force a smile.

"Like, what's the deal with Damon? Ooh, that man is *fine*. And that *ass*..." She shimmies her shoulders like a chill has run through her. "Is he seeing anyone special?"

Every muscle in my body tenses. My pulse slams in my neck as I flit a glance at my mother, who holds her hands up. She wants no parts of this, either.

The fact is, ever since we kissed, I've been dying to talk to Lea about us in full detail. She knows both of us, the way we are with each other, and how natural it would be for us to change the dynamic of our relationship. I want to gush to no end about how perfectly our lips fit together, how hot it was feeling him grow hard on my ass, and how I'm desperate to feel his body on mine again.

But then everything with Trish and the ChatVideo claim exploded, and I hopped on a plane with Damon. Suddenly, doing nothing felt hard. We spent the day in tight quarters on planes and laughing and playing in airport gardens. We created a friendship contract. I just didn't realize I'd need a noncompete clause.

But it looks like it's time to enforce it.

Version 1.0.

"He's seeing someone." I tamp down a fresh bout of tingles and say, "Me."

Now, in a movie or a book, I'd look like the total badass, letting Chelsea know she's barking up the wrong tree because the territory's been marked. *Objectify much?* But I don't get the sense she's the type to back down at the first roadblock.

"Oh, my goodness, that's so amazing." Impossibly, her mouth stretches wider. "From what Piper says, you two have been friends for like ever. Is this a recent development?" she asks.

Without a doubt, she's fishing.

Chelsea James sent one of the concerned Instagram notifications I received when Trish first posted. Yeah, so she's fully aware of everything that's happened with Kyle.

Over her shoulder, I catch sight of the sun dipping below the water. We've been out here for hours, and I've had a ton of fun. I might be a day late and a dollar short, but I'm learning to recognize when the party's over.

"We're pretty private," I say, polishing off the rest of my Peach Beach Bellini and pushing to my feet. "Piper, this was a blast. I'm going to head back to do all the check-in stuff and get our bags to the room then maybe rest a bit before the bachelorette party tonight."

Piper nods a couple of times. A flush spreads over her cheeks.

With every step toward the hotel—toward Damon—I feel my resolve waning. We desperately need a check-in with the friendship contract.

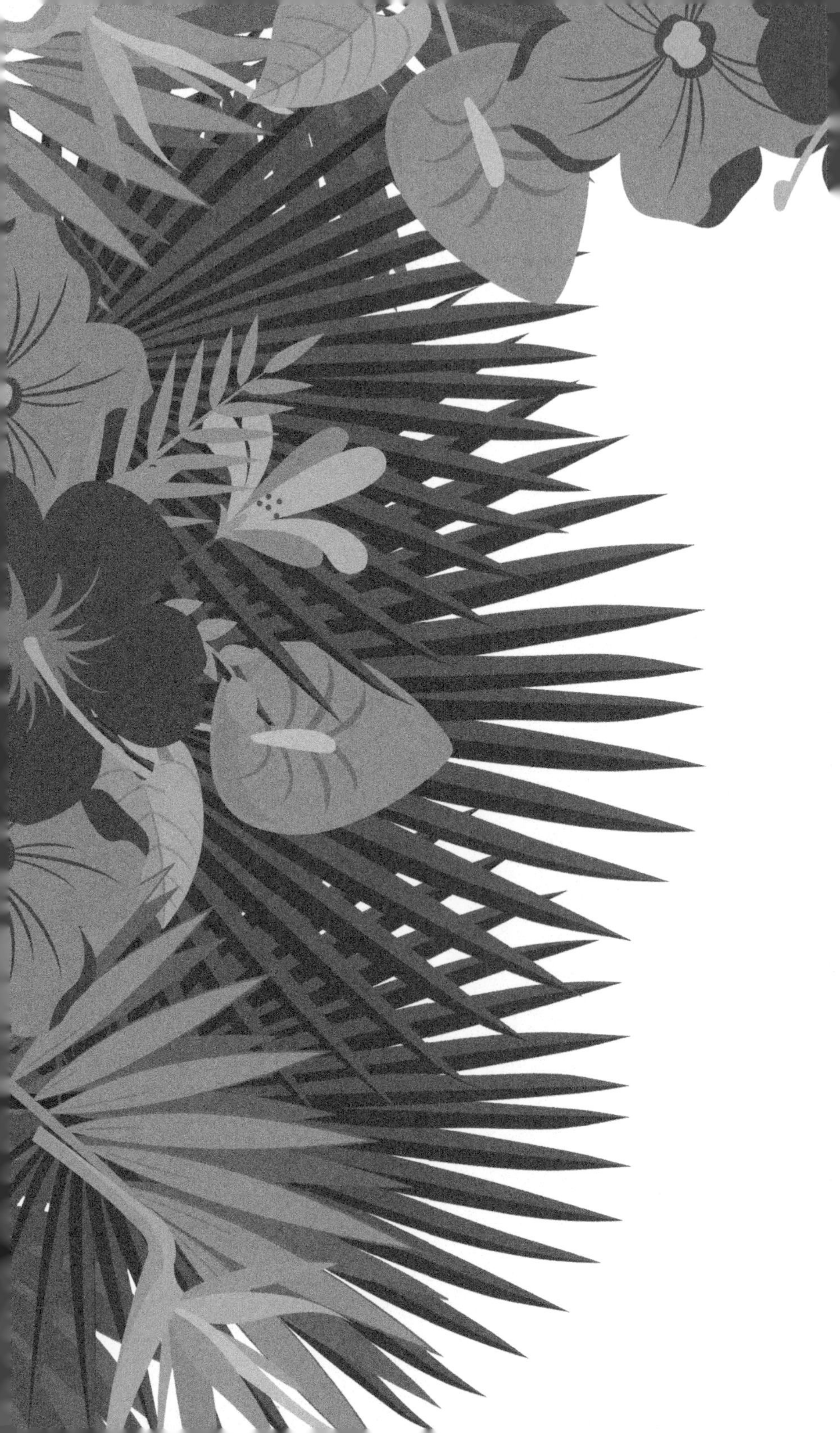

CHAPTER 8
Damon

Maybe I just don't think about weddings often enough, but I wasn't aware a groom roast was a real thing. Turns out, it's the modern male equivalent to a traditional bridal shower. "It's also referred to as the 'man shower' or the 'bro bath,'" Aaron explains like he's reading verbatim from a script Piper prepared for him.

"Seriously? Not one of you has ever heard of it?" He asks for maybe the tenth time today as he throws up his hands. His expression twists with mildly irritated disbelief. "Swear! Can't take y'all nowhere."

There are eleven of us total in the sleek, black, chartered van stocked with charcuterie boards and bottomless sparkling water. He keeps insisting we call it a party bus. The fact he's dead serious does nothing to cut down the snickers.

"Bro, give up. We're headed to the last of five bars on a local brewery tour and we're still not drunk," his best man, Mark, reasons. "It's cool, we'll save the debauchery for the bachelor party tonight."

A promise I'm sure Mark will make good on.

The groomsmen, Brian, Colin, and Duncan, aka Dunk

(I'm guessing that's based on his hoop skills or towering height), are wild guys. Pete, Nico, Steph, Kent, and Quincy, who are longtime friends, spouses of bridesmaids, or family of the Malones are likely wary of what gets back to their other halves and relatives.

One guy in the back, who sounds a lot like Dunk, coughs out, "Piper wears the pants!"

"Get him a 'groom' sash!" someone yells out from the general vicinity of Brian and Colin.

Laughter rumbles over the group again, and Mark guffaws, gripping Aaron's shoulders and reassuring him it's all in good fun.

That's what I keep telling myself. Just put Allegra out of my head. Enjoy this opportunity to get day drunk with a fun-loving group of men and celebrate Aaron, who, despite his tall, athletic frame, I've always affectionately referred to as my little brother. *I'd one day hoped to call him my brother-in-law.*

I've been avoiding Allegra because I haven't been honest with her. Maybe I never have been.

That needs to change.

I said I would do anything for her, so I'm here. But I can't afford to get confused about what's real.

As much as Allegra says the breakup was for the best, that she and Kyle were more roommates than soulmates, I saw her face. She stood there in the airport garden, so far gone, so lost in the life she must feel was swiped from her grasp. She didn't hear the timer go off or me talking to her. Her attention was fixed longingly on her phone—on Kyle and Trish.

It's understandable she needs time and closure.

I'm not insensitive about what she's gone through in just a few days. She's coming out of a years-long relationship, and her belongings are stacked in my living room, but I won't be Kyle's placeholder until he comes running back—or hers, when the contract ends after this weekend, and she eventually moves out of my place. *Moves on without me.*

For me, the garden was a glaring reminder not to get caught up.

When we arrive at the last bar on the tour, we walk in like a tribe of craft beer aficionados with a singular goal: Tipsy or bust.

It's a goal taken straight to heart by our man of the hour. Aaron, more determined than anyone not to go out like a punk whose "bro bath" lives on in blacktop whispers as a failure, orders double (pre-paid) wood paddle flights for everyone—we're not doing rounds in a place like Kauai Brew.

From outside, the place looked sketchy—rundown cars, boarded-up buildings, a few people walking around looking like they're looking for trouble, wrought iron bars on the windows and doors. It doesn't exactly seem like a luxury vacation spot for a bunch of tourists wearing pricey timepieces and expensive shoes getting out of a European-make charter van.

But once we cross the threshold, it's like we've entered an upscale alcoholic beverage experience for the person of refined taste.

Warm mahogany woods, galvanized metal, and stacked slate give the bar—*microbrewery*—a distinctly modern industrial feel with cool yet cozy vibes. Centered behind the sleek bar top is at least a ten-foot-long tap surrounded by pocket shelves featuring individual ales, pilsners, lagers, porters, stouts, I.P.A.s, and even an appetizing Saison.

The atmosphere is hype, too.

In no time, we are tossing them back to a live band whose beefy Polynesian front man has pipes for days.

"Dame," Dunk slaps a heavy hand on my back before calling out over the music, "Seven o'clock. Yellow dress."

I coolly swivel on the barstool, craning my neck. Off my left shoulder, a group of four women who are dressed carefree enough to be locals are huddled in a small circle, but only one is facing me. She's wearing a buttery yellow, second-skin dress and has loose, long dark hair, full red lips, and her brown-eyed gaze trained on me.

"She could be looking at any of us," I say, eyeing the rest of the guys.

The woman is undeniably a knockout, but she isn't Allegra, who I reassured earlier we were in a good place. The last thing I need is to add another layer to our complex equation.

Dunk pounds the bar with his fist to get the attention of the crew, then leans casually against the edge, facing the woman wedging past her friends and heading directly for us.

"Looks like we're about to find out," he says.

And we do.

"Hey, thought I'd come over and meet some new friends," she says, her words rolling off her tongue in a soft flutter.

The entire squad jerks their chins and murmurs their hellos, waiting to see what I do.

"Nice to meet you. Damon," I say, extending my hand, to which she gives me a hardy shake and tells me her name is Keilana.

For a moment, I wait to see what she says or does next. I don't want to be the asshole making assumptions about her intentions. She could genuinely want a new friend from the mainland. Or, when she peeks over her shoulder at her friends, I think maybe she walked over on a dare.

"So, what's the occasion?" She smiles, letting her soft gaze drift curiously over each guy in the crew. "Someone's birthday? Vacation?"

A fresh bout of snickers rumbles over us, and I'm all too happy to deflect the attention off me and onto Aaron.

"We're celebrating. *This*," I fan my hand out over the entire squad, "is what some would call an informal gathering of guy friends in honor of the groom's impending nuptials. Aaron, here, is getting married this weekend." I flash him a raised-brow "how'd I do" expression before returning my attention to Keilana.

"Wow." She gnaws her lower lip, the corner of her mouth twitching. "That's a new one. I've never heard of a... What did you say it was called again?"

The guys throw out the terms Aaron mentioned.

"Man shower!"

"Bro bath!"

"So, yeah. It's not a fad *at all*. Just a new progressive tradition for the evolved, modern male." I struggle to keep a straight face.

The entire squad breaks out in laughs.

"Okay, thank you. Bravo! You all should really take this act on the road. I'm sure it'll be a hit with the socially stagnant crowd."

As Aaron plops down on the barstool and flags down a bartender, everyone moves to huddle around him and let him know they're just giving him a hard time.

But while they're reassuring Aaron that they are indeed glad we have this chance to all be together in paradise before he embarks on a new life with Piper, Keilana takes the opportunity to lean in close and whisper in my ear, "Do you want to go somewhere?"

I lean back and look at her. Heat pools in her eyes, and her floral scent bands around me.

I'm tempted to be this beautiful woman's placeholder for the night and to let her help me forget how long I've wanted Allegra and the promises I made to my best friend, to myself. I could start moving on right here and now.

But the memory of kissing Allegra and knowing, not just

in theory anymore, that we'd be amazing together, is inescapable. No matter how hard I fight it, I still want her.

Even if I still don't know what she wants.

With all the focus on Aaron, I lean my head close to Keilana's ear. "Thanks for the compliment, but I'm here to support Aaron." *And his sister.*

After that encounter, I get ragged on the entire ride back to the hotel for passing on the local fare. Colin and Brian call me a corn boy for giving up the chance to be the first of us on the scoreboard. I wasn't even aware we were keeping score. They argue that it's a "scientific fact" weddings make women hornier than normal, and it's our job to capitalize on it.

Aaron and Mark give me loyalty points, and the rest of the squad do nothing more than share meaningful glances and nods of solidarity. They don't know Allegra's and my status, but they know most of the complications that go along with being here with her—couple or not.

Either way, when the van pulls up to the hotel, I'm both anticipating and dreading getting settled in the room. I double check the text Allegra sent earlier with our room number and confirming our bags have made it to the room. With a wave over my shoulder to the guys, I tell them I'll meet them in the lobby later tonight for the bachelor party.

Then, I hop on the elevator, select the third floor, and steel my nerves for the talk that Allegra and I are about to have that's twelve years overdue.

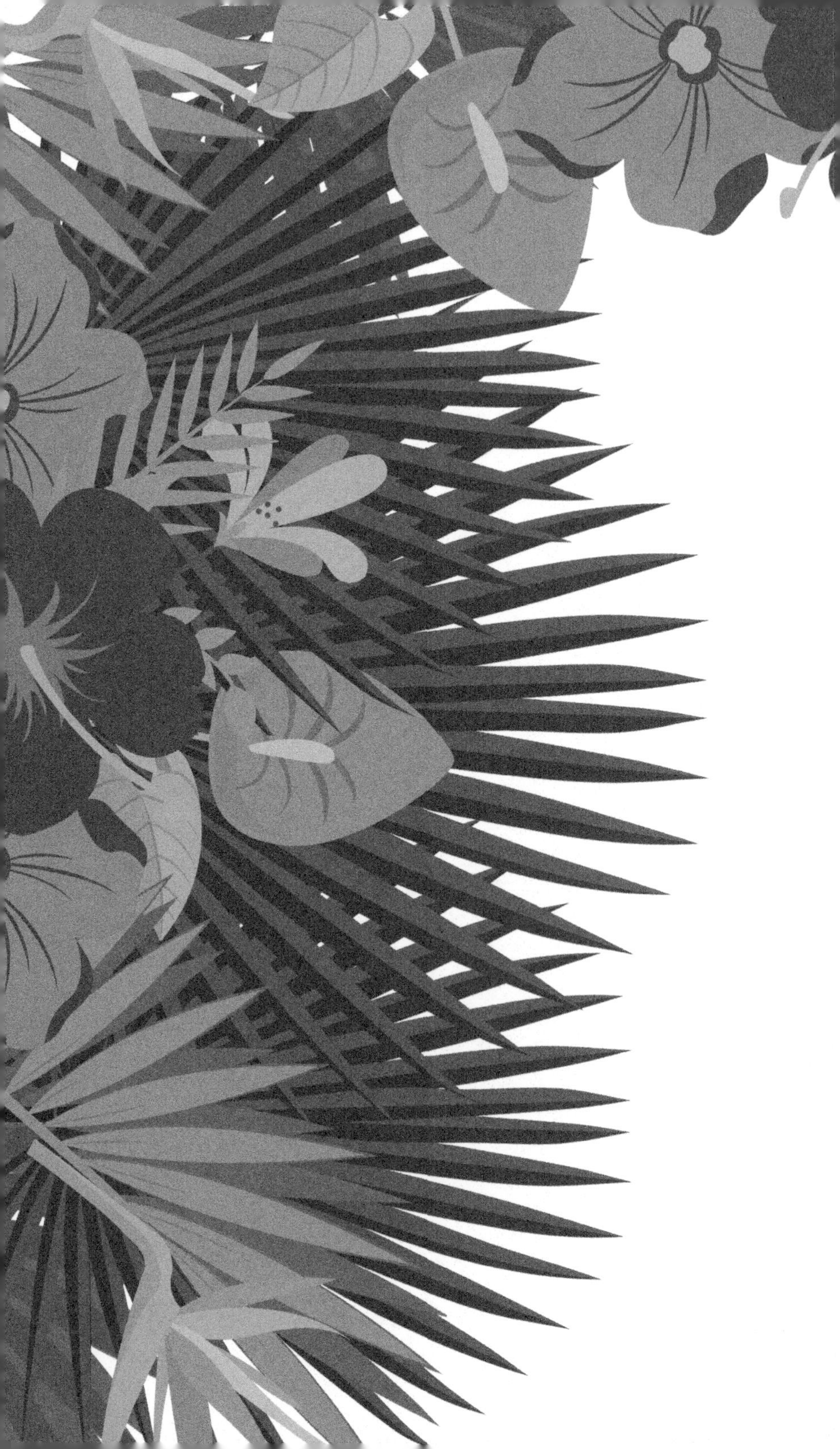

CHAPTER 9
Damon

I exit the elevator and take my time walking down the moonlit hotel hallway, unsure where to even start. How do I break the silence between us when I was closed up that entire last flight? *I've yet to even tell her why.*

When I reach the room, I knock lightly.

"Who is it?" Allegra calls out from the other side of the door.

I knead the back of my neck, "It's me."

A few seconds tick by before she swings the door open and flashes me a small smile.

"Hey, come on in," she says as she turns on her heel back into the room wearing a white terrycloth robe cinched at the waist—and not much else.

I swallow hard, averting my gaze to the book in her hand as she pads over to a coastal blue settee next to the open patio door.

"I hope it's okay I took the left side of the bed. I wanted to be closest to the patio when the morning sun comes in," she says, peeking up at me.

"It's cool. I don't mind."

"Your bags are in the closet, and I put the extra key card on your nightstand, too." She's rambling, and fidgeting, avoiding my gaze, and it kills me. I hate she seems unsure how to be around me and that I've wedged this uncertainty between us.

I walk over to the patio and peer out at the crashing waves. Under the night sky, the moon casts a mesmerizing glow on the water like diamonds sparkling in a depthless mine.

My heart thuds behind my ribs.

"Listen, Al. I've got a couple of hours until I said I'd be back down to the lobby for Aaron's bachelor party." I glance at her over my shoulder. "Can we talk?"

"Yeah, sure." Her voice is soft as she slides a bookmark between the pages. She sets the book on the nightstand then pushes to her feet, walking over to stand beside me.

"Lately, I've been thinking a lot about us."

In my periphery, I notice her posture stiffen. "Me, too."

"We're more than friends. To me, you're my family. You're my pers—"

Allegra's phone pings.

A second later, mine does, too.

"Lea," we both say, smiling.

"Shoot, with the luncheon and everything, I forgot to let her know we made it." Allegra reaches for her phone as I slip mine from my pocket.

Lea 5:27 pm
I'm FaceTiming you. Answer.

FaceTime, not ViddyChat. Shit.

Allegra must recognize the significance of Lea's choice, too, because she gives me an apologetic shrug. "Wait, what were you going to say? Before Lea texted?"

Both our phones ring, but we answer on Allegra's phone, leaning into the frame together.

"Hey, Le, what's up? We're both here," Allegra says. "Is everything okay?"

Lea nods, but digs her fingers into her scalp, taking a handful of her hair into her hand the way she always does when she's nervous. "Listen, I wouldn't have bothered you all since I know you're probably doing all sort of Piper-planned wedding activities." She laughs, shaking her head likes she's glad we're here instead of her. "I had a chance to review Trish's file for the claim against ViddyChat."

Allegra and I don't speak, we just listen for what's coming.

"It's a small, women-owned video communication startup. It's been around for three years in the Henderson area, doing grassroots, word-of-mouth-type referrals to build their clientele—mostly, the Greater Las Vegas area businesses. But they started getting some traction with small television spots." Lea pauses and types something on the keyboard before she looks back at the camera. "Look at the ads I just sent to you."

On her phone, Allegra swipes over to email, finding the most recent one from Lea with the subject line, ChatVideo vs. ViddyChat. In the message's body is a side-by-side comparison she put together reflecting the differences and similarities between the two companies.

Company	ViddyChat	ChatVideo
Years in Business	2	3
Slogan	Be Present Now.	Be Present.
Brand Logo	Orange-red one-dimensional computer monitor w/ company name inside	Deep red one-dimensional computer monitor w/ company name inside.
Television Spot	Mother and child both at school playground seemingly face to face but unable to locate one another. Camera pans to reveal they are talking on a phone (aired this year).	Two business executives seemingly speaking face to face at a conference table about making a business deal. Camera pans then turns to reveal they are talking via a computer (aired one year ago).
Target Client	Global individuals and businesses	Local businesses with five-year plan to gradually offer national then global services.

I'm not sure if I finish reading before Allegra, but she continues to stare at the screen.

"The owner of ChatVideo is gradually scaling, but she doesn't have the funding or network ViddyChat does, so the way it's looking...I'm inclined to say there's validity to this copyright infringement claim, and..."

"And?"

I lower my chin, massaging my temples between my thumb and middle finger. I know exactly where she's going with this because I should be fully on board with her thought process. We're founding partners working toward the same growth model goal. For a small intellectual property firm, a case as high profile as this one against ViddyChat could do wonders for our credibility and social proof...immeasurable. Plus, who knows how many larger firms ChatVideo consulted that didn't choose to take the claim seriously based on whatever liabilities they deemed too great?

Negative publicity is the least of a law firm's worries. It goes with the territory since most cases have a loser. There's also market, operational, liquidity, business, reputational, and systemic risk. The list goes on and on and on.

If the outcome is in favor of ViddyChat, some people will frame it as patriarchal favoritism over ChatVideo's women-owned business. With an unfavorable outcome and the corresponding financial implications, the firm who crippled a widely used video communication service could become the scapegoat or the black sheep of the industry.

The risks and rewards are clear.

Personally, and professionally, it would feel so fucking good to make Kyle pay for being a coward and a crook, but I selfishly just want to leave my past in the past. The Hammonds didn't want me when I was a kid. I have no desire to reconnect with my foster sister.

"Earlier, I spoke with Laura Hammond." Lea picks up a manila file and taps it against her desk. "She's got the retainer ready, but I let her know I needed to confer with my partners."

We don't make unilateral decisions. With the three of us, it has always been majority rules. Over the years, we've each won some and lost some.

A mix of annoyance and guilt flares in my gut. I've yet to tell Allegra and Lea about my ties with Laura, but I don't want it to sway our decision either way.

"So, what are you thinking, Le?" I ask, pressing my fist to my lips, knowing full well Allegra will be the tiebreaker.

Allegra flits a tentative glance at me. Worry creases her brow. It doesn't take a lot for her to see I'm not exactly chomping at the bit to deal with her ex. Even hinting that my reservations have to do with anything other than Allegra's past with Kyle, Lea will latch on it, and she won't stop.

Sure enough, she cocks her head at me and shoots me a "Seriously?" expression. For her, this is ninety-nine percent about business and one percent karma coming home to roost. Putting The Trio first means Lea and I should want Kyle to go down on Allegra's behalf.

The two of us turn to Allegra, expectantly.

"We wouldn't be us if Lea and I weren't in different camps, waiting for you to sway us. You know where I stand." I shrug, though she probably doesn't know where my head is. I've been acting jealous and juvenile since we got off that first flight. I didn't tell her how I really feel about us.

Al fidgets with her cuticles before she finally peeks up at me.

"Are you going to be mad if I say I want to do it?" she asks, but before I can answer, I feel the weight of Lea's attention come crashing down on me.

"Will *you* be mad if I say I don't want to do it?" I shoot back.

Answering a question with a question...fucking great.

"Excuse me, why would you be mad at Al if she committed to a case that will take our firm to the next level?" Lea blinks, her wild fringe of lashes flapping like wings. But then her gaze darts between Allegra and me, and she folds her arms across her chest. "Is this still The Trio, or did a little tropical vacation turn you two into a duo?"

Allegra huffs out an incredulous laugh like Lea is way off base as opposed to hitting it out of the park with her blood-hound instincts.

"Uh, no." The inflection in Al's voice spikes as she tosses me a telepathic S.O.S. with her raised-brow stare.

I don't have it in me to keep up the charade, though. I've still got too much on my mind and nowhere to unload.

"Mm-hmm," Lea grumbles. "Whatever. Since I'm apparently out of the loop, Damon, are you going to be mad at poor, helpless, little Allegra if she does what's best for our law firm?" She rests her chin on her hands and fixes a plastic smile in place.

I shake my head and flip my wrist to check the time. I still need to shower and dress before I head down to the lobby.

"Not at all," I say. "So, that's two out of three in favor. Majority rules. Set up an appointment for Wednesday morning. That'll give us a day to settle in back at home. We're going to need to have a powerful line of defense to deal with your boy, though."

"No, honey. That's Allegra's *ex*-boy. Don't even try me."

With that, I say my goodbyes to Lea, walk into the bathroom, and barely close the door before all my demons corner me.

* * *

Under the spray of the steaming hot shower, I flatten my hands against the tile basin, letting my frustration and uncertainty drain from my neck and shoulders. Anger swells inside me. What am I doing here? Who am I anymore? I'm willing to throw away a groundbreaking case to avoid dealing with Laura? Or is this about keeping Allegra from Kyle?

A groan claws its way from my throat.

Am I that fucking insecure about being her rebound because she looked at his social media and she wants to take him down in court like she should—like we should?

I should've started by being honest with her and myself—about Laura, the case, and about us.

I didn't turn down a woman willing to do God knows

what at that microbrewery because of a half-hatched friendship contract. Nor did I agree to fake a relationship during a Hawaiian wedding weekend to help my best friend save face with her family and friends. I opened my home to Allegra Marie Malone because I love her.

I love her.

On some level, I think part of me always knew what I share with Allegra isn't just love between friends. She was never *just* my friend.

Since the day she accidentally knocked my books off the table in the Boyd library stacks and made the rounds to every table to apologize for the noise, I've known. And every day after, I've learned she's not just a dream come true with full lips, golden skin, and those sweet intense green eyes.

I love her because she's unapologetically loyal and she acts with every corner of her heart leading her. She sees beneath the surface to the good in people. And when she learned I'd spent most of my life either in foster care or couch surfing to keep a roof over my head, she claimed me as her family. Then extended her family to me.

And I can't bring myself to tell her this one simple thing about a woman I once counted at my sister...

Fuck.

"D?" *Fuck.* Allegra's voice rips sharp and hard on the other side of the door, tearing me from my thoughts.

I squeeze my eyes closed, shoving aside my hang-ups. "I'll be out in a minute,"

Shit, how long have I been in here?

The creak of the door pierces the air, snagging my attention. I jerk my gaze toward a sliver of light stretched across the ceiling.

"We're not doing this anymore. We will not share this amazing room in *Hawaii*...at my brother's wedding with our family and friends, and not talk." Allegra blows out a shaky breath. "You said you were ready to talk. If this is where it must be because you keep running from me, then...so be it."

Her tone is uncertain and frustrated, but it's laced with determination.

I smile to myself because her barging into the bathroom while I'm in the shower is so Allegra. She faces her fears head-on, even if it means putting herself in the middle of it.

"Look, you said we had a thing about bathrooms..."

"Bathroom doorways," I chuckle. "This can't wait until I get out the shower?"

She says nothing at first, but I hear her soft inhale, the way she does before every case. She's building herself up for what's next.

But as light footsteps grow closer, followed by a quick, chilly rush of air, my body prickles with awareness.

"Allegra."

"Can I come in?" Allegra asks as she slides the steamy glass door further back. The conviction and determination that burns bright in her luminous green eyes is lost completely when her gaze drops. Her eyes widen when my dick twitches.

My breath gets caught in my chest.

Because I'm powerless to say no when my want outweighs my will, I watch her slowly tug her robe belt, letting the terrycloth gape open. She shrugs, letting it glide off her golden skin and fall to her feet in a puddle on the floor.

Allegra clears her throat, defiantly lifting her chin to me when I don't answer her.

"Please," she says as she steps in behind me.

Every inch of me hardens, and my pulse races with an aching need so strong, I'm rendered speechless. *Talking is overrated.*

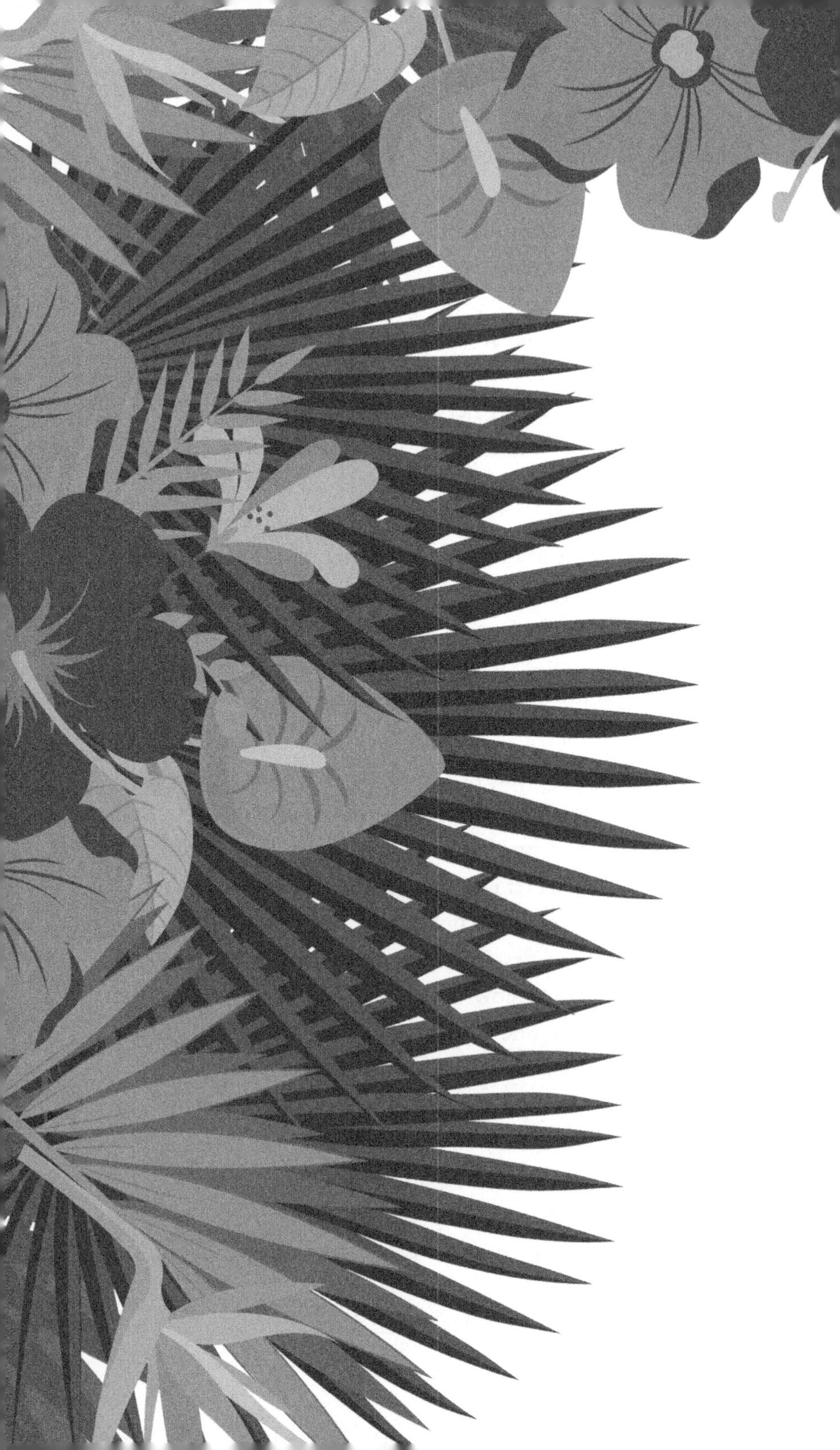

CHAPTER 10
Allegra

Damon's breath hitches as I step into the shower behind him and pull the glass door closed. He doesn't move or speak as I glide my hands over his abdomen, molding my body to his backside. There's only the sound of our shallow breathing synchronizing.

"It's okay," I whisper, my stomach churning. "We don't have to use words."

Just for tonight, I don't want to think about what sex with my best friend will mean for us on the other side of midnight or how much more I want us to be. I don't want to think about how jealous I was when Chelsea asked about Damon or the look on his face after we talked to Lea. I certainly don't want to think about how I couldn't make it twenty-four hours before breaking the one rule that could tank my "case."

Instead, I focus on the smooth, wet glide of his hard chest beneath my fingertips as I scrape my nails down his sides until I'm digging into his thick thighs. I'm so desperate to be closer. My attention is acutely centered on the round, toned muscle of his ass pressing into my stomach.

I blaze a trail of fiery, sweet kisses over his neck and

shoulder blades and down the curve of his back. My body is thrumming with a current of electricity so strong I might come undone from anticipation alone.

As he lets me revel in my wanderlust by roaming my hands freely over his body, I realize I've never needed the words.

The thing about Damon is, he's always been the quiet type. He listens and stews and broods, then he acts with intention. His silence is the unwritten fine print that he cares enough to keep you in his thoughts. With me, he laughs, and we enjoy each other's company, but he rarely needs to speak. Everything he does shows me how he feels.

I don't need Damon to tell me.

"Show me," I mouth into the kisses as I weave my hands along the lean curve of his torso. I take his dick into my hands, stretching and stroking him until he's hard and thick. His breaths are ragged as he trembles on the edge. "Show me everything you can't say."

A fierce hunger burns in Damon's eyes when he turns to face me. His wide, muscular chest rising and falling, he sets his sturdy hands on my hips, gently shifting us around so my back is against the cool, wet tile.

The bob of his Adam's apple as he swallows tells me he's barely holding onto his testimony.

But I don't move.

The way the steam billows around us, I could almost convince myself this is a dream and tell myself my head is just in the clouds. *This can't be real.* I probably stayed on the other side of the door just wishing he'd say what's on his mind...

My heart knows better, though, and it rattles my ribs like it's trying to break free from my chest to get to Damon. Every second his stare bores into me, I feel the tiny tears mending.

This moment isn't just about me taking what I want without romanticizing what comes next or deciphering

Damon's silence. I came into this bathroom to be with him and to reassure him he's not alone in this. Whatever we are—whether I can name it or not—I feel it, too.

My breaths quicken.

I catalogue every shadow and line and contour the warm glow of lights cast over his angular face—the coppery undertones of his smooth cinnamon complexion, the water beaded on his broad forehead and heat-stained cheeks, the way the new stubble adds a little roughness to the sharp set of his sculpted jaw.

When his lips part, he draws in a long breath. I stare unblinking at his slight overbite and the full pout I so badly want to kiss again.

"Damon—"

Tenderly, he takes my face in his hands. It surprises me, and I breathe harder. His touch on my cheek is unbearably familiar and foreign, and I feel like if he doesn't put his mouth on me and his hands on every part of my body, or if I don't feel him moving inside me very soon, I might die right here.

"Touch me," I beg. "Please show me."

Damon lowers his head, so his mouth is a whisper from mine, tormenting me as he stops to search my eyes.

"This isn't about the contract. I'm not pretending to be in love in front of your family and friends." He stiffens. His brows knit together as he struggles to get the rest out. The texture of his voice is rough and tortured when he bites out, "This is about you and me, Allegra."

Not big head. Not his friend, Al...Allegra. Our naked bodies are pressed so close together, I can feel the ridges of his hard length throbbing on my stomach. Our heartbeats play like drums over every nerve ending on my body.

It feels like closing arguments, leaving our fate for the judge and jury.

Warmth and longing curl down my spine as I nod and repeat, "You and me. Only, you and me."

A slow burn works its way through my chest, sparking into flames. Fire licks through me as he dips his chin and shows me with his lips all the words he can't express right now.

I feel this kiss down to my toes. It's demanding and relentless, sending shivers and tingles washing in waves over my aching body. He shows me with his tongue. In overwhelmingly addictive brushes, he alternates between gentle sweeps and rough, exploring sucks like he's torn between tasting and savoring.

I nibble at his lower lip, panting, wanting, needing him.

Damon drags his scorching tongue over my cheek, down my neck, until he finds the peaks of my small, round breasts. He takes them in his mouth one at a time, sucking and licking as he shows me more with two fingers. When he slips them inside my slick folds, he tells me with the strongest testimony that I come first in this.

My sex clenches round him as he adds a third finger, winding me up until my nipples are almost painfully hard.

This is the Damon I know—always so quiet but saying more in his silence than words could ever express.

He watches me with a desperate glint in his eyes as I thrust my hips, riding his hand, panting my satisfaction. His gaze grates over my aching flesh like even if I hadn't walked into his shower naked with no intention of talking, even if the need for him to be inside me wasn't so intense, he'd still want me.

I see how much he wants this, too.

His unabashed desire is my undoing.

But while he shows his feelings through quiet actions and mind-numbing physical touches, I sense he responds to words of affirmation.

"I need you, Damon. Only you," I moan. "Show me."

In response, Damon works his hands down to my ass, grinding his hips so I'm pinned between him and the wall. His expression is a tortured mess of lust and unspoken words clawing from his pores.

"I've got an IUD. I get tested regularly, and I haven't had sex in months," I say quickly between shallow breaths.

He searches my eyes. "My last test was negative, too. Are you sure about this, Al?"

"Yes."

His breaths come fast as we move in a blur of hands and limbs, twisting and positioning, sending electricity racing through my veins. Chills run down my spine at how good his rough grip feels at the cinch of my waist as he lifts me up and centers the head of his dick between my thighs, showing me from the inside out.

He surveys me the entire time as he guides me down the length of his hard, pulsing length and fills me so completely. *He's showing me with every inch of his body.*

"Oh, my sweet, sweet Lord," I gasp, loving how we've barely spoken two complete sentences but how utterly unnecessary words are at this point. I understand on a cellular level now that to fit this well, we must've been made for each other.

Damon must know, too, because he takes his time. He moves in slow, deliberate strides, creating sweet, delicious friction that drives me wild. As if fueled by my whimpers, he peppers petal-soft kisses over my throat that I've bared to him, sending waves of shudders washing over me.

And it's all the confession I need.

Our minds and bodies move in sync like a fine-tuned instrument, filling the air with a symphony of ragged breaths and sated moans.

I cling to his neck, my body pliant and pulsing as I let myself wilt in his grasp. I close my eyes, letting fireworks spark behind my lids. I fall into every electric pulse and flex of his fingers. I get wrapped up in his touch and the heady mixture of steam and Damon's clean scent. As he teases his tongue into my mouth, we kiss with an urgency that makes me feel like we're racing against a clock. Like if we don't hurry, the moment will be lost.

"Hurry," I whisper.

"You and me," he reminds me once more.

Damon and I move at a frenzied pace, chasing the sensation as an orgasm swells inside me. I clench my thighs around his waist, holding on as long as I can not to lose this feeling. But the room spins, and my entire world tilts on its axis. My pulse thunders as Damon pumps harder, drilling deeper into my aching flesh as I tighten around him.

When he pulses inside me, I'm drenched in emotions, my body trembling and quivering.

As we come down, he traces his tongue over my lips, tenderly nipping. Then he pins me with a soft, intense stare.

Without a single word, he says what he always says.

I'm right here. I'm always going to be right here.

As my brain autofills a happily ever after with my best friend, I choose to believe it.

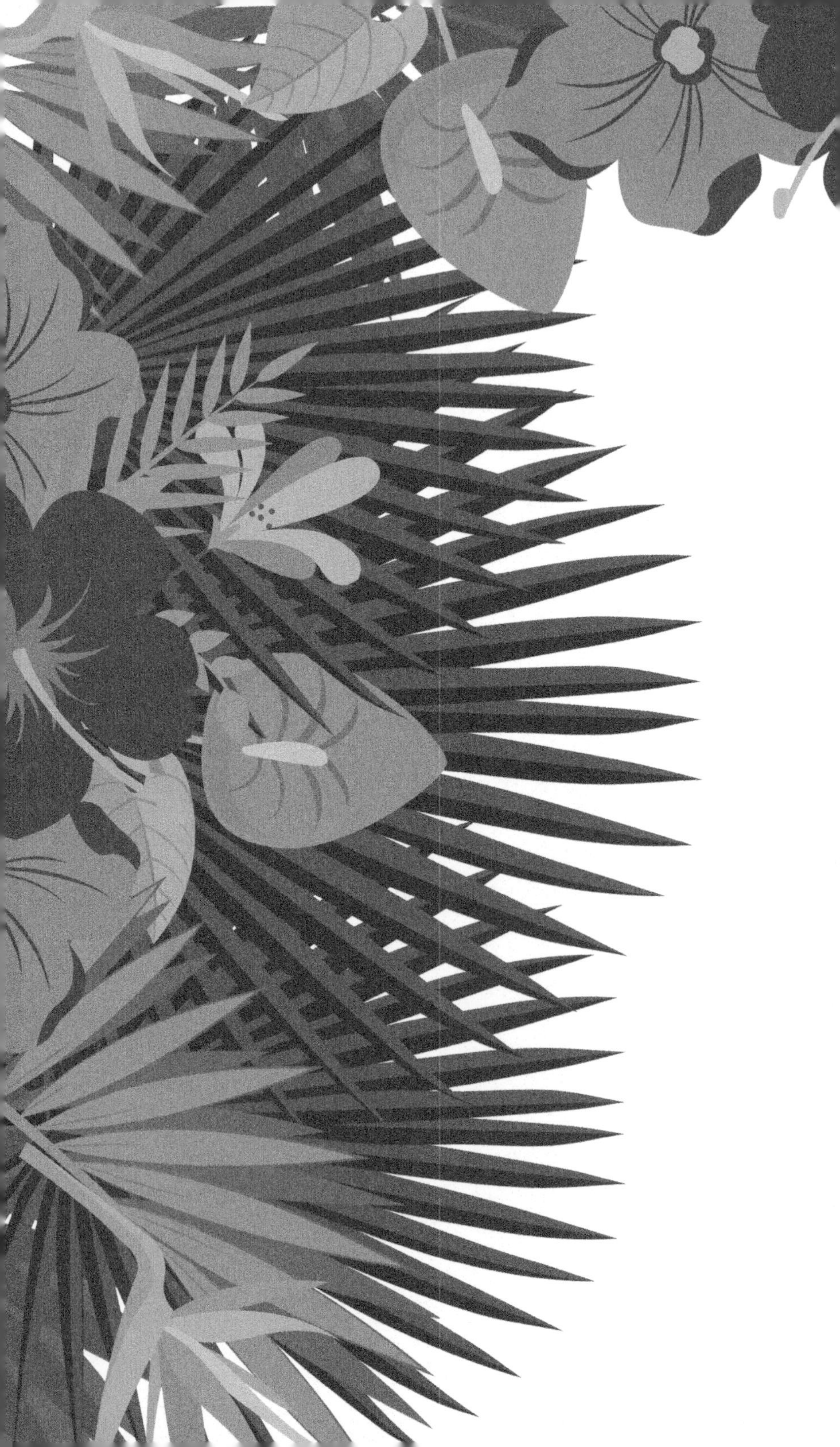

CHAPTER 11
Damon

By the time I make it down to the lobby, I'm the last straggler walking into a fog of cologne and slickly dressed guys in pressed suits who have no shame in letting me know I'm the holdup.

"What happened was—" I start, prepared to say anything other than how I had to drag myself out of the room rather than leaving Allegra in that robe asking if we could move things to the bed.

Dunk cuts me off.

"Yeah, yeah. *'What had happened was...'*" He mocks me, blowing out an exasperated breath. "Everyone knows there's an excuse coming next." His lanky frame sways as he throws his head back with a robust groan. "My dude, seriously? What were you doing? Your hair? We all know you're a pretty boy, but damn."

A few of the guys guffaw, joining in a collective laugh at my expense.

I don't explain or come up with anything remotely believable, because Aaron drops his head, laughing a mirthless laugh that says he already knows the answer, though I don't know how. His shoulders shake as his stutter step picks up to an easy gait until he's in the center of the huddle surrounding me.

"Let's just say my boy Damon has his hands full." He chuckles, rubbing his calloused hands together. Then he jerks an eyebrow up at me. "Would I be close if I said it's a thin line between friends and lovers?" he asks, sounding about as corny as they come by twisting the old love-hate saying.

The entire gang of guys grumbles something about Piper and gossip. I overhear a mention of the bridal luncheon as they walk past, one by one slapping me on the shoulder.

"So, Piper told him what?" I ask, lagging at the tail of the group.

They file into a line, heading out the main entrance of the hotel toward the valet line.

Colin and Brian hang back with me.

"Let me guess. You hooked up with yellow dress?" Colin asks with a smug grin smeared across his pudgy face.

Of course, because they're a two-for-one-deal, I get Brian's gutter-drenched two cents too. "You got her digits and had her meet you at the room, huh?"

Digits? What year is this?

"Uh, no. I didn't get the woman's *digits*. And I didn't bring her back to the room I'm sharing with *Allegra*." I enunciate her name to get through to these knuckleheads. Then I pick up my pace to stand beside Aaron in the valet line.

"What was that about?" I ask, jerking my chin up. "I've got my hands full?" I feel the crease between my eyebrows deepen as I shrug. "What exactly did Piper tell you?"

He smiles to himself, snickering. "You and Allegra?" His gaze darts to me before he looks out at the moonlit horizon.

I follow his gaze, remembering the view from the patio up in the room. How I'd been so tense, my mind racing through the endless possibilities of how things could go when I finally told Allegra how I feel about her and about Laura. I was nearly ready to tell all when Lea called.

"It's about time," Aaron says, taking my silence as confirmation.

I don't have to ask what he means. There's been no one else for me. I think the only one who doesn't know is Allegra.

Snippets of the past hour flash past my eyes like a 4-D experience. The moment she dropped her robe and asked to join me in the shower, I'd lost my words and the ability to do anything other than let her flood my senses. The moans spilling from her lips as I moved inside her fueling an uncontrollable fire, the feel of her hands roaming wildly over my chest the way I'd imagined a million times before, the spray of water over us...

But with Aaron, I don't know what he knows. *'About time'* Allegra and I are together or that we are more?

The thing is, even I still don't know how much more.

"Can I just say I've hated every guy she's ever been with? I don't know how much of what Piper said is true because it's Piper..." He laughs, scratching his head. "But if you and Allegra are really trying out this relationship thing...you have my blessing. I'd even say you have Mom's blessing. You are family. I wouldn't mind if you made it official."

My heart clenches.

I scrub my hand over my face, chewing the inside of my cheek to stifle the emotion threatening at my throat. Tears sting at the corners of my eyes, anyway. It's what I want. More than anything in this world, this beautiful family is what I want, and she's the only person who I want it with. Hearing Aaron—who I already think of as my brother—say it aloud touches my heart.

"Thanks, man." I suck in a deep breath, nodding to keep from emoting. "Sincerely."

"We love you." His half-grin returns in full effect. "Even if you and my sister are...you know..."

I bark out a belly laugh.

"So, uh...I'm just curious. What exactly did Piper say? Or should I ask, what did Piper say that Allegra said?"

A line of valet attendants driving golf carts pulls up in front of us, and Aaron jerks his eyebrows up as he shrugs. "Long story short, at the bridal luncheon, they were playing games, and Chelsea ended up asking Allegra what your story was."

"What did Allegra say?" I ask as I slide onto the back seat of the golf cart next to him.

"It was more like what she didn't say..." Aaron is interrupted when Mark taps him on the shoulder from the driver's seat. Dunk, seated beside him, calls back to the rest of the guys and instructs them to follow us and stay close. "Anyway," he continues as we pull into the lane, "Piper said Allegra looked like she was ready to jump on the table and pounce on Chelsea for even asking about you." Aaron throws his hands up. "In a nutshell, Allegra marked her territory."

"Uh, okay," I chuckle. "So, you're saying Chelsea asked what my deal was, and Allegra claimed me?"

Aaron shrugs, tilting his head from side to side like he'd prefer a little more color to my word. "That's about the size of it."

I nod, considering how much weight I should give to a story from Aaron via Piper. It's borderline adult telephone game. But there's got to be a piece of truth in there somewhere.

"Thanks." I nod, but I'm already planning what I'm going to ask Allegra when I get back to the room.

After a couple of miles of zigzagging turns through the grounds, the golf carts pull onto a secluded lawn almost completely surrounded by what looks like towering pine-line hedges. It's dark, and it's hard to tell what anything is by the light of only the few strategically placed torches.

I scan the area for women in grass skirts or hogs rotating and roasting over a fiery pit. But there are only ten chairs set up in a semi-circle surrounding a makeshift parquet dance floor.

"What's the plan here?' I ask Aaron as we step off the golf cart and find two open chairs in the middle.

As soon as Aaron sits, Mark comes over, shaking his head.

"Nope. We have a special seat for the man of the hour," he says, taking Aaron by his elbow toward the center of the dance floor.

"There's no chair..." Aaron looks genuinely confused. Really, it's sort of hard to watch. I've only been around him and his best man twice, and I've already caught on to what's happening. "Mark, seriously? What are we doing out here?"

As if on cue, four skylights illuminate the edges of the space.

If Aaron hasn't caught on yet, I know he's at least figuring out how mad Piper is going to be when she finds out what her fiancé's best man has planned.

"Look, this isn't cool," he says, already marching back toward the golf carts.

The rest of the crew block him from leaving.

"Relax," Pete says, pressing his palms against the air.

"Yeah, Aaron, it's fine. Piper thinks we're in the saloon smoking cigars and drinking whiskey just like she planned." I can't see if it's Quincy, Steph, Kent, or Nico, but it's one guy whose other half is out with Piper and likely believes the same story.

It's not drums or ukuleles that snatch Aaron's attention. The bass of hip-hop blasts through the quiet. Rhyme and verse collide in ass-shaking music, and six hula girls sashay onto the dance floor, waggling their hips in dizzying circles.

Except they're not hula girls. Or even hula women. At least not by trade. The grass skirts are quickly unfastened, followed by their giant purple bikini-top shells, and then there are a half-dozen buck-naked women in nothing but feathery headdresses and green leaf anklets.

"Holy shit." I blow out a breath, clamping my hand on Aaron's shoulders as I bite into my lower lip.

Mark, Brian, Colin, and Dunk are already cutting a parquet rug with their hands in places Piper would certainly not appreciate Aaron's hands going.

"I can't fucking do this," he says in a wide-eyed panic.

"Aaron!" Mark yells, waving him over. "They want to give the groom a proper sendoff into celibacy. He cackles like a grade-A asshole.

Still shaking his head, Aaron looks on. His expression is a combination of pissed, shocked, and horny as hell. There's no telling how long Piper has been making him wait for their big wedding weekend based on some etiquette book or rite of passage.

He looks like he's in physical pain seeing all the ass and breasts bouncing freely.

"What is happening?" Aaron bites out. His jaw tightens as he swallows. I could be wrong, but he looks like he might cry.

Based on the position of Mark's hand between the thighs of the woman he's "dancing" with, I really couldn't say, but I'm getting hard just thinking about slipping back into the room early to be with Allegra.

Maybe this time we'll try the bed or the patio...

Giving his shoulders another squeeze, I say, "I think the nine of them will fit in two carts if someone stands or laps it..."

Aaron turns to me with a relieved expression, like I'm an actual savior here to deliver him from this den of sin on the eve of his wedding eve.

On the far end of the floor, I catch sight of a woman unzipping Quincey's pants as he unbuttons his shirt, officially turning this party clothing optional.

"Two more days," I reassure Aaron, swiping the keys jingling from Dunk's pocket as he buries his face between a woman's breasts and motor-boats her. "Holy fuck. I cannot stay here and see how far things go."

In full agreement, Aaron follows suit, sneaking onto the golf cart beside me as we burn beautiful sod to get out.

After I drop him off at the hotel entrance, I tap out a quick text to Allegra asking how the bachelorette party is going, then tuck the phone in my pocket without sending. She's at a party I assume is going swimmingly, so I leave the talking for later and wander around the shops in the lobby.

In the window of a fine jewelry shop, a pair of small diamond hoops catch my eye. The setting is simple, diamonds on a white-gold band, but they sparkle like Allegra. *She claimed me,* I think as I enter the store and spend a few minutes talking with the saleswoman who assures me, "They're perfect when you love someone but aren't quite ready for 'I do.'" As she slips the box into a small velvet bag, I thank her for her help and head off, following posted signs to the water.

Two signposts in, I change course for the "renowned gardens," fondly remembering the Honolulu Airport gardens Allegra and I discovered together, minus the last few minutes.

With a quick glance over my shoulder, I step over the rope closing it off for the night. Among the colorful flowers and tropical foliage, I'm transported back there—towering pines, banana palms, monstera, swaying willow trees tucked between koi-filled waterways and sparkling lanterns. I feel like time turned back, and I wish Allegra was here to see how magical it is.

We'd wondered what the gardens would look like at night

and how the vibrant birds of paradise and cascading waterfalls over lava walls would come alive in the shadows.

Slipping my phone from my pocket again, I stare at her name on the screen, debating whether to press send, when three small ellipses appear. I wait with bated breath and struggle not to smile too hard when the message populates.

Allegra Malone 10:21 pm
Thinking about you.

I laugh. The fish and trees are my only witnesses. I wonder if they sense my joy. I wait a sec before typing out a response.

Damon Dawson 10:22 pm
I'm thinking about you too.

Allegra Malone 10:22 pm
Are the guys behaving? I hope Aaron knows Piper tracks his phone. LOL.

I laugh giddily. A fresh energy fills me.

Damon Dawson 10:24 pm
Rest assured. I delivered the package safely to the saloon. I cannot speak for any of the other guys...especially the NC-17 surprise Mark is probably enjoying right now.

Allegra Malone 10:25 pm
You think that's bad? Do you know who Gemma is?

Damon Dawson 10:25 pm
Is she the quiet one with the bangs, always with Chelsea?

Allegra Malone 10:26 pm
Okay, yes. She's one of Piper's bridesmaids. Super quiet. Sweet. Stays in Chelsea's shadow. Also, total lightweight. I'm talking like one wine cooler and bam! Can't remember her name. DRUNK.

Allegra Malone 10:27 pm
So, Chelsea made the executive decision not to bar hop and instead had us all meet in her room where there was a stripper waiting. Since Piper wouldn't have some "random man touching her," she told the girls to have at it. Four Peach Beach Bellinis later, Gemma pushed the guy down on his little performance chair like he was her personal submissive, mauled him, then ground herself on top of him with everyone in the room taking incriminating pictures.

Allegra Malone 10:29pm
She's going to die in the morning when she realizes she slipped her panties to the side and rode him like a goddamned stallion.

Holy shit. This conversation is not going where I thought it was. Maybe weddings do make people hornier.

Damon Dawson 10:32 pm
Yeah, I think some wild hedonistic shit is happening tonight.

I facepalm when I realize she might think I'm talking about us. So, I quickly tap out follow-up message.

Damon Dawson 10:32 pm
I think Mark, Dunk, and at least four other guys are hooking up with the "strippers." Aaron couldn't get out of there fast enough. We both know Piper would've had his ass. LOL. So what's happening now that Gemma hijacked the entertainment?

Allegra Malone 10:32 pm
Sir, when I tell you I had to get out of there... Not my scene at all. LOL. Shit is going to go down at the rehearsal tomorrow. How about you? Did you head back to the room after dropping off Aaron?

Damon Dawson 10:33 pm
I was just thinking I wish you could be here with me in the gardens.

The three ellipses appear, then disappear.

A few seconds later, the faint click-clack of heels grows louder on the slate pathway.

"Bright side?"

I turn to her voice. "Bright side..."

Allegra tucks her phone in her purse and follows the winding garden path toward me. "Great minds," she says, beaming and coming in for a hug. She bands her arms around my waist and squeezes with her entire body.

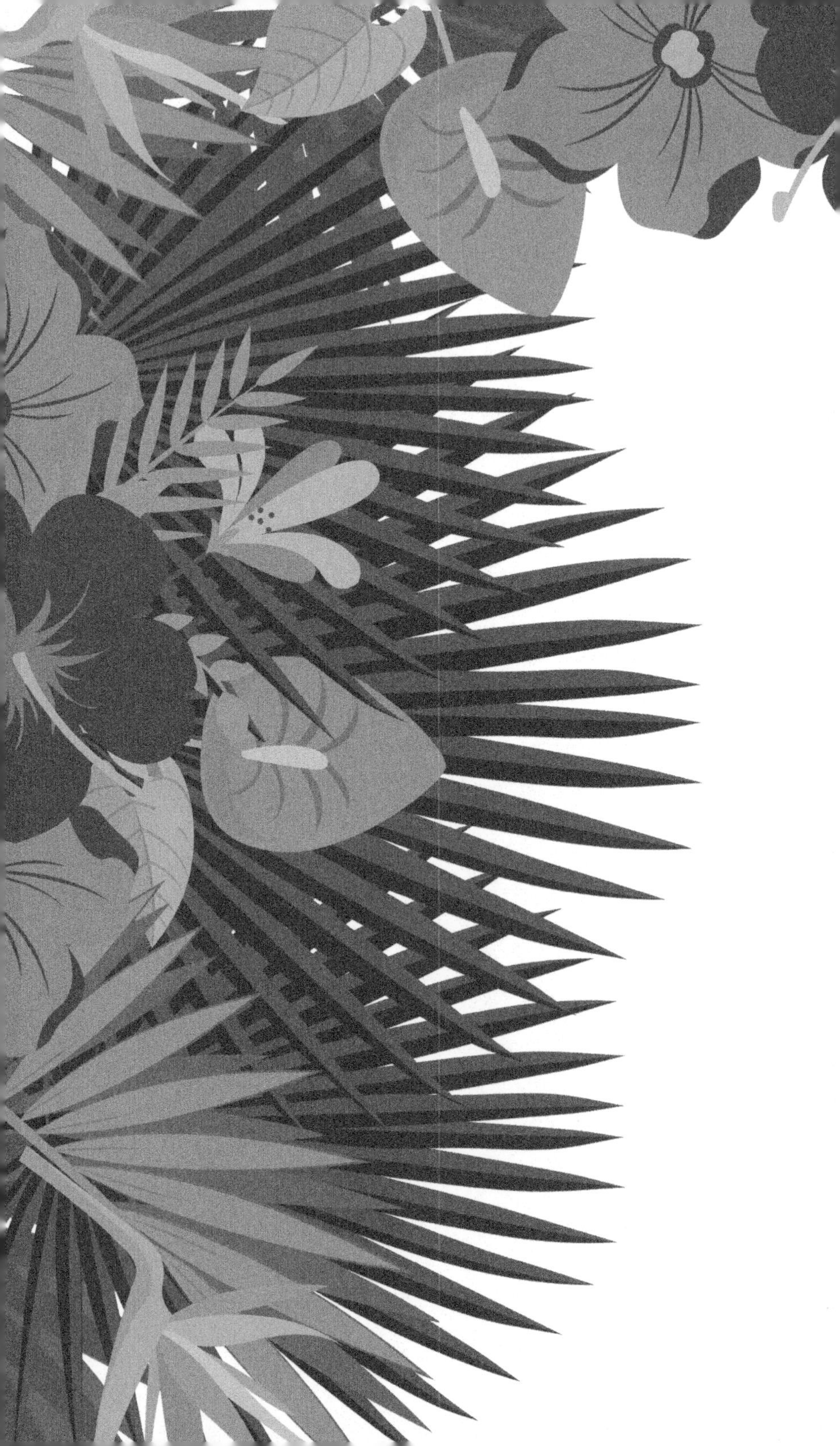

CHAPTER 12
Damon

"How did you know I was here?" I'm cheesing as Allegra hugs me tighter.

"I didn't. I just...I didn't want to go back to the room by myself. Then I remembered the cashier at Chow-Mein Express talking about how gorgeous the gardens were, so, here I am. Here *we* are." Allegra nips the corner of her mouth sheepishly, looking up at me.

I rub my hands in slow circles over her back. "No stripper hookup for you tonight?"

"Nah, I've got my heart set on someone already."

My pulse kicks up, my heart skittering hopefully. "Oh, yeah?"

Resting her head on my chest, Allegra scrapes her fingertips over my stomach. "Yeah, he's sort of a tall, dark, and brooding quiet type. Great friend. Seriously nice ass."

I bark out a laugh. "Thanks, I think."

"Oh, you are welcome. Thank *you*," she chuckles, lifting her chin to kiss my neck before loosening her grip and walking further into the garden. "This place is...just magical. It really reminds me of the Honolulu gardens. But on a larger, bigger-budget scale." She muses.

She stops in front of a koi pond, staring with a faraway gaze at the water that's illuminated an electric blue.

Allegra, standing there rubbing her hands over her forearms, surrounded by brightly colored flowers and lush trees. I can't help feeling like tonight is some kind of warped dejá vu. It's still us. We're still playful and free in paradise. But it feels like Laura, Trish, and Kyle are all fading into the background, especially with Allegra in that red dress that's molded to her golden-brown curves.

This time, I'm not walking away.

As I close the distance between us, settling in behind her, and I rest my chin on the crown of her head, clasping my hands at the cinch of her waist. For a few minutes, I soak up the sounds and the breezes, the easiness of this second chance, and pray we're not still pretending.

We both start speaking at the same time, eager to remove any lingering boundaries between us.

"You go. I didn't exactly let you talk back in the room," Allegra says through a giggle.

We both laugh because sex is certainly an effective—preferred—method of communication. We said a lot of things back there that have irrevocably changed our dynamic.

"No, you can go. Mine will take a little longer," I murmur.

Allegra nods, releasing a soft breath, then she asks, "Why do you think I want to take the ChatVideo case?"

Her voice is low and tentative, like she's afraid of my answer, as she settles easily into my embrace.

It's not that I don't want to talk about ChatVideo and tell Allegra everything about Laura and the Hammonds. I was just hoping we could talk about us first.

"Honestly, I don't blame you, Al, or Lea. I know what it'll do for the firm's future, so I should be on board, too, but—"

"This isn't about revenge, D." She drops her head into her hand, her thumb massaging her temple. "When I think about ChatVideo and the hours she must have spent away from family in front of a computer—spinning her wheels and brainstorming to come up with an idea that sticks—only to have it swiped from underneath her. I know we haven't reviewed the full claim yet. However fresh or innovative the brand and marketing, Laura Hammond figured out a way to meet the needs of her customers the same way Mom did. She deserves to have someone on her side, you know?"

I feel like a complete asshole.

Here I am thinking about myself and passing on the case because of my connection with Laura, when I know what Allegra, Aaron, and Mama Malone went through. Mama Malone was tired of using chemical-laced products not meant for a wide variety of natural hair textures, so she rolled up her sleeves, pulled out her pots and pans, and made her own homemade recipes. She put in the legwork to sell them at county fairs and flea markets and built something tangible to pass on to her kids. Then a big-name haircare company took advantage of their network to swipe her ideas while her patents were pending. As a startup, she didn't have the money to sue once her patent was issued.

They were counting on it.

For Allegra, her career is built on righting the wrongs of the past. She fights for the dreamers and the hopeless romantics.

This isn't about me.

"I know. I'm so sorry, Al." I kiss her forehead. "My head is all over the place. It was selfish, but in the back of my mind—"

"Do you think I still want to be with Kyle?" She blurts out, getting straight to the crux of my rambling.

The weight of her question crushes down on my chest.

No matter how good this feels, the fact of the matter is, days ago Allegra was in a relationship with a man who she thought she was going to marry. And now she's here with me. More than life itself, I want these whirlwind days, twelve years in the making, to mean we're supposed to be together. But the thought I could be her placeholder until she finds something better...it steals my air.

Allegra takes my silence as agreement, turning in my arms to read the heavy expression on my face.

"D, look at me." She reaches up, curving her hand over my jaw, brushing the pad of her thumb over my bottom lip. "When we were in the gardens, I was looking at those pictures because I needed it to sink in. Before I unfollowed and blocked them, I wanted to remember they were two people who don't deserve to be a part of my life."

"I get that."

"Do you, though? It bothered you the same way it bothered me to see the hurt etched on your face. You're a beautiful surprise in the middle of all this chaos."

"That's just it. Everything is happening so fast. You haven't dealt with your feelings about the breakup or moving or Trish, none of it. As amazing as all this is, I feel like I'm just complicating things for you."

Allegra cups my face with both hands and stands on her toes to brush a soft kiss over my lips. "Listen to me. Yes, there are a bunch of moving parts right now, but you're not complicating my life. You're the only thing in my life that makes any sense." A laugh spills into the kiss.

"Did I miss something?" I ask.

"So, um... I didn't get to tell you, but earlier at the bridal luncheon, we were playing games. Then Piper's maid of honor, Chelsea, asked about you, and I don't know what happened, but I got so jealous." Allegra buries her face in my chest. "I wanted to climb across that table, shake her, and warn her if she didn't stay away from you, I'd—"

A deep, robust laugh rocks my body.

"You'd do what?" I ask, stepping back to survey Allegra's face.

She shakes her head as she pinches the bridge of her nose. "Ooh, the death glare I shot her... It was so embarrassing, and I really couldn't tell you what I would've done, but she was going to feel the pain and the wrath."

I tug Allegra to my chest as my heart does cartwheels. "I'm flattered, but also I'm glad you chose nonviolence."

"Barely." She giggles.

The lightness of the mood somehow empowers me.

"It's okay. I've been harboring a soft spot for you too." I give her a quick peck, then slip my arm around her shoulder, veering on the path. "I can't tell you how many times I've wanted to deck some of the guys you've chosen clear in the throat."

Allegra tilts her head to give me a sidelong glance. "Exactly how long are we talking here?"

"Let's see." I pretend to run a mental tally. "About twelve years." I feel my chest tighten with apprehension as I set the words free after all this time. At her soft gasp, the need to qualify my response gnaws at me. "I never wanted to risk losing our friendship, Al. You're my family, and that's worth more to me than anything else."

We walk quietly for a bit, letting everything I've said, and everything I didn't say in the shower, seep in.

She knows I was the quiet kid in the corner for half my life, passed over and passed around from family to family, waiting to be chosen, and looking for my forever home. I'm still working through how I'm going to let her know *she* is my home.

The earrings burn a hole in my pocket, so I fish out the small bag.

"This is for you." She eyes the velvet bag for a beat before she finally takes it from my hand.

"It's not a ring or two-carat studs, but they reminded me of you."

Allegra slows to stroll, removes the box from the bag, and stares at them without saying a word.

When the silence gets too thick, I do my best to lighten the mood.

"So, your friendship contract...yeah, I've been living it all this time. We're going to need some amendments or a new version altogether." I try to laugh it off.

The humor doesn't seem to translate, though.

Allegra comes to a full stop, squaring her body to mine.

"Fuck the contract, D. I can't pretend with you." Her expression is grave as she searches my eyes. "You think I'm not scared of how I feel about you, and that I haven't seen you all these years and felt something?"

I lower my head, but she chucks up my chin.

A warm drizzle carried on the summer breeze and charged with electricity dapples my skin, but we don't run for cover.

"I didn't trust myself not to screw everything up with the only man who matters to me," she says.

Thank God the gardens are closed and we're the only trespassers. Lust and something like love pulses between us as we kiss under the tropical sky blanketed with a million stars. With all the fish and flowers and low-lit trees surrounding us, Allegra slips her greedy hands beneath my shirt. She deepens the kiss, teasing her fingers over the waistband of my pants. With a relentless urgency, she yanks at my zipper, freeing me from my pants as she strokes my aching flesh.

The only man who matters to me.

I let her words fuel me as I tug her dress hem over her thighs and round ass up to her waist. The need to feel myself moving inside her is almost too overwhelming. Then I discover she isn't wearing panties.

"Fucking hell, Al." I take her lower lip into my mouth, sucking and teasing as I glide my fingers between her thighs, grazing her tender flesh before dipping two, then three, fingers inside. "You feel so fucking good."

She moans her approval and tells me how much she needs to feel me inside her, and it's too much to hear and do nothing about.

I lower myself onto my knees and replace my fingers with my mouth, worshipping at her altar.

"Oh my God, D."

Her breaths come fast and shallow as I pry her open with my tongue, sucking and tasting her salty sweetness. I lift one leg over my shoulder, and my hands grip her ass as I dip my tongue deeper and harder, impaling her slick, warm folds. Her fingers dig into my shoulders, and she lets her head fall back. Her breaths are ragged as she whimpers with approval.

As I swirl my tongue and dart it against her swollen flesh, an orgasm ripples through her as she comes for me.

She's winded and sated as I push to my feet and tug her over to a grassy area where I lay down my shirt. Settling on the cool fabric, I hold my hand out to her. Without taking her eyes off me, she straddles me, slowly lowering herself down my shaft until her sex clenches around me. And as we move, slowly rocking to a gentle steady rhythm, kissing, and falling headfirst. I think I'm finally ready to tell Allegra.

She beats me to the chase, though.

"I love you, Damon," she says, slowing as she presses her fingers to my lips. "I know you must think I'm all over the place with my head and my heart or that I'm just out of one relationship and now I'm jumping in with both feet with you, but this is different." She winds her hips, releasing a soft gasp. "Finally, after all these years, we're together, and we're different, D.".

"Only you and me," I remind her.

We kiss and hold each other. It's soft, sensual sex. We love on each other as we stare longingly into each other's eyes. As we rock and grind, every sensation is heightened. Our warm breath swirls around our necks and ears until we're both numb and raw and unraveling together.

After, as we fix our clothes and follow the path toward the garden exit, Allegra asks me to put the earrings on her. Then, I take her hand in mine and kiss the back. When she looks at me, I hope she knows I won't ever let it go.

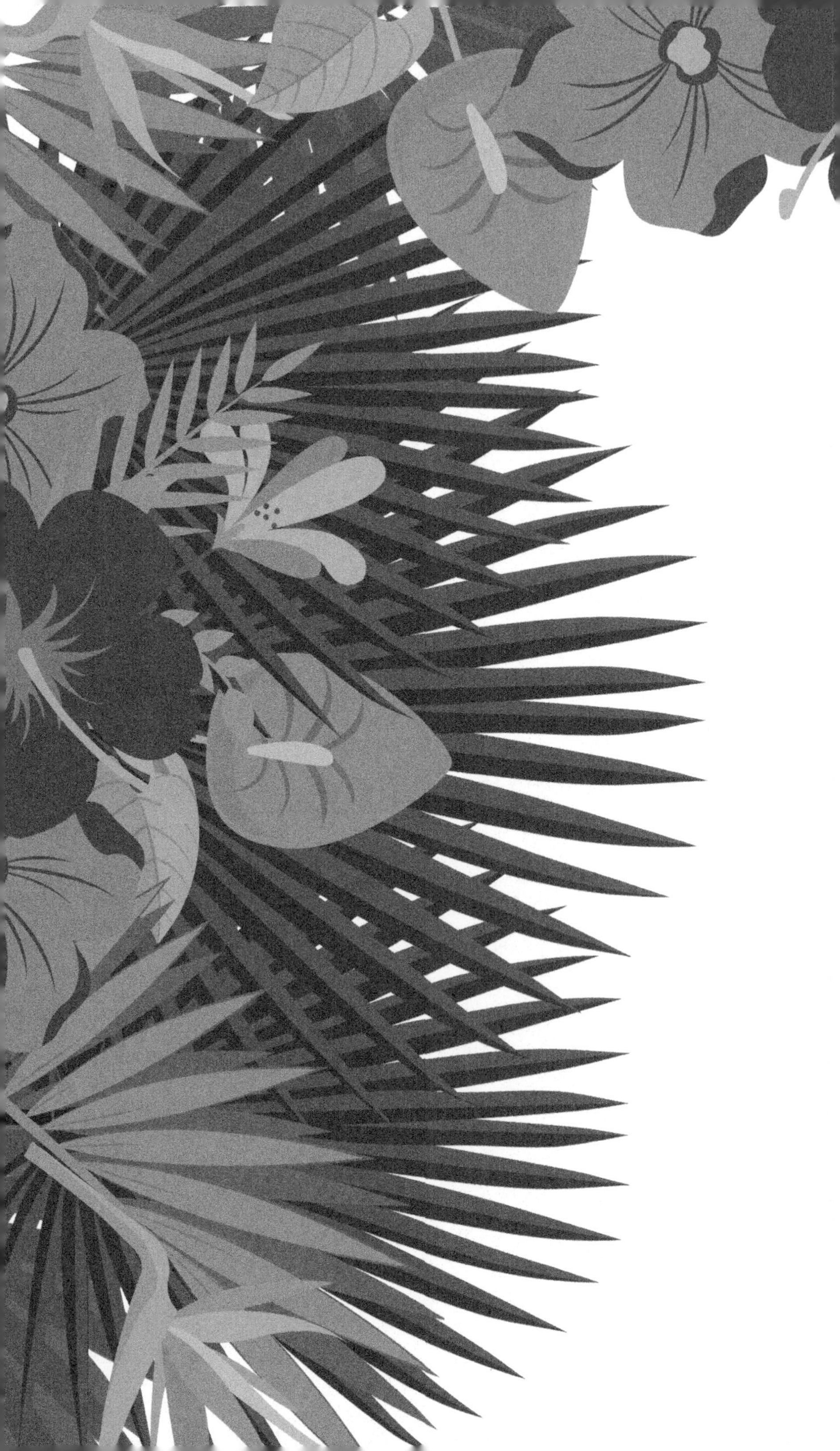

CHAPTER 13
Allegra

According to Piper's binder, the rehearsal is supposed to be an opportunity for the wedding party, their dates, and immediate family to practice the ceremony before the actual event. They want all hands on deck for a brief run-through to work out any last-minute kinks and tweak accordingly.

Key word: brief.

The agenda in the binder has the rehearsal set at an hour or less, but we are now going on two full hours with no end in sight.

I don't know who's worse between the hungover bridesmaids or the rowdy, horny groomsmen guffawing and making side jokes about the shenanigans of last night.

Everyone is laughing up and down the aisle, playing grab-ass, and looking at their phones like this is an adult daycare instead of a formal wedding rehearsal—which is going terribly wrong.

"Okay, let's do this once more, and try, *try*, to get it right this time." Piper drags in a deep breath, closing her eyes for a few seconds as she lets her arms dangle at her sides. Tucking a flyaway strand of sleek ebony hair behind her ear, she slowly exhales, then plasters on her "all is well" smile as if nothing is bothering her.

The show must go on, but I see the fraying edges at the corners of her mouth, the tightness of her forehead, and her rigid stance.

That's the part that pulls at my heartstrings.

I know what it's like to put a smiling on your face when you feel like doing anything but.

Damon, fed up like me, and apparently willing to do something about it, pushes to his feet in a storm of fury.

"That's enough!" He marches to the front of the aisle and starts barking out orders, binder in hand. "Aaron, Mark, Dunk, Colin, and Brian, in that order. You're here." His tone is hard and no-nonsense as he shoots them a challenging stare, daring them to keep playing around on his watch. "Look, I know we're all tired. Some of us are hungover and regretting ill-advised decisions from last night, but I'm not about to sit around and let you all ruin Aaron and Piper's wedding."

Damn.

Damon is amazing when he's sweet and tender, but when he's taking charge and putting an entire room full of immature adults in their places, he is sexy beyond belief.

I tamp down my urge to swoon as he draws his broad shoulders back, baring his throat to them.

"Thanks, but it's okay." Piper sets her hand on Damon's arm, but he is undeterred in his mission.

"It's not okay." He turns to face the guys, who are still snickering. "You think it's funny for her to stand here and watch her dream wedding go down the tubes? We're hoping the weather lets up, but if it doesn't, she and Aaron are going to need your help to make sure tomorrow is special. They're going to need *you* to remind them why they chose you to help them celebrate..." He trails off, staring each person down. He's letting them know in no uncertain terms that their behavior makes him question why they were chosen.

The laughter dissolves.

The light drizzle spraying Damon's and my skin last night turned into a tropical weather system threatening to become a hurricane. So, the late-afternoon rehearsal that was supposed to be outdoors overlooking the water with a breathtaking view of the sun setting over paradise was canceled, as was team karaoke poolside and the property-wide scavenger hunt. The only two things left on the agenda are the rehearsal and the promise of fun and games over dinner with drinks to follow. So, I get why Piper's looking forward to the only two events not lost to inclement weather.

Her fairytale destination wedding may end up in a stuffy, beige hotel ballroom, after all, with no background sounds of waves crashing against the shore or sweet-scented breezes. If we lose power, no music for the reception, either.

A dream wedding hinged on the power of backup generators.

Not if Damon has anything to say about it, though.

He turns his stony gaze on the bridesmaids, making it plain they're not exempt.

"Chelsea, Gemma," Damon drops his attention to the binder, appearing to double-check the names, "Serena, Tiffany, in that order. You're here." He fans his hand out to the left, waiting as they fall in line. "Is this where you want everyone? Are they in their correct pairs?" He turns to Piper, who sheepishly nods, and the beginnings of a genuine smile quirks the corners of her mouth.

Then she tosses a glance over her shoulder at me.

Her look is unmistakably in agreement with my earlier assessment of take-charge Damon. *You did good, girl.* She gets exactly why I'm falling so hard for my best friend.

The thing is, I'm still shocked myself about how real my feelings are for Damon. It's like I finally took off the blinders, and everything I've ever wanted feels within reach. What could be better than love with a man with whom I share the same values, history, and goals? And who is also amazing in a bed? *I assume.*

He's amazing in steamy showers and moonlit tropical gardens, so it only stands to reason.

I let my gaze drift over his broad shoulders, the thick cords of his neck, and the way his rigid stance hardens his muscles. In a flash, every touch, kiss, and moan from last night replays in my head, and I'm struck by the turn my thoughts take. It feels like a point of no return. We've come this far, and we can't go back to being just friends...if we ever were "just" anything.

You and me.

That's all I want.

After doling out instructions and answering questions, Damon sends everyone except Aaron and Mark, who are positioned at the altar at the front of the room, out to the hallway for a last run of the day.

Once the grandparents and parents have been seated, Piper's adorably fierce six-year-old niece shows us all how it's done. She struts her stuff, tosses imaginary flower petals at each row marker, and gives us good face at the end of the aisle. Chelsea, her arm linked in Mark's, flashes Damon a smile as Dunk and Gemma, Colin and Serena, and Brian and Tiffany enter. Damon just gives her a steely stare in return.

Piper is now being escorted down the aisle by her dad, so I don't pounce.

After the mock ceremony, Damon confirms that the people reading poems and passages indeed have copies in large, easy-to-read fonts and that they're included in the binder to have on hand for the day of. Because of the number of attendees and possible weather advisories, the receiving line is nixed.

At 7:15, we finally make it to the restaurant's private room reserved for large parties. Damon volunteered for us to man the doors to help Piper and Aaron, so we wait for everyone to file inside and find seats. I can't take my eyes off of him the entire time.

Lord, the way I'm in love with this man...

Mrs. Yates stops to thank Damon for helping her daughter get the wedding party in line and moving the rehearsal along and tells him what a handsome young man he is before she turns to face me.

"You two make such a lovely couple. Maybe we'll be hearing more wedding bells from you all soon..." She leans in to kiss my cheek, and whispers, *"Don't let that one get away. He's a cutie."*

"I'm working on it," I say, laughing as she enters the room and finds a seat next to her husband.

"What was all that about?" Damon tosses me a half-grin, and a crease appears between his eyebrows.

I shake my head. "She just appreciates your finer assets."

He lets out a deep, throaty laugh that does inappropriate things to my insides. "Is that so?"

"Yup. She told me I needed to snatch you up quick."

Tracing his teeth over his full lower lip, he nods and points a finger at me. "She sounds like a wise woman. You should definitely listen to her."

"Oh, I'm listening, all right." My cheeks heat just as Chelsea traipses in front of us, lingering a little too long in front of Damon for my comfort.

After what I told him last night about wanting to crawl on the table and shake her, I sense that's the image going through his head when he catches me glaring at her. As she passes, he fixes me with an amused stare.

"*Non*violence." His lips twitch as he enunciates the word.

"First Mrs. Yates, then Chelsea. You're turning into a hot commodity..."

"Oh, yeah?"

When the last of the group is seated, he glides his hand over the small of my back and guides me to the two open chairs between. Damon seeks out my hand under the table without missing a beat. He intertwines our fingers, tenderly rubbing the pad of his thumb over my palm. He's constantly showing me, even when we're not the center of each other's focus, that I'm still in his thoughts and we're still connected.

"Someone's happy today." Mom hikes up an eyebrow and gives me a sidelong glance. Her gaze skates over our interlaced hands.

Mom, please let this be.

"Yes, someone is," I agree, staring straight ahead and struggling to bite back the joy bubbling up from my toes to my chest. The buzzing happiness I feel when I'm with Damon and the soft, playful intimacy and comfort we share can't be contained or concealed, though.

We both smile politely as the servers make their way around to each person. They take our entrée orders and top off our water glasses and champagne flutes to prepare for the toasts.

I'm saved from Mom's inquisition by Serena and Tiffany pulling me into a conversation about last night and "the event which shall not be named." They go on about lightweights and the dangers of sexual droughts then laugh about how it's always the "quiet ones."

I just nod and say little in response. I know Gemma is mortified enough without the gossip mill running alongside the incriminating photos.

Despite the distraction, I still feel Mom's eyes on me. So, of course, the instant her seared ono with honey soy glaze and my grilled salmon arrive, Mom dips her chin to her chest. A grin stretching her lips as she leans in close to me.

"I'm so happy for you, baby…" she says. I sense the silent "but" dying on her tongue. There's warning in her tone, and I want to both cover my ears and listen to what she has to say.

Whatever it is, she's lived it.

I tilt my head to her, weary and tense.

"No, there's nothing to worry about," she says. "I just want you to be careful with him. Take things slow if you can." The inflection in her voice rises slightly, snagging on "if I can," like she's confused whether she's making a statement or asking a question. *If* I can take things slow. *If* I'm capable of not rushing into a relationship.

"Like I said, we've known each other forever, but it's new," I say. "We're still feeling our way around."

I hate how slick the words feel on my tongue, sliding from the truth.

"You've just learned about his feelings, but he's loved you for as long as he's known you, baby," Mom continues. "He won't bounce back the way we do."

Bounce back?

This was the reason for the warning I heard in her tone. Those words crawl over my skin, dig beneath my flesh, and settle there. They're the same words Kyle used when he ruthlessly severed all ties. And now, Mom. But is that what I'm doing with Damon? Bouncing back? Latching on to my next rebound? Have faulty instincts taught Mom and me how to bounce back after a tough break?

No, what Damon and I share isn't me falling into my old habits…is it?

He's sitting next to me, so I can't be too loud, but I lean

close to Mom's ear and pray she'll receive what I'm about to tell her.

"I love him." It's a whisper and a plea for her to hear me as I let this amazing, warm, and sweet feeling wash over me. Before mom can ask me how I know, I add, "Love isn't living together or how much time has been spent in a relationship. It's not about finances or travel or sex or how bad I want it. I think I've been so used to what love isn't that I lost sight of what it is. Damon shows me every chance he gets."

It's all the evidence I need.

He's it for me. I don't want anyone else.

I turn to Damon and study his beautiful profile—the sweet, full lips that kissed me thoroughly through the night, his serious expression etched in the lines of his smooth, coppery skin, his warm brown eyes. When he looks at me intensely, I still feel it on my flesh hours later.

He's perfect, and the idea we could be anything less, that I could hurt him, leave him broken with no spring left, reaches right inside my chest and wrenches my aching heart.

A loud clinking rips me from my thoughts as Mark taps his fork against his champagne flute. He stands and flashes the table his trademark smoldering eyes.

"Most of you all know me, but for those who don't, I'm Mark, Aaron's best man. The *best* man," he quips, winking at the line of ladies on the other side of the table before breaking out into a chuckle. "Nah, I'm just playing around."

I smile despite the heavy sensation in my chest, struggling to be present for my brother.

"Because Chelsea will probably be up here forever with her toast"—Mark jests— "I'm going to keep this short and sweet." He dives into a high school homecoming story completely unrelated to Piper.

My throat tightens when Damon squeezes my hand to get my attention.

You okay? He mouths.

I nod too many times to be convincing, then tilt my head to either side, letting him know I'm just emotional, and not to worry. He removes his hand from mine and scoots his chair closer to curve me to his shoulder, so I'm hugging him from behind as he gingerly rubs my thigh.

The closeness is unbearably intoxicating and shamelessly reassuring. I'm drunk on his touch and his clean, heady scent banding around me. There's an easiness in knowing he really sees me...us. An unrelenting, desperate ache to be closer still crashes down on me, leaving me totaled.

I have no control as my heart and my brain work in collusion, filling my head with all the possibilities. Hope and fear blend seamlessly. What if I'm not hopping into the next relationship? What if I don't lose Damon? Instead, what if I'm right about us and he's everything I've hoped and dreamed all wrapped up into one amazing man who doesn't need to tell me he loves me because he shows me every day? What if I open my heart and let him all the way in?

Damon tilts his head to me.

"Bright side?" He slips his hand into mine when I tip my chin up. "I've been thinking, when we get back, I've got extra closet space and I clean out a few drawers... Maybe you'll consider staying with me?" He sucks in a small breath. "You've always been my home, Al. I love you."

And just like that, my entire heart is gone.

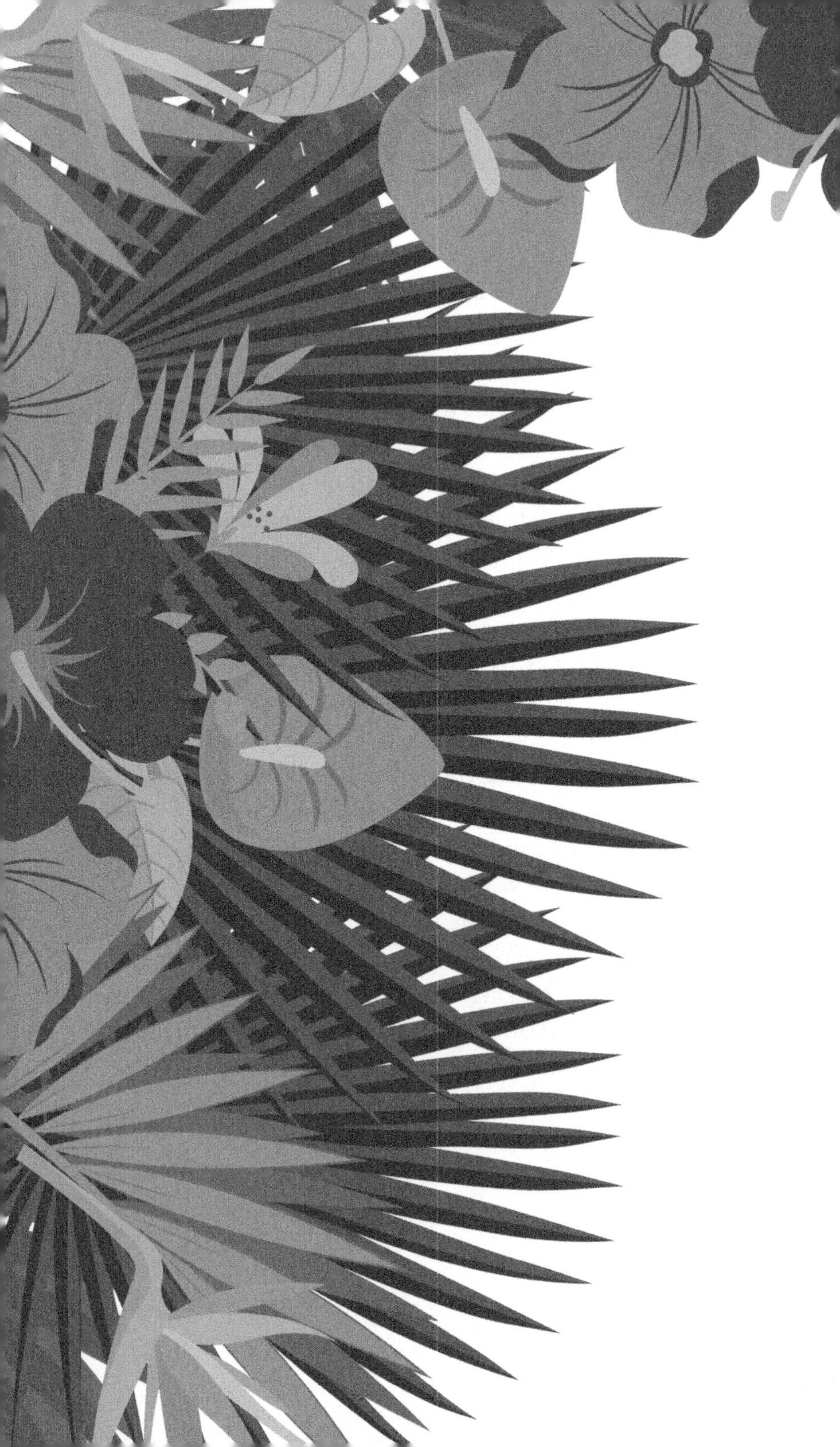

CHAPTER 14

Damon

"I'm serious, D. I've got to go. I promised Piper I'd help keep the women in line, and you know what happened last time..." Allegra steps out into the hallway, still staring unblinking at me like she wants to push me into the room and back into bed.

She licks her kiss-swollen, beaming, and beautiful lips.

I throw up my hands in surrender, and my towel inches lower around my waist, threatening to come off.

"That wasn't on purpose." I bow my head, smiling and hoping she'll cave and come lose track of time with me.

"Sure, it wasn't." She groans, wedging herself into the doorway to kiss me again, this time with the hungry desperation of knowing we'll be dragged through photos and getting dressed for the ceremony before we get to be together again. Her hands roam freely over my bare chest before she hooks her fingers over the top of the towel to feel the hard evidence of how much she'll be missed.

"Stay." A low growl claws from my throat as I kiss her lips and cheek, working my way behind her ear. "Stay with me." I drag my tongue over the sensitive skin, reveling in the moan I've coaxed from her. "Please, just five more minutes."

Her lips part as I slide my hand between her thighs and feel how hot and wet she is already.

"You are not playing fair." She closes her eyes against the rising sensation, subtly swaying with my movements.

My pulse races and electricity jolts through me.

We're halfway into the hall, and at any second, someone could walk out and see us.

I don't care.

This is what it's been like since we left the rehearsal dinner. I let her in on the secret that's been weighing on me all these years and told her I loved her. Then we had to wait through an hour of toasts and glass clinking before we finally made up an excuse about needing to be in the room for a work call with Lea.

We skipped the room altogether, resorting to clawing off each other's clothes in a family bathroom and fucking on the sink. Both times before had been tentative as we felt our way around our feelings. But in that bathroom, it was desperate and needy playful sex complete with snort laughs, clothing malfunctions missed mouths as we fumbled into our rhythm.

Only as we came down in ragged breaths with our racing hearts and trembling bodies did we stop to assess how amazing our sloppy thirds were. It wasn't like we were in a high-rise. We fucked in a bathroom because we were too desperate to wait for an elevator to go up three floors.

That's the good stuff.

That stuff makes me feel like I'm floating. It's the euphoric stuff that drives a man to finger fuck his woman in a hotel hallway, chasing touches just to keep the caffeine buzz thrumming through his blood.

I'm so high, I'm afraid to look down.

It wasn't until we were in bed on the verge of sleep last night when Allegra mentioned the irony of having one unchristened bed after two days into a hotel stay together. We'd checked off the shower, the gardens, and a public restroom stall that smelled vaguely of baby powder and butt paste.

Rectifying that tragic irony has taken us through the night and into the hallway.

"That's it...let go for me." I hold Allegra to my chest as she trembles against me. "While you're having girl talk about fucking strippers and wedding-night lingerie, I want you to think about how you let me get you off with the maid watching from the end of the hall."

She gasps, jerking her head toward the elevator where an older, velvet-skin woman with her hair piled in a dark bun on her head watches us endearingly. Allegra's mouth is wide open when she meets my gaze.

"Relax, from where she's standing, we look like a couple, hugging and so desperately in love we can't bear to leave each other's sides." I press a kiss to her lips, lingering. "She's not wrong about that part."

One more kiss, and I slap Allegra's ass, sending her on her way.

"Go put some clothes on, and stop teasing me," she says, tucking her lower lip between her teeth.

Her open-mouthed smile as she backs away is priceless, and the inspiration for another cold shower before I brush my teeth, dress, and head out to meet the guys in Mark's room, the bachelors' suite for the day.

The second I step foot off the elevator, I hear the music. Bass thumps behind a muffled old-school hip-hop verse blended with the roar of laughter. I knock twice before Dunk answers, and the noise hits me like a gust of whiskey-laced wind.

The people in the surrounding rooms must love them.

"Oh, shit." He cups his mouth with his hand, craning his neck back to stare me up and down. "Look at Kosher Crew coming through with the cold white linen pants, looking like he wants to give Stella her groove back!"

For the sake of my rep, I give him a cross-jump bounce and dip into a grind.

A whole mess of disbelieving, awestruck oohs and aahs ensue over me missing my chance on the old hip-hop and R&B music video countdown show. They spread out into a huddle, encircling me like I'm about to break into more moves.

"Chill. I don't think you all can handle this level of swag," I say, holding out my hands, bent over with laughter. "It's not right to show Aaron up like this on his wedding day."

Another wave of raucous laughter falls over the guys.

Eventually, they find their way over to the minibar, stocked with liquor and thick Cuban cigars, set to hang out on the balcony until their call times for the photographer and videographer.

Dunk holds one out for me, but I decline. He shrugs as if I'm missing out.

"Brian rolled a fatty if that's more your speed."

But I'm good.

I don't need a cigar or weed to get me high. I'm still weightless. My head is still in the clouds over these past few days with Allegra. It feels like I'm living a dream, and any minute I'll wake up.

Fingers snap next to my ear, jolting me out of my thoughts.

"You good?" Aaron asks.

He's still in blue chino shorts and a white t-shirt, looking preppy casual and unaffected that his nuptials are only a handful of hours away.

"Are you?" I retort, my lips still quivering with a stifled

laugh. "Piper hasn't planned your prep time down to the second?"

He chuckles, nodding. "She tried, but Mark wasn't having it." He empties a can of Coke into a glass already filled two fingers high with rum. "I owe you thanks, too. I appreciate you reeling everyone in yesterday at rehearsal."

"I got you." Slapping my hand on his shoulder, I toss him a mock-serious expression. "We can't have you starting this marriage out on the wrong foot because of a bunch of shenanigans. Piper will have that ass..."

Aaron barks out a laugh.

"Okay, I can see how you might think that, but Pipe and I...we pick our battles. We agree to disagree on some things and argue about others. But I suspect you'll learn marriage isn't always about who's in charge of what. Wherever she's strong, I let her lead, and vice versa. It's about complementing each other."

The corners of my mouth tug downward, and my lower lip protrudes as I nod. "It sounds like...like a load of bullshit she fed you."

We laugh. Digging on each other is all part of the fun.

"You've got jokes." He nods, smiling. "It's cool, but I see you and my sister making googly eyes and the longing stares and constant touching. That part slows over time as you get more comfortable, but hopefully, you're left with the feeling of belonging, you know? Like, the connection you've made together was all worth it." His voice lowers to a wistful bass. "Somehow, you've found someone with whom you really fit well. That's the shit that really matters."

Aaron gets this far off stare like he's seeing himself and Piper somewhere happy together in the future, but my mind snags on an unraveling thread.

Belonging.

I don't have a response.

If these past few days have proven anything, it's that Allegra and I have an undeniable, insatiable chemistry. We can't keep our hands off each other. It's a dream I keep thinking I'm going to wake up from. *Maybe it* is *just a dream.*

I spent too many years learning to focus on what's real and not getting too comfortable trying to belong.

Will what Al and I share translate when we get back to Vegas? What if Aaron is right, and this weightless, high-flying feeling fades? Will we still feel like we belong together?

I'm afraid to believe in forever homes. With the Hammonds, I learned nothing lasts forever. I want so badly for Allegra to prove eighteen years of foster care wrong.

The thought weighs on me as Aaron makes me a rum and Coke, too. I try to focus on his blessing of Allegra's and my relationship and the blessing he extended from Mama Malone. I hold tight to the idea he counts me as family, shoving aside my fear of loving Allegra only to one day lose her.

But as we talk about the plans for the day and the guys get dressed for photos, the anxiety lingers, swirling in the back of my mind.

Even as guests fill the rows of wooden folding chairs flanking the long white aisle runner, it's still there, gnawing at me, twisting my gut, telling me I'm unworthy of a place—or a person—to call home.

Just before the processional begins, Allegra plops down in the seat I saved for her, slipping her hand into mine as she kisses my cheek.

"Phew, that was a close call. Gemma stepped on the back of Piper's dress and all hell broke loose, but we worked it out. The friendship is on thin ice. The jury's still out whether it's the dress or sex with the entertainment that did it, but..." She blows out her cheeks, slowly releasing a breath. "I'm here."

I squeeze her hand, forcing a smile.

She picks up on the tension immediately. "What's wrong? What did I miss?"

"What did you miss?" I repeat.

Over the speakers, a soft ballad fills the air, and the shuffle as everyone stands to receive the bride saves me.

Allegra's eyebrows dip with concern as she twists to survey me over her shoulder.

"D?"

Because I don't have the words to tell her what's really in my heart, I pull her into my arms and clasp my hands around her waist. A wave of fear and sadness wash over me as we watch the bridesmaids and groomsmen approach the altar, smiling happily. *Belonging.*

"I missed you today, that's all."

My throat tightens as I cling to Allegra, trying against everything I've known not to let my hopes disintegrate. But as Piper glides toward Aaron, beaming and excited about the journey they're about to embark on together, the risk of losing my best friend, the only person who feels like home, it overwhelms me.

I'd never want to take away everything that's happened between Allegra and me this weekend, but I knew how deeply rooted my feelings were for her.

I can't lose her.

The corners of my eyes singe as I bite back tears. "I love you, Al."

Sensing the tension in my chest and the movement of my stuttered breathing against her back, Allegra whisks her fingertips over my forearm until Piper reaches the altar. Only once we're seated does she turn to look at me.

"I love you so much. Please don't shut down on me." She's still looking straight ahead as her brother and Piper vow to love each other for better or worse. "Please."

I shake my head, putting my arm around her shoulders to tuck her into my chest. As she tips up her chin, I cover her lips with mine briefly, closing my eyes against the fall.

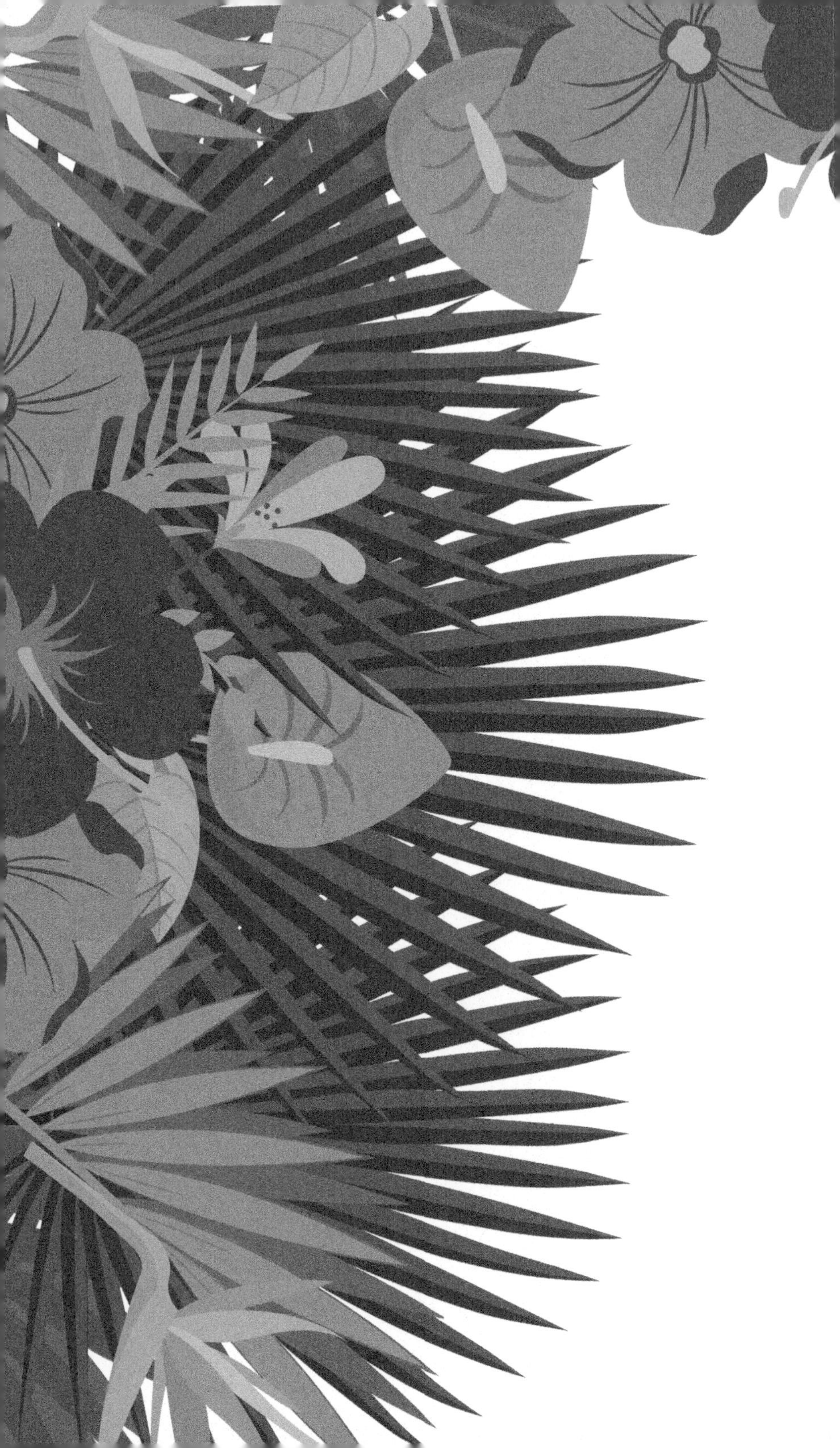

CHAPTER 15
Allegra

The instant we're airborne, I twist to face the window seat where Damon is slouched against the armrest and his balled-up neck pillow. Somehow, he looks both boyishly adorable and slightly hungover.

"Remember when I said, 'fuck the contract?' Yeah...so I'm thinking we maybe need to rethink that decision."

"Is this something we can talk about when my head isn't pounding? Maybe, when we aren't in a metal tube flying over an ocean?"

Valid point.

But I didn't spend my brother's wedding ceremony and most of the reception stress-eating buttercream cake and wondering what's happening between a drunken Damon and me just to sit through another six hours—plus a two-hour layover in LAX—and let the silent treatment continue.

Not happening.

"First, answering my question with a question is proof that you're guilty. Second, that's precisely what I want to talk about...the reason your head is pounding." I clarify.

Because he's intent on lying there with his eyes closed, I

lightly tap him on the shoulder, determined to get this off my chest before I can't.

"Seriously, D? I really can't believe you're going to this length."

"What are we talking about?" He groans, like he's the least bit innocent.

I stretch up to press the button to turn on his overhead light. It glares down on his sleepy face, and he squints in horror as I snap my fingers near his ear. He jerks his head toward me like it was a brass gong instead of my fingers.

"We're talking about the last twenty-four hours and how you've been ignoring me," I say, folding my arms across my chest as I shake my head. "I'm talking about how we went from doing what we did in the hallway yesterday morning to you taking full advantage of cocktail hour after the ceremony. You drank like a fish, then you turned out the dance floor with your stupid Kosher Crew dance battle moves—"

"No, I didn't."

"Uh, yes, you did." I release a mirthless laugh, irritation bubbling up inside. "That's not all you did. Add in the Cupid Shuffle with your own *cha cha dip to the ground and turn around*. You had everyone doing it. Ugh." I roll my eyes. "Don't forget the electric slide where you showed not only my mother but Piper's mom how to do the 'midnight version.'" My tone drips with distaste because, *come on*. "What is with you?"

Damon scrubs a hand over his face, wincing as last night's memories—before he passed out across our bed—seem to come rushing back all at once.

That's right, let's get on the same page here.

"Meanwhile," I raise my palms against the stuffy airplane cabin air. "When I wasn't persuading you not to show us your 80s break dance moves, lest you break a hip or knee, I spent most of cocktail hour and the reception hunting down the guys who were with you in the bachelor suite. I was hoping they'd have the balls to tell me what the hell happened in the mere five hours we spent apart."

At this, Damon sits up, finally giving me some legitimate eye contact, likely, and accurately, sensing this is going to get worse before it gets better. But there's a mix of shock and shame in those deep, dark brown irises.

"You did all that because of me?" A look of disbelief and a faint flush creep over his stubbled cheeks.

I heave a sigh, righting myself in my seat and staring at the muted movie playing on the seatback in front of me. Fittingly, Rachel McAdams is about to discover the seatmate she's been flirting with on the red-eye is a domestic terrorist.

Not today, Satan. Do not kill your best friend, Allegra.

When I nod, Damon shucks off the blanket he'd been nestled in and grips the armrest between us.

"Al?" He waits until I toss him a sidelong glance—as murderous as it may be. "I didn't realize how bad I was at hiding things from you."

So, he is hiding something.

"What things, D? I deserve to know what could make you go from fifty shades of hallway seducer to *The Quiet Place* in a handful of hours."

Damon sucks in a lungful of air then lifts the armrest so there's nothing between us but his sealed lips. Taking my hand in his, he kisses the back, holding it to his chest.

"On a surface level, it all boils down to something as simple as—" *You don't trust me.* "I'm scared."

"And you think I'm not?" For a few seconds, I close my eyes and breathe against the annoyance flaring in my gut before I start again. "You think that being with you doesn't feel like everything I've ever wanted *and* the greatest risk? I was considering marrying a guy who was carrying around a ring for someone else. I'd say I don't have the best track record with trusting people. The man was a user. I don't trust my heart or my body, but I trust *you*."

"Why?"

I chew the inside of my cheek to keep my emotions in check as I bite out, "I can't lose you, D. I don't know what I'd do without you." My throat tightens and the last words are barely above a whisper. Heat swarms my cheeks as I blink back tears, imagining the void he'd leave in my life.

With his free hand, Damon swipes the curve of my cheek and cups my face.

Shutting my eyes against his warmth, I lean into his touch.

"D, I shouldn't have to get you 30,000 miles in the air to find out what's bothering you. I don't think we'll be okay if you shut down on me again."

"I'm not. I was just trying to figure it out myself."

A small laugh bubbles up from my chest. "You do this, you know? You clam up when something is bothering you, and I go crazy racking my brain trying to figure out what's wrong, who hurt you, what I've done—"

"You did nothing."

"Then, *please.*" I shift to face him, inwardly hoping he can see how much his silence makes me feel like I'm to blame. "It's still me, D. I'm still your best friend, and you can tell me whatever's giving you reservations about us." Pecking his lips, I linger. My eyes bore into his. "What scares you most?"

He lets the silence buoy on the surface of our emotions for a moment, like he's considering how much he wants to say.

"Losing you," he mutters, finally. "Losing my best friend and the only home I've known."

The shame etched on his solemn face reaches inside my chest and wrenches my heart.

Taking his face in my hands, I tip up his chin, needing him to really see me when I tell him like he's told me too many times to count, "Damon Dawson, I'm not going anywhere. You're my best friend and the love of my life. We're connected. We're family. You are my eternal bright side."

A faint smile quirks his lips.

"Yeah?"

"You and me. That's all this has ever been about. Whether you like it or not, our bond is binding and irrevocable, sir. Did you not read the fine print in the contract? We belong together. Yes, I said *belong*."

Damon tugs me closer, blindly reaching up to turn off his overhead light before he kisses me slowly and thoroughly. The fiery sweeps of his tongue and gentle sparks of his fingertips on my neck to the curve of my cheek set my skin ablaze. He tips my head back to deepen the kiss, and a low growl spills from his full lips.

"I love you, Al."

"When we get home, no more clamming up, that's my stipulation," I say, punctuating each phrase with kisses all over his face. "We overhaul the entire contract for Version 2.0. I see you, so you don't get to be the quiet kid in the corner waiting to be noticed anymore. Not with me."

"No more," he whispers, his lips finding mine.

"Promise me you'll trust me with your worries, and I'll be your forever home. Those are my enforceable terms and conditions, Mr. Dawson. Our love is the consideration."

"I promise."

Pulling back slightly, I squint my eyes. "Since your hangover is still painfully evident, I'm going to cut you some slack right now, but just so you know, I fully intend to get that in writing."

We kiss, rocked by turbulence as the plane crosses the

Pacific. Above us, the "fasten seatbelt" sign illuminates, and the captain instructs all passengers to remain seated while we pass through it.

Damon and I sit back in our respective seats, buckling our seatbelts and replacing the armrest between us. But he digs into his carry-on, fishing out his EarPods and gives me the second one so we can watch the movie together.

He drapes his blanket over us then finds my hand underneath and holds it, letting me rest my head on his shoulder.

A little while later when the turbulence evens out and the cabin is dark and quiet, he squeezes my hand, and I think he's going to say something poignant and meaningful.

I couldn't be more wrong.

"So, did I do anything else regretful last night?"

The smile tugging at the corners of my mouth is real. The shift is almost imperceptible, but I feel the easiness settling again between Damon and me.

I missed it.

"Before or after you passed out lying horizontal on the bed in all your clothes while drooling?"

"Damn."

"Exactly." I giggle. "By the time Aaron and Piper entered, you were at least one platter of fancy hors d'oeuvres and three drinks in. Plus, Tiffany's husband Quincy said you'd been downing rum and Coke with Aaron before the ceremony, so..."

"Look, I figured if I was going to be stuck in my head, maybe I could drown out my anxiety."

I huff out a laugh, sliding my feet close to his and running my socks up his calf.

"How'd that work out for you?"

Damon cranes his neck back. "Did you really go into full investigator mode, asking around about what the guys were up to?"

"Yes. I was so confused because when I left the room in the morning, we were two seconds from going at it in the hallway. I couldn't figure out why you were suddenly clamming up again after you'd scandalized the housekeeping staff by whispering dirty sweet nothings in my ear. So, desperate times..." I shrug, but Damon nuzzles his face into the bend of my neck. "Long story short, I did a mental run-through of Piper's timeline for the guys, retracing your steps through breakfast and disbursing the groomsmen gifts before I realized you all were meeting back at the 'bachelors' suite.'"

"I see... So, when you said you needed to go talk with your cousin Terry, you'd narrowed down the guys who weren't in the wedding party but who were in the room and hunted them down?"

"Yup. In a nutshell, I needed answers."

"Remind me to never do a crime. CIA has nothing on you." Laughter rumbles over Damon's shoulders. "You're something else. Well, what facts did you gather during your reception shakedown?"

"A whole bunch of nothing."

This time I laugh because beyond a few dances and buttercream cake, my efforts were basically fruitless.

"Unless you count the invite that we scored to Terry's end-of-summer cookout Saturday after next. Despite my cousin's affinity for fresh gossip, it should be fun—dominoes, spades, good music, barbecue."

"I'm down."

"She probably just wants to see if we're going to last that long." I roll my eyes, sighing good-naturedly. "As far as the fact-gathering goes, I'm sorry to report most of the guys were paying you zero attention. Drinks, cigars, shooting the shit, that about sums it up what they did while you and Aaron were talking. I didn't want to bother him on his wedding day, but I fully intended to call him the second he and Piper got back from the honeymoon."

Damon rubs circles on my back. "The final verdict?"

"If you were going to that length to maintain your silence, I had to go further to find out why. I put my investigation on hold and danced with you until you could barely stand upright. I knew I had 30,000 feet and six-plus hours to corner you." I boop his nose. "Dawson, Friendship Contract Version 2.0 will be memorialized in ink when we get home."

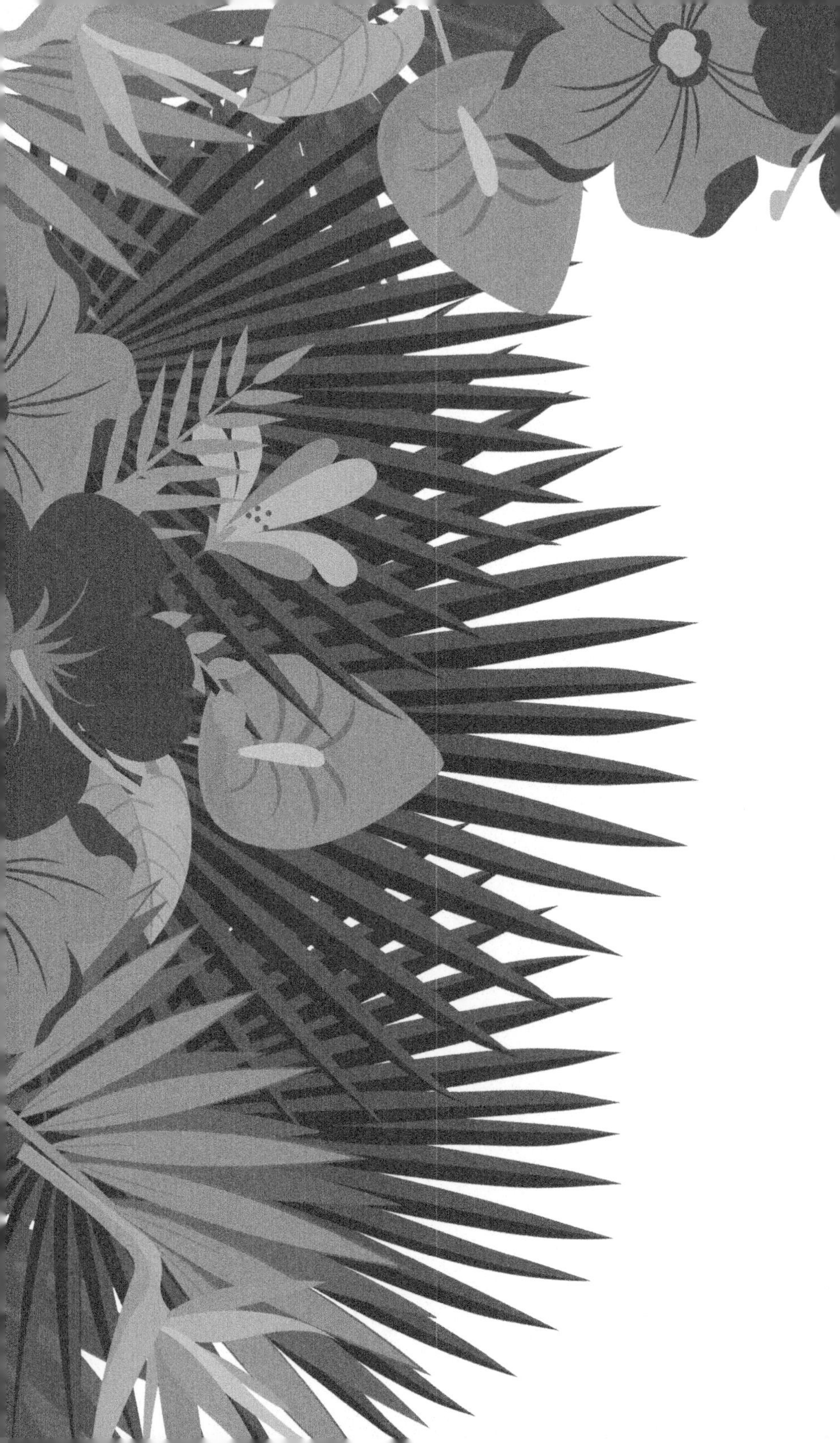

CHAPTER 16
Allegra

The rest of the flight and through the L.A. layover, I'm still high on the grandeur of what "home" means to me—to "us"—now. *We're an us.* Naturally, my heart hijacks my brain, and its autofill duties work overtime. Thus, I get lost between semantics and my vivid imagination, visualizing our cute, personalized welcome mat.

It will say, "Welcome to *Our* Home" in a swirly script with red roses or a trendy damask pattern. I figure we'll need one of those coffee mug sets that reads, "I like her butt," and "I like his beard," too.

Adorbs.

The way my brain functions, it does not stop at home decor.

As we leave the airport terminal and the shuttle drops us off at long-term parking, I'm thinking about how I'll answer *our* home phone. *Who in the heck even has a landline anymore unless it's a business?*

But still.

Thanks for calling our home. Let me get the Mister for you...

Our blessed nest. Okay, maybe I've been watching too many

old sitcoms and home remodel shows. That's super Claire Huxtable.

You've reached the home of Damon and Allegra.
Nah.

But it's that last one that ultimately leads me to the dilemma of last names. And this is the part where I get way too carried away way too fast. I strike "the Dawson-Malone" residence the second it fills my head because it sounds more like a trendy hotel chain or a clothing line. I finally settle on "the Dawson home."

Suddenly, everything isn't just a daydream and notebook doodling fodder.

I'm struck with the realization that I don't want to just be Damon's best friend and roommate. I don't want to be housemates and coworkers or in a short-lived affair that lasts a couple of years and ends with him proposing to a bootleg version of me with a gaudy ring. Damon and I might have leaped over a bunch of steps on the relationship roadmap, but I want to skip straight to the end. I want more world-shattering kisses and toe-curling sex and more handholding and promises to each other. I want to mark this moment as the nanosecond I realized: I. Want. To. Marry. Damon. Dawson.

Shit.

If I was still beating around the bush, I'd silence my brain. But on cue, like an overzealous version of autocorrect bullying my words before I can finish typing them, it autofills:

Allegra Marie Malone Dawson.
Allegra Marie ~~Malone~~ Dawson.
Shit, shit, shit.

But, if you look up "marriage material" in the dictionary...

"Here, you take the keys and call the elevator. I'll grab the bags," Damon says as he passes me the key ring before he hops out to heft our suitcases from the trunk. It's an exclamation point of my autofill.

Breathe.

"Are you sure? I can carry—"

"I've got you," he says, like my personal, sexy hero.

Sigh.

When we finally make it up to Damon's loft—*home*—we are beat. *Some of us, mentally and physically.* He leaves our suitcases at the door, and we weave through my mountain of boxes, and strip off our clothes before we drag our tired bodies into the shower—separately. It's an act of self-love on my part. I need to think *without* Damon's forearms and sexy lip-biting grin fogging the speck of clarity in my useless brain.

After we brush our teeth, I let Lea know we made it back safely, then wander out to the living room to rifle through my clothing boxes for a pair of clean, comfy pajamas. But as I'm standing next to the stacked boxes with all my worldly possessions, I feel the freak-out descending upon me like a looming tidal wave followed by a blaring alarm.

Warning: Reality ahead.

Damon and I are not a half-hatched, meaningless contract I scrawled across my notebook. Cute door mats, phone greetings, a sweet message on my outgoing voice recording—none of it matters. Our relationship is genuine, and so are the consequences of every decision we make from here on out.

Now more than ever, I've got to think logically.

When I finally fall into bed next to Damon, I roll onto my side to face him, and he gives me the sweetest kiss through the biggest grin.

"What are you cheesing about?" I ask.

"Nothing, I'm just happy," he says, adorably.

My mouth is so dry.

"Me too…" I laugh, letting some of the tension drain with

the small breath I release. "Okay, don't laugh at me. It's probably residual wedding feelings, but I *might've* gotten carried away thinking about us and where this relationship is headed..." I trail off, bracing myself for the rest.

But Damon's slow smile is everything.

"You can't just say something generic like that and not tell me the specifics. A man needs to know these things." He traces his teeth over his lower lip, scooting closer to band his arm around my waist.

I squeeze my eyes closed.

"I got hung up on the word 'home,' and it sort of spiraled from there—doormats, coffee mugs, outgoing voicemail recordings—all with some version of *'our home'* or 'The Dawson Home.'" I cringe as heat warms my neck and cheeks.

"Look at me," Damon says.

When I do, a sliver of moonlight coming from the blinds crosses his face, so it looks like glitter sparkling in his eyes. As much as I'm mortified, I'm so mesmerized.

"That might be the sexiest thing I've ever heard." He squeezes me closer still.

"Yeah? Because I thought it was sort of corny..."

Damon chuckles. "It is, but corny from you is my favorite kind." He kisses my forehead, beaming. "Now, what are we talking here with the doormat? Hearts and flowers or are we going rogue with a 'Welcome with tacos and wine' sort of thing because I'm down for all of it."

I swat his chest and he catches my wrist, using it for leverage to roll and tug me on top of him.

"No, seriously, though." Concern shifts the shadows and lines of his features. "What's on your mind, Al?"

"Are you sure this is what you want? Is losing me the whole of your worries; are you having second thoughts?" I cringe. *Because I'm freaking the freak out. We live and work together, so we just committed to what? What's the fine print here?* "You know me. Taking things slow? My heart and brain are already conspiring to share more than a bed and a doormat, D. I want to share rings, vows, last names. Give me a few hours, and I could have our entire wedding planned down to the place settings and registry." I groan, lowering my forehead to his chest. "God, why am I so extra?"

Hugging me to his chest, Damon kisses my hair.

"Listen, if you think that doesn't warm my heart to hear you say that about us, you're wrong. Al, I want everything with you. But we need to learn to navigate these fresh waters before we go full speed."

"Welcome to 'The Dangers of Leading with Your Heart 101.'" I laugh, feeling more hopeless than romantic.

My stomach is in knots as worry gnaws at me.

Damon, seeming to sense neither of us will probably get any sleep tonight if we don't find some sort of bright side, rolls on his side, taking me with him.

"Where's your purse?" he asks, pushing off the bed. His posture is filled with a renewed energy. He holds up his palms at the curious expression I flash him. "Relax, big head, I have an idea."

He goes into the living room for a minute and returns flipping through the pages of my notebook.

As he settles on the edge of the mattress, I crawl over to him, sitting back on my knees to look over his shoulder as he drags a pen over the page, crossing a giant X through the Friendship Contract.

"Okay, that was extreme, but..." I laugh.

"You said you wanted it in writing. Now, let's really put some thought into Version 3.0." He jots the full title in all caps at the top of the page, qualifying his statement. "Though important, that one promise we made on the plane isn't enough. Maybe this will help us figure out how to proceed *slowly*," he drags out the word comically slow.

"I'm listening."

Recognizing the seriousness of our intentions—and the fragility of our hearts— Damon and I spend a good hour drawing up an entirely new contract by moonlight. We both concede it is necessary, given our miserable failure with the first version—and my admittedly weak inflight second version.

Complete with legalese and smart-sounding words, we come up with new terms.

This time, it feels official.

THE FRIENDSHIP CONTRACT (VER. 3.0)

This contract is entered into by and between Allegra Malone and Damon Dawson. The term of this agreement shall begin immediately and continue through a termination date of never.

The terms are as follows:

1. Be open and forthcoming with each other. Address all worries at first available convenience to avoid festering problems, assumptions, and miscommunication.

2. This is a long-term relationship based on love, with the intention of eventual matrimony, shared home ownership (The Dawson Home), and (2+) children.

3. Immediately upon return to work, inform necessary parties (Lea Cook) about the aforementioned relationship and intentions to avoid further conflict of interest. Furthermore, as both parties are partners in a shared legal firm, a separation of business and personal life must be instated during work hours.

4. With regards to the studio residence located at 1000 Summer Skye Lane #306, Allegra Malone (future Allegra Malone Dawson or Allegra Dawson) has permission to freely

"make it feel like a home" with artwork, plants, scents, furniture (with dual approval from both parties), and home decor items not limited to bookends, throw blankets, pillows, wreaths, doormats, and coffee mugs. She is free to use red or pink and put "female products" in the medicine cabinet and under the sink, if she agrees not to complain about shavers, hair in or around sinks, clothes near or around the hamper, and unfinished White Claw cans discovered about the premises. No landline phone will be obtained.

5. Both will discuss the possibility of a limited-use television in the primary bedroom. Sleep sound machine will remain.

In consideration of the mutual promises set forth herein, both parties agree that if at any time changes are required, they will reconvene to determine necessary amendments. This contract shall be binding and may not be modified in any manner unless in writing and signed by both parties.

x Allegra Malone

x Damon Dawson

It's amazing what a little fine print can do to ease the uncertainty. It turns out fully-hatched, meaningful contracts are a balm to my trigger-happy brain.

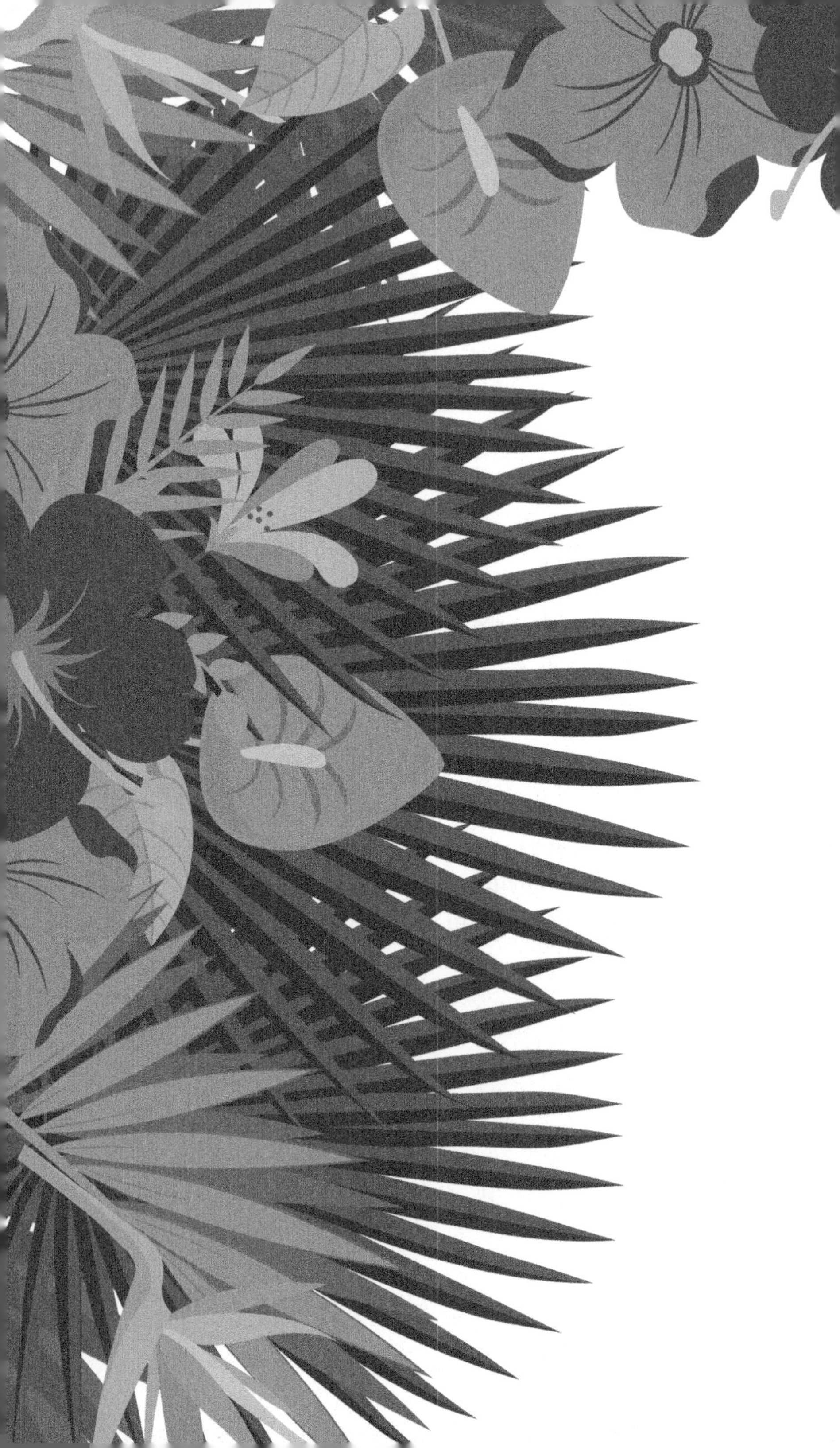

CHAPTER 17
Damon

It's Tuesday, but Lea insisted she doesn't need us back to work until tomorrow, so Allegra and I spend the day unpacking until Lea sends her case notes for us to review. After we unload our suitcases and throw in a load of laundry, we move into the kitchen. I whip up some egg and cheese omelets for energy, most of which we exert as we kiss and taste test each other between bites until our plates and the countertop are cleared for a morning quickie. Then, Allegra puts on her 70s R&B Soul playlist, and we get to work tackling her boxes.

As she empties, I break them down and add them to the growing recycling pile. It's the same place, but with Allegra in it, it feels different—warmer, welcoming, alive with music and laughs and the scent of comfort food and her shea butter lotion. Slowly, the loft begins to look like our home.

"Midnight Train to Georgia" blares through the Bluetooth speakers as Allegra, with her hands full of toiletries and hair products, hits Gladys' low, sultry notes on the way to the bathroom. I surprise her and come in Pip-style on the bass-filled backup vocals.

"Damn, that's sexy!" she calls out.

I chuckle to myself.

The whole day is lighthearted and underlined with love and lust as we fall into a comfortable rhythm.

I'm so relaxed, I almost forget our brief vacation ends tomorrow.

While in Hawaii, I was able to push work to the back of my mind. But in less than twenty-four hours I'll see my foster sister for the first time after two-and-a-half decades. I can't ignore my anxiety any longer.

I don't know Laura anymore. She's probably not the girl with braids who I played Nintendo with or the girl who snuck into the kitchen with me to eat cereal in the middle of the night because I was still hungry. I doubt she missed letting me comb her My Little Pony's hair to calm me down after nightmares. I know nothing about the person she's grown into—if she's married or has kids of her own now. She may not even remember me, though I suspect it's been her behind the PI contact requests.

My anxiety isn't over seeing Laura Hammond. It's about the memories she'll bring with her that constantly remind me I wasn't worth keeping around or loving. I don't want to feel unworthy in front of Allegra.

Why does she love me when no one else did?

"Earth to Damon." Allegra is a few inches from me holding out an empty box. I have no clue how long she's been standing there, but I feel the weight of her stare on me. "What's going on in that head of yours?" she uses one of my trademark lines.

Distracted, I take the box and tug off the strip of tape from the bottom seam, bending the cardboard flat.

"Nothing, I was just um... thinking we'll probably need to add storage cubes and a pack of hangers to the shopping list for today."

"Look at me."

Hiking up my eyebrows, I slowly turn to meet her curious gaze. "What's up?"

She's quiet for a beat, still searching. "You can talk to me, you know. We said we were going to be open and forthcoming with each other."

I shove all thoughts of my past and of seeing Laura tomorrow aside, determined to keep busy and be present with Al.

I'll tell her tonight.

"We did, and I honestly think we need to get some more hangers if we're going to fit your entire wardrobe and extensive shoe collection into the bedroom." I do my best to shake off my worries and settle back into the easy mood.

Allegra folds her arms over her chest, rolling her eyes as she laughs before turning away. I slap her on the ass as she shuffles over toward the last of the boxes, giggling.

Later, in Walmart, we move like a well-oiled machine. Our rhythm is seamless as we check off food items to restock the fridge, then make our way over to the houseware section. Allegra grabs the hangers and storage cubes, then picks up plants, throw blankets in soft brown and bold red to meet both our aesthetics, coffee mugs, and wine glasses. We even check out some reasonably sized televisions for the bedroom and compromise on a forty-inch set.

By the time we finish shopping, neither of us is looking forward to cooking, so we pick up McDonald's drive-thru—nuggets with ranch dressing for her and a Big Mac meal for me.

We settle on the couch and kick up our feet to watch *Love & Basketball* on TV. Well, I do. Allegra is only half paying attention as Q and Monica roll on the floor, fighting as kids. She's too busy scouring the depths of the internet to track down the perfect doormat when her phone pings.

Allegra turns to me. Her expression is a mix of amusement and pride when she says, "Oh, my goodness, look at your friend."

Lea Cook 3:27 pm
REMINDER: Our appointment with Laura Hammond from ChatVideo is tomorrow at 9:00 am. Both of you need to be here before she gets here. I've reviewed the full file. Attached, find your copy, and be prepared to wave at your boy going down because Malone, Dawson, & Cook, LLP is about to take off.

Allegra takes a long pull on her soda straw, then stuffs a ranch-drenched nugget into her mouth. "Your friend is still at work, hyping herself up for tomorrow."

I laugh through a mouth full of my fries.

"You know, for her, it's about the principle just as much as it is retaliation for daring to hurt her friend."

Shit, I really need to tell them about Laura before tomorrow. Ping.

Lea Cook 3:27 pm
Be prepared for lunch at Francesco's following, during which I expect all the salacious trip details and gossip. Visual aids and incriminating photos much appreciated.

Allegra flips the screen back to read the second text message and shoots me a wide-eyed look of panic.

"Hey, rule #3." I shrug. "We agreed to 'immediately' tell Lea when we got back to work."

"Technically, she knows our feelings are mutual," Al grumbles, scraping a hand through her hair. "Does she need to know all the steamy details?"

Ping.
We lean in to read the next message.

Lea Cook 3:27 pm
I will know if either of you is lying, so don't even think about it. And Trio Wednesday is at Damon's this week, so tidy up. I'll bring wine.

"Does that answer your question?" I ask, dusting my hands off. I dab a napkin at the crumbs around my mouth, stifling my anxiety because I don't want to think about what dinner tomorrow night will be like after our appointment with Laura.

Allegra pushes her food aside, jolts upright, and pulls her knee onto the cushion to face me. "We're supposed to be proceeding slowly. If we say anything, she's going to be all geeked up. Do we have to tell her about us, you know...?"

"Having sex?" I supply the rest of Allegra's thought, chuckling. "But she's going to take one look at us and know. Especially with that look you get when you're...all the way in."

Allegra swats me playfully, sitting back against the cushion. "Whatever." She faces the television, but her quiet demeanor tells me she isn't watching the movie. I sense she's mentally weighing all the possible effects our changing relationship could have on The Trio.

"Plus...Lea has known how I feel about you for the last decade. She's been pretty clear she'd be in favor of us finally 'connecting.'"

A huge gasp of a laugh spills from Allegra's lips.

"Okay...so, you two have shared this knowledge all these years and were totally fine with leaving me out?" Pressing her fingers to her lips, she mumbles sarcastically under her breath, "Good to know."

Scrubbing a hand over my face, I release an amused groan.

"Listen, Al, I wasn't just trying to smash. I also was not trying to be your consolation prize or your rebound after you ended things with one of your corny dudes."

She huffs out a laugh, blinking, and the tension in my shoulders drains a little.

"Oh, that's rich. First, except for Mitch, who dealt with his anxiety by telling jokes, no one I dated has ever been corny. As I recall, you were the one who invited him to open mic night, so don't even try it." She crumples a napkin and tosses it at me before twisting to prop her feet back up. "And another thing, stop talking like there were so many guys."

I should let this go, but she's making it sound like there were so many opportunities for me to take my shot with her when the gaps in her dating life were few and far between.

Because I'm not trying to argue, I choose the higher road.

"So, I'm clear, you're saying that back at Boyd, Eric Reid—who was about yea high with the politician side part, starched pants, and a Michael J. Fox obsession—was cool?"

"Um, who doesn't love *Back to the Future?*"

Touché.

I nod. "Every twenty-one-year-old guy has posters of 'MJF.' covering every inch of space in his apartment." I cough out the word *loser* and nod half-seriously. "Oh, and driving a DeLorean isn't corny at all."

Allegra rolls her eyes, but her lips twitch as she stares at the television. She's got a faraway stare as she watches Q give Monica a ride home from his basketball game and ask about her date, Spaulding.

"Whatever, D."

"Ooh, but Eric had nothing on the British guy, Pierce. If I'm remembering correctly, you had a thing for boy band look-alikes. There was a Backstreet Boy, an NSYNCer, a Boyz II Man, and one of the Directions." I blow out an impressed breath. "Shoot, with that sort of collection, you could've started your own group."

Allegra takes one look at me and pinches the bridge of her nose. "You about done?"

"What about that guy with those sweeping lashes and that rugged guitar..." I trail off wistfully. "He only wanted to make music, but his selfish family wanted him to run their hotel chain. Tragic."

She gives me a slow clap, and I think it's the end of our comedy hour. But she jolts around, folding her arms over her chest, pinning me with an annoyed stare.

"Is this one of your worries? Do we need to be address this before it 'festers into a problem?'" She throws up air quotes, exasperation bleeding into her shaky tone. "Like, do we need to reconvene over this?"

Throwing my hands up, I say, "Not at all. I'm merely being open and forthcoming like we promised we'd be with each other."

I just wish I didn't feel like such a dick for letting my frustrations about tomorrow inch into what I have with Allegra.

But I also need her to recognize how many times she *didn't* notice me between relationships.

"It doesn't change how much I love you, Al. But the fact remains, our timing was always off before. It's important to realize that..." I say, leaving an opening for a subject change.

"And now it's right, I hope," she spits out. "I mean, I didn't realize how closely you followed my dating life."

"I've been here the entire time. You just assumed I wasn't paying attention." I tug her into my lap, dragging the pads of my fingers over her cheek "But none of that matters because it's in the past. I was just playing around with you. I wished you would've noticed me sooner, is all. But we're together now, and I'm the lucky one here."

"Damn straight you are." Allegra pouts, but a smile threatens at the corners of her beautiful mouth.

"I get to be in a long-term relationship based on love," I say, reciting verbatim the contract language she suggested. "One day, I get to marry the woman of my dreams and share a home and kids. Honestly, I still can't believe after all this time this is real. I'm with *the* Allegra Malone. And she enjoys having sex with me." I make a big production of pinching my forearm and waiting to wake up. "Go figure."

This earns me a warm, infectious laugh I feel all over my skin.

It still feels like a dream.

As Maxwell croons *"This Woman's Work"* and Monica and Q make love for the first time, Allegra cups her hands to my jaw, pulling me down to cover her mouth with mine. I slip my tongue between her parted lips, deepening the kiss as I unravel my body from hers to fit myself between her thighs.

She tilts her pelvis, arching her back to meet my semi that's quickly hardening into a full erection. Already, she's yanking my shirt over my head and tugging my sweats and boxer briefs over my hips, and I'm hard pressed to keep going at this pace.

I slip my hands under her sundress to grip her ass. Scooting her down flat, I hook my thumbs over the sides of her panties and slowly drag down the thin fabric with the careful resignation of disarming a bomb.

My muscles tick and harden with restraint.

"Dang, you're looking at me like I've been a bad girl and you want to punish me." Allegra jokes.

My dick twitches and hardens, almost painfully so.

Allegra does not know how fucking sexy it is to hear her tease me. We've been sharing sweet, tender kisses and professing our love at every turn. That's been by design. My body tightens with pent up need so fierce I'm teetering on the edge. I want rough, messy, hard fucking in a way I don't know if she can handle. I need to lose myself in her.

But what will she think about this side of me?

I hike up an eyebrow, stifling the urge to just let go. "Are you saying you think you can handle it?"

Her half-lidded gaze darts to my hand gripping and stroking my dick. She traces her tongue over the swell of her lip with a mischievous glint in her eyes. "I'm saying not only can I handle it, but it has been highly anticipated."

"Is that so?"

"Entirely so," she purrs. "Trust me..."

I crack my neck on either side.

"In that case..." I flip Allegra onto her stomach, gripping the dips of her waist as I circle my fingers over her clit until she's slick and ready. Then I center my erection between her thighs. I smack her ass and dig my fingers into the thickness of her round curves as she squirms beneath me. Spreading her open, I thrust my hips hard and fast, watching as she takes me whole, and I'm so deep inside her I can't move just yet.

"Tell me how you want it," I say.

She releases a breathy moan, hardly able to string together words. "Hard."

And I drive harder, deeper, faster until I'm sweating and hoarse. I use all my frustration and anxiety to let go. She tightens around me until an orgasm ripples through her. And then I'm unraveling inside her. We're a mess of grunts and whimpers as we come undone in shivers and shakes.

"Shit." Allegra stares unfocused at the ceiling. Her tone is wistful. "First, bravo. And second, we need to quickly figure out an amendment to the 'separating business and personal' clause because...how am I not going to think about you bending me over my desk every second I'm at work?"

I manage to laugh between shallow breaths.

"And third," she continues, craning her neck to look back at me, "this is exactly what I was talking about on the plane."

"We talked about a lot of things during the flight. You're going to have to elaborate." I pull out and slide in between her and the couch.

"Rule number one."

I hike up an eyebrow, signaling I still need further clarification on that vague comment.

"D, you've obviously been holding back. Something's been bothering you all day, and it's fine if you're not ready to talk about it, but at least tell me that. The way you just turned me out..." She moans her approval. "That was amazing and delicious, but it felt like stress relief."

"I get that," I say, shame flaring in my gut.

"No, you don't. Not completely anyway. We need mutual trust, including all the doubts and dark little secrets, especially the sexy ones like the magnificent display you just put on, if this is going to work. You certainly don't have to hide anything from me."

It's the perfect segue to tell her why I'm so bent out of shape. I should just tell her about my foster sister and get it over with instead of allowing my partners to walk into a meeting at a disadvantage because I'm knowingly withholding my connection to Laura from them. But I just got out of my funk. I'm not eager to jump back in with both feet, so it'll have to wait until morning.

"Look, emotions have been high. I just didn't know if you could handle, or whether you'd want, hard fucking with me."

She purses her lips, blinking.

"Excuse me, why would you assume I wouldn't? As I recall, I'm the one who intruded on your shower in the hotel. That took balls. Yes, I want it soft and sensual sometimes. But I also like it hard and rough, too. I want to try every way with you," she says, extending her pinky finger.

"Oh, well, you know once we pinky swear…" I smile and hook a finger around hers, and we seal the promise by pressing our thumbs together until the pinky link releases. "It's settled," I say.

Starting tomorrow, it's all about trust. All I've got to do is make it through the appointment with Laura.

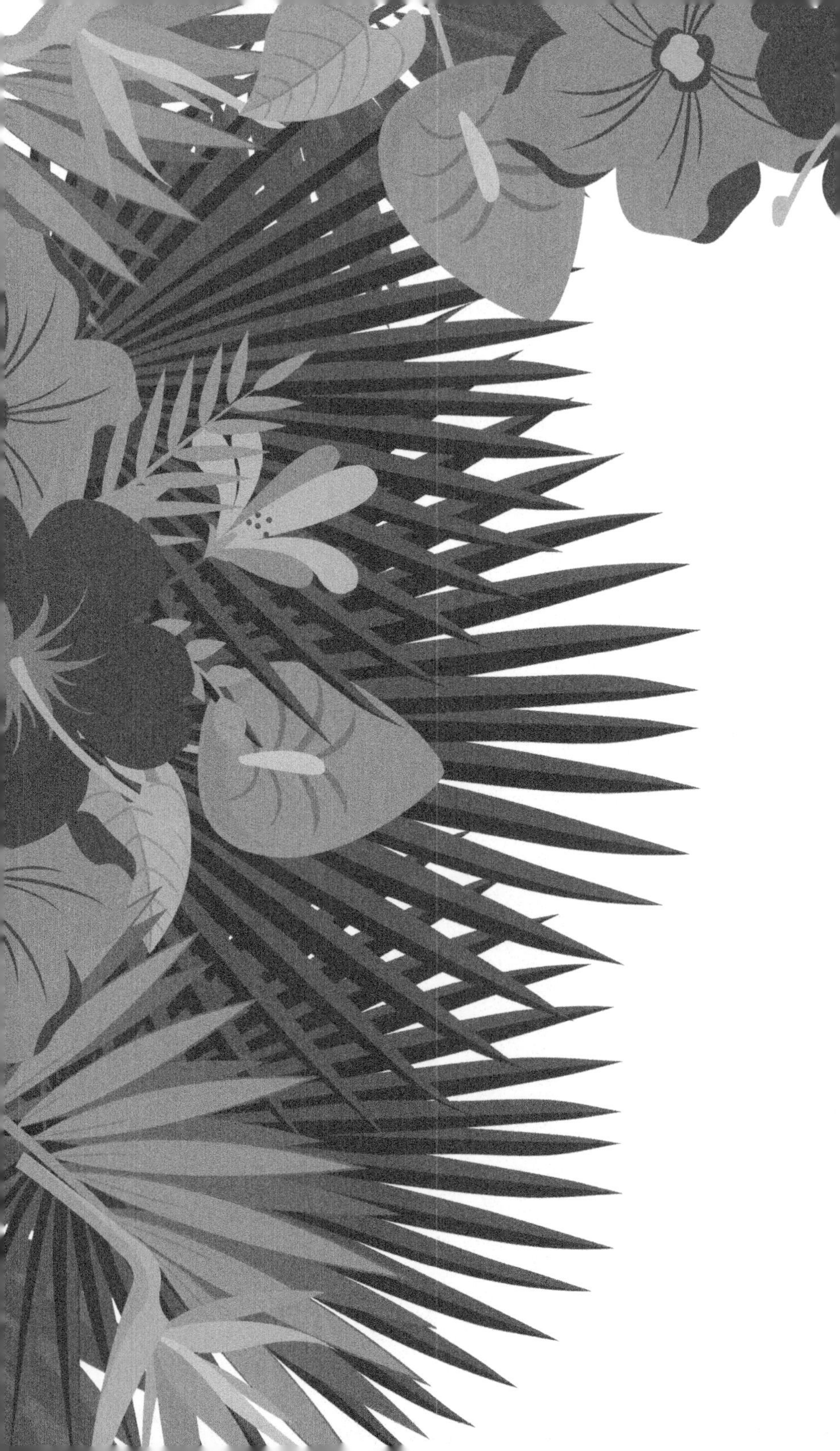

CHAPTER 18
Allegra

Damon and I step onto the high-rise elevator at our office building. As the door closes, he reaches to press the button for the sixth floor, then slips his hand in mine, intertwining our fingers like we've being doing this forever. There's a weighted tension to his grip, though.

"You're sure you're okay?" I ask, looking up to search his eyes.

He flashes me a reassuring smile. "Yeah, I'm good. I'm just eager to get in there and chat with you and Lea before the client arrives."

Except his posture is a rigid line, and the muscles at his jaw are hardened. The crease etched between his eyebrows from last night never left.

"I'm sorry about the alarm," I say, fishing for the source of his anxiety. Instead of hitting snooze, I turned the alarm off, and now we're running late. Maybe it's simple as panic from being roused from sleep.

When we finally realized the time, we tore out of the blankets, took quick—separate—showers, scrambled around for clothes, and grabbed fruit off the counter as we rushed out of the loft. This entire morning, we've barely exchanged a handful of words.

He nudges his shoulder against mine, sensing me studying him.

"Babe, stop worrying. I said I'm fine. We're a little late, but I'm just getting my head in the game for this meeting," Damon says. "We really need to discuss the...details of the case."

With my free hand, I reach up to remove the red-dotted tissue scrap on his chin from where he nicked himself shaving this morning.

"Oh, yeah. I uh...got a little too close." A shaky smile stretches his full lips.

For the dozenth time, I'm tempted to ask if he needs to get anything off his chest. Deep down, I sense there's more bothering him than arriving seven minutes late. I just can't figure out what or why he's holding onto it so tight.

In Hawaii, he'd voted not to take the ChatVideo case. Is he really that nervous about our appointment with Laura Hammond? Why?

We reviewed the documents Lea sent over last night, so we're prepared for the meeting. We still need something concrete to prove Kyle's motives with ViddyChat. Trademark infringement cases are arguably hard to prove. Is Damon worried about losing and letting Laura Hammond down?

As the neon red analog numbers slow to the number six, I mutter, "We've winged it before off Lea's case notes., It'll be fine. We've got this" just in case that's what's gnawing at him.

The doors glide open, and Lea is waiting.

Her body is halfway between the reception desk and the door to the conference room, like she was mid-conversation with Alyssa as she peers over at us. Then, with all the slow-motion drama, her gaze drops to Damon's and my interlocked fingers, and she lights up like the Fourth of July.

It starts with a couple of slaps on the desk, then she throws her hands up like the holy ghost is working its way through her and she needs to testify to his divine glory.

"Won't he do it! Lord, won't he do it!" she exclaims.

There are springs in her feet as she turns on her six-inch black patent leather heels, dipping her chin to her chest with her hands raised high. She walks over and wraps us both in a full-on bear hug.

"Damn, I was worried. D, I didn't think you were going to man up. But thank goodness for forced proximity in a tropical paradise and destination weddings because you came *through*."

Damon and I erupt in laughter, hugging her back.

It's been a long time since the three of us have been away from each other for any good amount of time. Already, Lea's presence feels like the missing link, strengthening our bond. Even Damon seems to loosen up.

"We missed you, too." He laughs, squeezing her tighter.

But she pulls away, careful not to get makeup up on his shirt or blazer. We wouldn't want to make a bad first impression. Lea straightens her sleeveless, knee-length, wine-colored sheath dress before she pins her stare on me, blinking.

The corners of her mouth twitch conspiratorially.

The woman is a bloodhound who can sniff out details with her eyes closed. Damon said she'd see right through us, and of course, she does. She loves us as much as we love her. Why wouldn't she want us to 'connect'?

I roll my eyes, struggling to hide my smile.

"What?" I ask, sheepishly.

"Don't 'what' me." Her smile is wide. "With that silly, guilty grin, glowing all up in here, stars in your eyes like you're a dang Disney princess... Shit, I know all about tales as old as time and kissing frogs to find your prince..." And she's dead serious as she reads me like a book entitled *Lies My Best Friend Tries to Hide from Me.*

Stating the obvious, I shrug and say, "So, as you can see, something happened while we were gone."

Lea folds her arms across her chest, darting her questioning gaze to Damon for less vague details.

Then, cool as a cucumber, Damon surprises us both when he tells her in concise, definitive terms, "We're in love and living together with long-term intentions. We'd appreciate your verbal blessing."

Well, damn. How open and forthcoming.

He lifts my hand to his lips and presses a soft kiss to the back, meeting my gaze. *You and me,* he says without a word. His expression reassures me not to worry about Lea or us or anything, and that I can trust him. Hopefully that means whatever's bothering him won't affect his love for me.

With a small smile, I let relief wash over me.

Now, I'm officially ready to separate personal and business when I turn to see Lea's face.

If a little handholding stirred up prayers and testimony, this confession is basically the resurrection. I mean, it might as well be Easter because she presses her hand over her mouth, ecstatic about the second coming of Damon and Allegra. Not giving a flying fuck about messing up her YouTube tutorial perfect makeup, she blubbers incoherent gibberish. *Are those tears in her eyes?*

"Lea..." I trail off as she scoops me into a hug.

Over the next few minutes, she freaks all the way out physically and emotionally. There are more tears, more hugs, more testifying. We are given her highest blessing, which she offers in extension from the man above. Apparently, the good lord was tired of using a gentle hand to guide us toward each other and opted for Lea to do his good work.

I'm sure she wants all the calendar events and milestones that go with finding love for herself, but I secretly think she wants them for me more since she'll get to help plan them. Hearing Damon speak so freely about love and long-term intentions is major for us girls.

Somewhere in all the haze, I'm guessing Lea's strategically plotting our social media relationship status update, a housewarming, engagement announcements, wedding save the dates, the font on our wedding invitations...all of it.

Naturally, with Damon and I arriving late and such a world-changing event right before we meet with a potential client, Lea is too flustered to sit still at the conference room table.

"Don't take too long, Lea," Damon calls after her as she leaves us to our own devices, informing us she'll need a few minutes in the restroom to compose herself.

Damon and I hang in the lobby talking with Alyssa from Fallon Events about Hawaii, telling her how amazing the resort, water, sunsets, and gardens were. All the while, he rubs circles on the small of my back, and I'm reminded of the rehearsal dinner. Just like then, I cling to him, his clean heady scent, and our connection, reassuring.

As his posture stiffens again, I want to be here for him in the same way. I want him to know that I'm here. If he needs me to earn his trust, I'll do it.

"Okay, I'm human again. Let's do this. Conference room." Lea announces as she reappears. She shakes out her arms and flexes her fingers. She's refreshed her lipstick and smoothed the flyaways into submission, so she's ready to lead.

She's tactical, but not ruthless. For her, it's about discerning the truth while maintaining her focus on the person she's helping rather than the recipient of her wrath. Take Simon Cowell's earnest assessment and intentions about musical talent, replace it with a sage-plus-hood human bullshit detector in sexier shoes and a badass wardrobe, and hello, Lea Cook attorney at law.

"I've got everything already set up." She enters the floor-to-ceiling glass room and settles in the sleek ergonomic chair at the head of the long wooden table closest to the door. It's fully prepped with frosted water glasses, a coffee tray, and hard-copy packets set in front of the four chairs where we'll confer with Laura Hammond.

"Oh, so you're not playing around?" I laugh.

By the sheer amount of individually wrapped chocolate in the snack bowl, it appears Lea will be in rare form today.

"Lea Cook does not play in her place of business," she says, waving us over to the two seats at her right and leaving the one at left for Laura. That's a tactical move to see her coming.

"Does Lea Cook plan on referring to herself in third person for the rest of the appointment or...?" I snicker.

Damon's nerves seem to reemerge in full force as he scoots his chair forward and thumbs through the packet, so I do the same.

In anticipation of Kyle asserting the defenses of fair and collateral use, Lea put together documents to establish a trademark infringement violation. Under the Lanham Act, the similarity between ChatVideo's and ViddyChat's type of goods, logos, company names, and marketing channels creates commercial confusion for the consuming public. She's contending Kyle's initial intent was to capitalize on ChatVideo's already growing client base.

She's thorough.

Damon and I reviewed the packet last night, but there's something weighty about seeing Kyle's name listed on the paper as the "infringer." It makes it even more sobering. This is what he does. He takes and takes without remorse or recourse.

Having been on the receiving end, my urge to fight for Laura Hammond is overwhelming.

People like Kyle are the reason I pursued a legal career.

I leaf through the packet, scanning the laches, estoppel, and unclean hands doctrines. "If Laura moves forward with us, Kyle's only chance to prove he's not liable for infringement is asserting fair use. Period."

Lea nods her agreement as she pours herself a cup of coffee and rips the top off three packets of sugar. "Do you have any questions or comments after reviewing the packet?"

"Did Laura get a response from ViddyChat?" I ask.

"No, but I spoke with her a few days ago," Lea replies. "She said he posted on social media using the term 'the original' regarding ViddyChat the same day she contacted them. No direct response, though. He's basically baiting her." Lea huffs out a mirthless laugh, and I'm right there with her.

Damon lifts his chin and steeples his fingers in front of him. "Guys, I'm glad we have a few minutes because I really need to discuss—"

Through the open door, the elevator pings, reverberating off the glass walls.

"Table it until lunch." Lea straightens her posture. "She's here."

I don't know what I was expecting Laura Hammond to look like, but she steps out into the lobby, and I already feel more protective than I did reading the claim about her business. A real human jumps off the page.

At first glance, anyone would see a lady suit. She's an average-height white woman with light makeup and soft blonde curls pulled away from her angular face. Her black suit fits well, tapering modestly around her lean curves. And the leather briefcase just about seals the image of a businesswoman—small or otherwise.

But as Alyssa points her in our direction, Laura's face lights up with a genuine smile. As she approaches the conference room, I get a glimpse behind the suit of armor at the tired lines around her eyes. Her firm hands and chipped opaque nail polish bear the mark of all the nights she's stayed up perfecting, working through ideas, then scrapping ninety percent before she settles on the one she's about 99.9% comfortable putting her logo on. The one she's researched down to the finest details and logistics to fit her niche target audience.

In person, Laura Hammond looks sweet and nice, and in no way appears to be a doormat.

Damon stiffens at my side. His posture is ramrod straight with clasped hands on the table.

I shoot him a curious glance, but his focus is on Laura.

After we exchange greetings and pleasantries, Lea welcomes her to settle into the chair to her left. With a fresh cup of coffee and the chocolates strategically inched toward Laura, Lea gets straight to it. But I'm more interested in Damon's stilted breathing and the tightness in his expression.

"First, thank you for the opportunity to handle your claim, Mrs. Hammond—" Lea starts, but Laura cuts her off.

"Ms. now," she clarifies. "My husband passed on a few years back. It's just me running the entire show…wearing all the hats." She lowers her gaze and presses her thin pink lips into a nostalgic smile.

"I'm so sorry for your loss," I say, but she waves it off.

"Ten years we had. ChatVideo was our brainchild—our only child." My heartstrings are pulled. I'm on pins and needles to learn more about this woman who Damon can't take his eyes off of.

"Brian and I had an accounting firm years back. Many of our clients were from all over the place, so it wasn't workable for them to fly in every time we needed to run something by them. Secretly, Brian was a grassroots garage techie. He loved to fiddle and tinker if you know what I mean."

Damon leans back into his chair, glancing down at the table where beneath it I feel the vibration of his knee bouncing.

Laura is still lost somewhere in her memory as she continues. "He was a tinkerer like my late father." The bouncing stops and Damon centers his attention on her, the sides of his jaw jutting as if under clenched teeth. "He could fix anything—broken watch, television, dishwasher. I even got him to sew on a button or two for me over the years," she muses.

"You'll have to share your secrets on how you landed him." Lea jests. "At some point—*way* down the road," she clarifies. "I want to fall in love and stay married like you and Brian."

I toss her a reassuring smile but dart my gaze to Damon, and Lea seems to catch on to his uneasiness.

"It'll happen when it's right," Laura adds. "Brian and I were best friends for as long as I can remember."

Damon glances over at me as I slide my hand in his beneath the table. His expression is a tormented mess of pent-up anxiety, and I'm halfway inclined to excuse us to the lobby so he can tell me what's happening.

I draw my eyebrows together, only half listening to Laura, but silently pleading with Damon to let me in.

"So, once we fell for each other romantically, he was hesitant. And who wouldn't be? He was afraid to trust his instincts, and I was afraid to lose my best friend, but it all worked out in the end. We married and built businesses together. ChatVideo was the one he never got to see realized."

"Well, let's do this for Brian," Lea says, respectfully dragging us back on track.

Over the next few minutes, as Lea goes over each page of the packet, Laura provides us with copies of her thorough attempts to reach ViddyChat—unanswered and time-stamped email contact on the company website, postmarked handwritten correspondence to the physical business address, and recorded voicemails she left.

For the sake of establishing a timeline—and hurrying this meeting along—I ask about the dates of conception and execution of ChatVideo's formation and compare them with a spruced-up version of the graph Lea sent when we were in Hawaii.

I'm cross-referencing the business filing dates with the Secretary of State when a mental alarm goes off.

Cutting Lea off, I ask, "Did you have any previous correspondence with Kyle Andrews directly? You mentioned you'd recognized his face when you saw his picture online when you first discovered ViddyChat."

"Just once," she says, "at a networking event shortly after my launch. I was being honored at a 'Las Vegas' Ones to Watch in Business' event, and he was there. He asked a ton of questions, wanted to know how I secured financing, and what types of services I offered. I figured he was just another eager young person looking for insight." She stifles a curious laugh. "The man even flirted with me once he found out I was widowed. Thankfully, I had the good sense to turn him down."

Alarm rings again in the back of my mind.

As much as I wanted this meeting to be over five minutes ago so I can talk to Damon, now I'm intrigued. I remember Kyle attending that event. We'd just started dating, maybe two dates in. He'd had no business plan, no logo, no slogan, no ideas for marketing and advertising. He was still uncertain about his business concept, let alone a name. The only thing he had in stone was where his funding would come from—his dad.

Shit.

When we'd met up downtown for drinks the next night,

Kyle was reenergized. Not only had he come up with a logo, slogan, and terms for marketing, he had logistics and a fresh brand to go with the funding.

I'd chalked it up to inspiration from being surrounded by a creative community—like minds and all that.

Anxiety swirls around me, my cheeks heating. I force down the sick feeling rising inside me, thinking of what Kyle did to this woman.

"And Trish Santos? Do you know or have you had any interactions with her?" I rush to add.

"Only when I called to inquire about the claim. I believe her words were 'baseless,' 'mostly circumstantial,' and 'won't carry a lot of weight.'"

As if connected, Damon, Lea, and I shake our heads in disgust, embarrassed that we ever trusted Trish. *I vouched for her!*

In no uncertain terms, we assure Laura that Trish is no longer employed temporarily or otherwise with Malone, Dawson, & Cook. We tell her Lea has reviewed her claim again. Then, when we're satisfied of our position of disagreement with Trish's statement has been drilled down enough, I tell her about Trish's recent engagement to Kyle.

As I warn Laura about the public perceptions some people may form of her, she tells us she's already defied entry into a primarily male-dominated field and refuses to sit back while someone takes credit for her and Brian's handiwork.

"Let them say what they want. They'll want to keep this out of the public eye, but I've got nothing to hide. Let's shout it from the rooftops if necessary."

On that note, Lea tells her that with the retainer and any additional documents she deems helpful, we'll file the claim today.

Just as Laura agrees, the bloodhound in Lea goes in for the detail.

"If you don't mind me asking, how did you hear about Malone, Dawson, and Cook?" Lea asks. "Were you referred, or did you check out any other firms?"

Laura sits up and clasps her hands on the table with a huge smile. "I heard about your firm after reading that article about you representing Bliss & Makeup Co." She flattens her hands on the table, pressing them into the cool wood. "Kiss & Makeup Co. What kind of stuff is that? Even if it is different packaging, they're trying to muddy the waters for customers with similar business names—using Crimson Queen for their red lipstick, too. That's how I knew I had a leg to stand on. ViddyChat was doing the same thing to me."

"Yes, exactly correct," I say.

Laura pushes to her feet. "I like your firm is small—not a bunch of faceless suits who'll treat my case like another number. Yours is the only firm I've spoken with." She nods at Lea and me before settling her unblinking stare on Damon. "Plus, it seemed like a simple decision to go with family."

Damon's grip on my hand tightens.

My thoughts spin. Something inside me breaks, and I'm shutting down. Lea and I don't ask questions, but instinctively, I know.

As my heartbeat slows, it feels like time stops to allow the dots to connect. The blonde hair, the tinkering dad... They were the nameless foster family who almost adopted Damon. Now everything makes sense.

I know a private investigator's been reaching out to him for a while, but he ignores the calls. Those people he let in twenty-five years ago still want to reconnect, but he won't let them. They gave him back, he'd said. He's been holding on so tight to

The Trio all these years, he doesn't know how to let anyone else in.

Lea and I share a meaningful stare. Now both of us are ready to wrap up this appointment.

"Thanks so much. I'll contact you once the filing is done," Lea says, escorting Laura to the lobby and waiting with her at the elevator.

"Al," Damon turns to me and every nerve ending in my body pulses.

My mouth goes dry as Damon's gaze skates over me. I can't read his subtext or tell whether he's restacking bricks or taking them down. But I know without a doubt this is what's been bothering him. This is why he didn't want to take the case and why he's been so uptight and tense since Hawaii. The whole time, I've felt like there was still a wall between us.

He doesn't trust me.

He's known since before we left Vegas that Laura Hammond was his foster sister, and he didn't tell me.

I put my trust in him, and he didn't return it.

"Al, I wanted to tell you," Damon says, but I'm too much in my head to focus on anything he says or does after he sat through the meeting and said nothing. This whole time, he's let me sleep restlessly and wake up questioning what I'd done. When I asked him over and over what was bothering him, he clammed up.

Ignoring him, I gather my copies and my purse and jolt to my feet as Lea reenters the conference room. I'm flustered and angry, but I can't go home. Damon will just follow me there. It's his house. *The Dawson home.*

"I'm going to skip lunch and order out," I say. "If you need me, I'll be in my office. Otherwise, I'll see you all at dinner tonight."

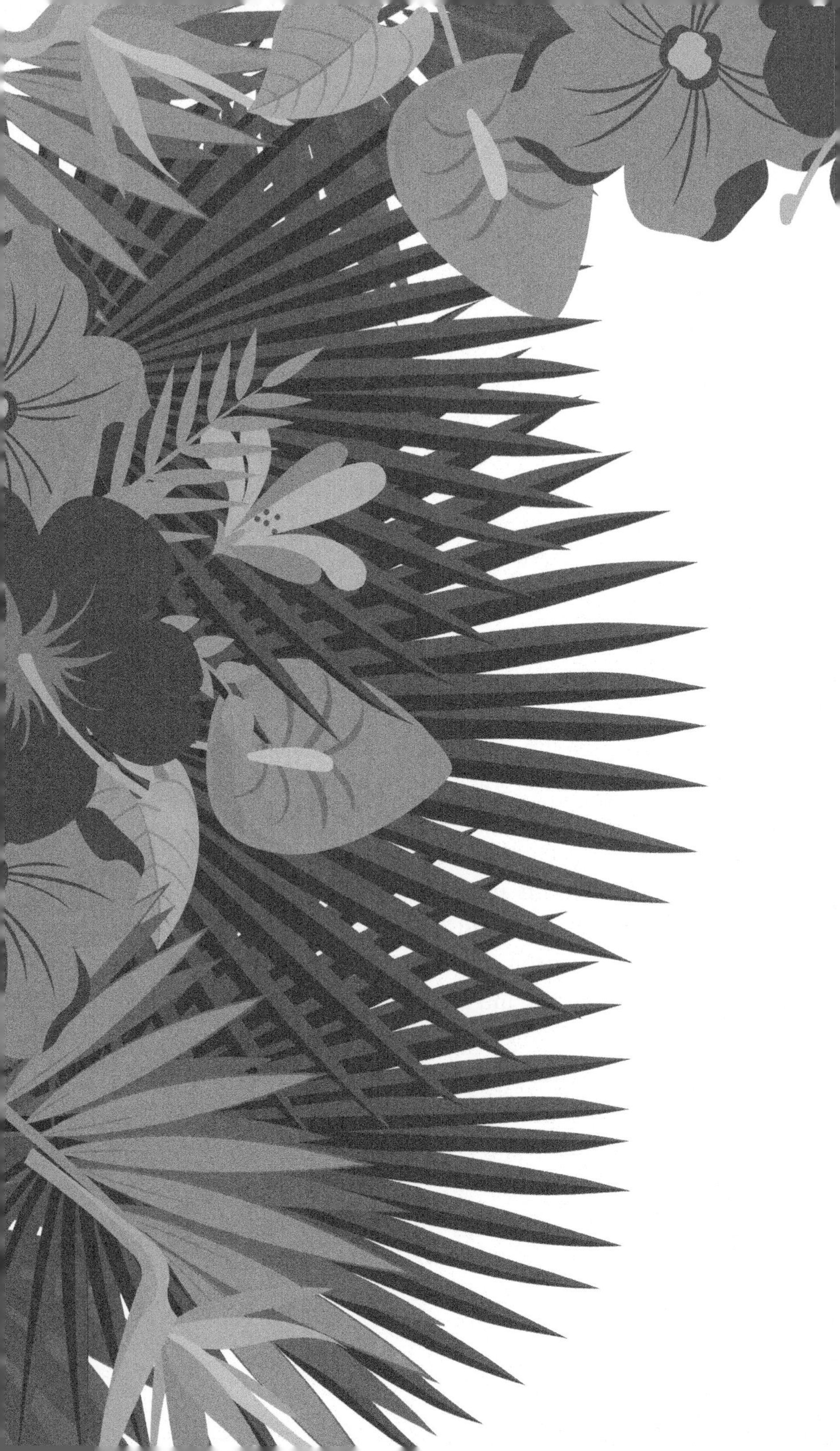

CHAPTER 19
Allegra

Damon and I don't talk the rest of the afternoon. We're at the office, and now I'm fully on board with separating business and personal. Whatever the hell that was back there with Laura Hammond, we can talk about it when we get home.

I turn off the music that's been playing low on my phone as I prepare to leave for the day. A knock sounds at my door, and Lea pops her head inside.

"Got a minute before you head out?"

"Sure." I force a smile, then I clarify, just in case she has any ideas of talking about Damon. "Should we do a recap of what we learned at the meeting and figure out some directives for each of us?"

The corners of Lea's mouth tug downward, and her lower lip protrudes as she nods. Then she says, "Noted." She's aware I'm not ready to talk about Laura's bomb drop and Damon's ensuing silence.

Not that my readiness has ever been a factor when Lea's in fix-it mode.

She plops down into the chair facing my desk, searching

my eyes a little too long for my comfort. I log off my computer and set my purse on the desk, signaling I'm ready for her to get to the point.

"Before I file anything, is there any reason you think we shouldn't pursue the case?" she asks. I've got to wonder if this is Damon speaking through her, and if he asked her not to take the case.

I think about Mom and all the hard work she put into building her business. There were so many late nights where she hunkered over the stovetop or her desk, figuring it out along the way. There was pride in her shoulders and smile with every sale or email from a happy customer. She held her head high as she shared her success with Aaron and me because she was so proud of what she'd built.

Drawing my eyebrows together, I shrug. "Why wouldn't we?"

She shoots me a pursed lip *don't play dumb* expression. But if Damon's reservations weren't strong enough to voice his concerns when we voted back in Hawaii, why should they matter now? At any point prior to this morning, he could've told us about his ties to Laura and we would've undoubtedly understood.

But he didn't.

Now we've got a professional responsibility to a woman and to our business mission statement, regardless of her connection to Damon.

"All I'm saying is, before you and I had any sign or reason not to help Laura Hammond, we felt strongly enough to meet with her, hear her story, review her supporting documents, and help her take down ViddyChat...because it was the right thing to do. What's changed?"

Lea slouches against the chair, absently scrutinizing her cuticles. She's weighing my words against everything that's happened today, this past week, and whatever she talked about with Damon at lunch.

When she meets my gaze again, I sense something isn't adding up for her.

"What made you ask about Laura's personal interactions with Kyle and Trish?" Lea asks.

I suck in a lungful of air, blowing out my cheeks.

"Look, I was going to tell you both at dinner tonight, but I guess now's as good a time as any. Kyle and I had just started dating when he went to the 'Ones to Watch' networking event..."

I take a few minutes to recount everything I remember from the beginning of our relationship and his supposed "epiphany" following the event. Even after I tell Lea I deleted Kyle's contact and text messages, the light in Lea's eyes still brightens at the prospect of having a concrete timeline to pin down exact dates and times for a stronger case.

With the wheels in her head spinning, she gets right down to business. She enlists me to check the filing and trademark dates for ViddyChat's logo and slogan. She's hopeful that after recalling the time Kyle asked me to review his trademark documents and logo back then, I might be able to recover something in my email, too.

She continues down her mental checklist. She'll have Damon check the company website verbiage, business formation documents with the Nevada Secretary of State, and any pending litigation against his company. Since she's not cooking tonight, she'll hang back and start drawing up the claim and prep to file.

"Laura's definitely right about him wanting to keep this out of the public eye. I've got a few press contacts I can keep on standby for an exclusive, should it come to that." Her smile is hopeful and challenging. "If I'm right about this, by tomorrow, we could hear from his counsel about mediation."

* * *

I left work early because I'm stressed and I need comfort food in the worst way. I'm frying chicken wings and fries in olive oil.

I've got Frankie Beverly and Maze blasting from the speakers as I duck into the refrigerator, searching for ranch dressing and hot sauce. Thank God, Damon buys the stuff in bulk.

My heart squeezes a bit, thinking about how thoughtful he can be.

Soon, I'm using long tongs to take out the chicken when the click of the front door lock sends me into swift panic. We live and work together. There's no way we can hide from each other or prolong this.

"Hey," Damon says. His tone is tentative as he glances over at me and locks the door behind him. "Smells good."

My heart races and my mouth runs dry.

"Can't go wrong with wings and fries, right?"

He sets his keys and phone on the entry table and shrugs off his navy-blue blazer, draping it over the back of the sofa as he walks over to the island. For a beat, he scans the counter and the stovetop.

"Need any help?" he asks.

"Nope. Everything is already done."

Damon pinches the bridge of his nose like that's as far as he got when he pictured us talking.

The air feels thick with tension and uncertainty, and I hate things are like this between us.

"So, am I right in assuming Laura Hammond is your foster sister from the family who tried to adopt you?"

"They didn't, though." *Try hard enough to adopt, love him enough.* I fill in the rest of his sentence. I'm not here to argue about his foster family, though. This is about us.

"I'm just trying to understand why you didn't tell us who she was."

Damon heaves an exasperated sigh. "Why are you so eager to take this case? What's the difference if she goes with another firm?"

Because it's not right. Because she could just as easily be my mom or some other person trying to pursue a dream, then someone pulls the rug from underneath them. Because she's your family.

"Ugh." I say, flattening my palms on the cool granite. "Just for a second, forget about who owns these two companies and how they're connected to us. Why is it okay for ViddyChat to get away with cherry-picking off the little guy, huh? If it were my business, would you fight for me?"

"You know I would," he grumbles.

"Then what's the difference?"

"Because she's nothing to me," he says through his teeth with forced restraint. His expression is pinched. He's every bit frustrated as he lets his head fall back into his clasped hands. "I don't know her anymore. I haven't seen or talked to the Hammonds since I was eleven years old. What was there to tell you? That I know *of* her?"

"If it was no big deal, then why not just tell us so we could—"

"You could, what?" Damon hisses. His eyes are cold and hard with a dark sort of glee just under the surface. "Huh? So, you and Lea could feel sorry for me? You don't know how it felt for Child and Family Services to drag me away crying because I was so desperate for love and affection, I clung to them like life. That's what you want to know about? How they made me feel so unworthy of love it makes me wonder how you could love me?" He barks out a hysterical laugh, jabbing his finger through the air. "See, this..."

"D?"

He stares at me unblinking with his nostrils flared and his lips quivering in a scowl. I've never seen him so angry.

My cheeks heat, and I don't know how to be right now.

"This shit is for the fucking birds." He turns and walks into the living room to sit on the couch, slouching into the cushions and closing his eyes.

"No. That's not what I wanted at all." My lungs constrict, making it hard to breathe as I bite back tears. "All I ever wanted was your trust and to be there for you the way you've always been there for me." He says nothing, but he tilts his head slightly in my direction. "I see all the calls you ignore from the private investigator and the way you shut down when something is bothering you. But we sat in that bed Monday—and on this couch last night—talking about trust and being open."

"I know," he mutters.

"What hurts me the most is you knew about her since before we left Las Vegas for Hawaii when Lea brought up the case, and you kept it to yourself. I had to learn about the man I love from a stranger. Deep down, I didn't want to believe it after all the years we've known each other, but now I know. You don't trust me."

An overwhelming sadness rips through my chest and my vision blurs with unshed tears.

"Allegra." He stands, but I can't look at him right now.

Rather than keep going, I round the island, excuse myself, and dart into the bathroom, locking the door behind me.

Not even a minute later, his footsteps grow closer until the shadow of his feet appears beneath the door. A laugh bubbles inside me because here we are again. What does it say about us as a couple that our most tender moments are always with a bathroom door between us?

The temptation to speak first niggles at me, but I force myself to sit on the cool tiled floor and listen.

"I know you're mad at me and why this case is important to you, Al." The emotion-thick voice taunts me. More than anything, I want to open the door so we can say our apologies and make all this go away. Somewhere in my heart, I know he needs this, though—hard love and the chance to confront his own demons—as much as I need to hear it.

"I should've just told you about Laura instead of shutting you out, and I'm sorry. You and Lea are the only family who have ever loved me without conditions, and I love you so much…"

The door shifts under his weight as he leans on it.

"I never knew my biological parents. Honestly, I never talk about the Hammonds because I've been trying to forget them for more than half my life. But since keeping my past from you is going to put a wedge between us, I guess I have to."

My chest tightens and I feel like I'm overheating as I let my head fall back against the side of the tub. I stare at the ceiling.

Do I want to know what shaped Damon into the person he is now? Yes. Absolutely, yes. But not because he feels like I've given him some warped ultimatum. I want him to tell me because he trusts me with his truth.

I'm pushing to my feet to open the door and tell him as much when he starts talking.

"I'd say I'd been in at least five homes by the time I turned eleven," he says. "Mostly they were nice people. Some even had pets and beautiful, white, picket-fenced homes. They smelled of fresh-baked cookies and had enormous yards to play and run in like they were straight out of the movies. Then there were also some small, run-down houses with closet-sized bedrooms and some run with regimented military-style rules."

"I'm listening," I mutter so he knows to continue.

"I never felt like I belonged in any of those places, though," he says. "Whenever I'd arrive at a new house, I'd find my bed and shove my garbage bag full of everything I owned in this world right under my pillow. I never unpacked." He releases a shallow sigh. "I knew I was a paycheck tucked away in a room, someone's idea of a religious repentance, or a temporary chore to be dealt with until I could be passed on to the next family." There's a short pause while he seems to pick away at his old scars. "It was a hard lesson, but it taught me to keep to myself, be quiet, and never let my hopes get too high. That's what got me through it."

My heart wrenches.

His voice is so tender I feel like I can almost touch the memories. I can almost see eleven-year-old Damon living his life in time-out and yearning for someone to talk to or to tell him he was loved.

"But then I got placed with the Hammonds." Levity twists his tone. "The house was small and not much to look at, really, but I still remember this funny little garden gnome on the side of the paved walkway beneath an overgrown hedge. He wore a red and white polka dot hat, and his pudgy little hand was raised in a wave like he was welcoming me inside."

We both release a subdued laugh, and my eyes prickle with tears for what he's been through.

He was just a kid.

"God, as much as I tried to use my old tricks, Jan and Gary did everything in their power to pull me out of my shell. Gary was a tall, barrel-chested guy with thick blond hair, stark blue eyes, and a cartoonish pointy nose. To look at him, you'd think he was mean as all get out, but no...big old sap." Damon releases a melancholy laugh to himself, and I can almost imagine his unfocused gaze as he flips through the memories like old pictures. "He used to be in the garage coughing and crossing wires and building computers from scratch. No matter how many times I said 'no, I'm good,' he'd ask me to come with him. When I finally did, he taught me all the tools and their names."

"He taught you what?" I ask incredulously, my tone laced with humor.

"Okay, you and I both know the only thing I know how to fix is a plate, but at the time...I looked forward to being out in that garage with him calling me son. He was very nonchalant about it, but every time he said it, I plucked it like a flower petal and shoved it in my pocket for later."

The tears fall freely now as I listen. I'm angry, sad, and numb at the same time. It's no wonder Damon's been holding this all in. When all you want is someone to love you and then you get to feel it and bask in someone's light, it hurts like hell when it's taken away.

"Now, Jan, she was baking or in her garden with Laura. Once, I made the mistake of telling the two of them those things were for girls. *Shit.* Jan was feisty and take-no-mess, and she blew flour in my face so fast... She told me to put on an apron and prove whoever said that wrong or live a lie. That's how I remember her."

He's quiet for a few beats. My heart wrenches for him dealing with so much hurt and regret.

When he continues, his voice is so faint I can barely make it out. "Laura and I were the closest, though. She had two long golden braids and a bright Pollyanna smile. She always looked for the good in people. She reminds me of you in that way."

"Don't try to get on my good side." I chastise him, biting back a laugh. "Finish telling the story."

He chuckles.

"She used to beat the dog-snot out of me at Mario Brothers." He barks out a belly laugh. "She was so cool, funny, and smart. Forget lemonade. She had a cookie stand. For a couple of bucks, she bought the generic pack with like fifty of those sandwich cookies in it and sold them for a quarter each."

This time, I laugh as I reconcile the woman I met today with this fun-sized version from Damon's memories.

"Like I said, she was smart, but she had a huge heart, too. The first time I had a nightmare, she snuck into my room with a tiny comb and this goofy looking My Little Pony with bright neon pink hair. She thought combing its hair soothed me, but it was talking with Laura that calmed me down." He stops there, and part of me wants to beg him to continue. Hearing these stories only makes me love him so much more.

The other part of me is just thankful he trusted me with this much.

"I had a sister and two adults who treated me like their kid. It was in me to resist how much I wanted to be part of this family, but when they started the adoption process...they always told me I belonged with them. For the first time, I let myself dream about living in that little house with the friendly-looking garden gnome, about what gadget Gary and I would build together, and the delicious cakes and beautiful gardens Jan, Laura, and I would create."

"Maybe you still can," I say.

He continues his train of thought. "These people made me feel like I was worth something, like I belonged. They made me dream about being Damon Hammond. So, when Child and Family Services showed up a year in, you can imagine how devastated and let down I was and why I never wanted to feel like that again."

Damon clears his throat. When he continues, it's with full

restraint in his voice. "She said Gary is gone. After twenty-five years, it still hurts because he was the only man who ever called me his son."

At this, I jolt to my feet and rush the door. I swing it open and let him pull me into his arms because he needs me. We need each other.

He glides his hands up the sides of my neck, letting his lips crash down with an insatiable fervor. I get an excited flutter in my belly to be back in his arms and let my needy hands roam wildly on his back as he arches into me.

"I love you, Al."

I tug him closer still, sinking into his touch. "I love you, too." Even as I savor the familiar comfort of his arms banded around me, I understand, though I know this changes nothing about what he needs to do.

More than before, I know Laura isn't nothing to Damon. We need to take her case. And at some point, they need to talk because that's what family does when we matter to each other. We work through our problems, we acknowledge each other's hurts, and when we can, we fight for each other.

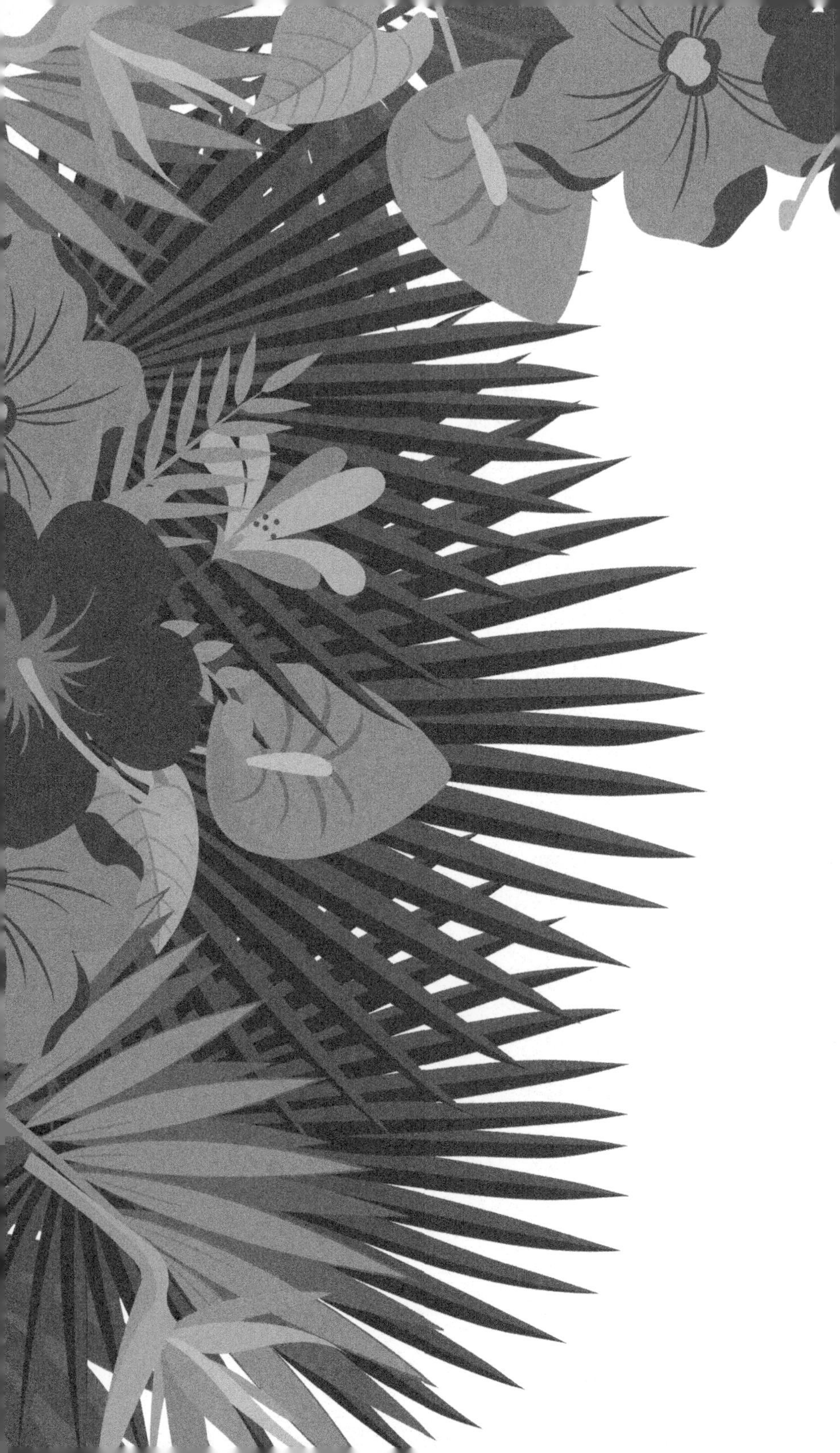

CHAPTER 20
Damon

True to form, Lea knocks on the door, effectively putting an end to Allegra's and my latest bathroom door confessional. She's double-fisting bottles of red and white wine and ready to kick off an awkward and stilted Trio Dinner. Over semi-cold chicken and limp fries, we play a full sheet of Yahtzee, letting the loud clink of dice clapping against a plastic cup fill the silence between us. Lea is unwilling to start another sheet since Allegra and I "failed to resolve our shit" and coolly cuts dinner short, warning us to shape up by tomorrow.

We do, mostly.

Allegra and I are back to normal-ish. All of Thursday, we're attentive, even though it feels like there's a six-foot marker between us. At home, I still feel her watching and being careful with me—testing my trust in her. I hate that I lied to her and Lea, but especially to Allegra considering the terms of our contract.

At work, she and Lea stick to their guns about the Chat-Video claim.

"I'm like, 'excuse me, but who in the hell are you?'" Lea

says dramatically. For the second time today, she's telling the story of Brandon Yu to Fallon, the wedding planner and owner of Fallon Events from across the lobby.

"Right? He has no clue who he's talking to," Allegra adds. During one of the few times we've talked today, Allegra told me she's already heard the story, as have I. Lea gets louder and more animated with each retelling.

They're all crammed in Lea's office across from mine, so whether I want to hear the story again or not, it comes in surround sound. With the glass walls, I get a 360-view of the whole scene.

I'm still waiting for Lea's big reveal when she says his name and lands her rather inventive punchline.

Brandon Yu is the Chief Legal Counsel for Andrews Enterprises, Incorporated. Or, as I like to refer to him, Kyle's daddy's problem solver. *Can't have your fuck up of a son blemishing daddy's good "billionaire" name, now can we?* So, Brandon Yu has been assigned to make all Kyle's problems go bye-bye.

When he called here first thing this beautiful Friday morning—I'm presuming after the papers were served bright and early Thursday—he unfortunately connected with Lea. Then, promptly, and stupidly told her, if she were "any good of a lawyer" she'd abandon all thoughts of going to court and agree to an immediate private mediation this coming Tuesday.

It's sad, really. This is Lea Cook, Attorney at Law, top of the class at Boyd, and all-around bossy Leo. She's highly efficient and results driven. The mere audacity of someone challenging her skill and intellect is both a personal affront and a pure turn-on.

Poor, unsuspecting Brandon Yu. He thought he was just playing hardball with some other suit. Little does he know keeping things under wraps and out of the public eye for daddy's fuck up will be his own downfall. I wouldn't be surprised if Lea agreed to mediation solely for the opportunity to get him in the same room and reduce him down to a grain of salt.

She can make a grown man cry.

"No!" Fallon slaps her hand over her mouth, and her bone-straight onyx hair spills over her shoulders.

"Yes, girl." Lea's lips are pressed together in a slight grimace. "It's like he doesn't get how satisfying it will be for me to ruin him." She huffs out a laugh, shaking her head. "Got me over here Googling the company just to have a visual of the man. He's fine as hell, but I'm going to make it my goal to take him down."

"She will, too." Allegra agrees.

"Mr. Bold on the Phone is not ready."

"Oh, my goodness, this guy sounds like a total asshole," Fallon adds, completely invested in the story. "So, what did he say when you told him you'd need to speak with your client before committing to mediation?"

Lea closes her eyes, pressing her fingertips to her lips—this time with extra head dip and a prolonged sigh. Then Allegra, takes the cue and answers for her.

"She was like, look here, Brandon Yu—"

Fallon's gasp is extra loud, abruptly cutting the theatrics short. "Fucking shitballs! Are you serious?"

They both eye her like she's ruining the best part when Fallon pinches the bridge of her nose, mumbling, "No, no, no, no. This is all bad." She squeezes her eyes closed with a groan. "Please tell me you're not talking about the ViddyChat case?"

"Oh, you mean the *ChatVideo* case?" Lea corrects her. Suddenly, I sense everything depends on which side they're on.

I swivel my chair around from where I've been watching them from an angle to face her office directly, reclining to see exactly how this unfolds.

Lea, Allegra, and Fallon have been friends since the second we stepped onto the sixth floor to check out the spaces. They'd walked around the empty floor envisioning colors, surface textures, and the type of furniture and signs they were going to purchase to embody our brands. Most of the time, Fallon is in the field making the vision of someone's marital dreams come true, but when she's in the office, this is what they do. It's all gossip, talking about fabrics, and catching up over chocolate—or wings with hot sauce, if Allegra has any say. Loud female bonding.

I see Fallon drop her head into her hands.

"This is not happening," she grumbles. When neither Allegra nor Lea fill the silence, she peeks up at them through her dainty fingers. "I'm totally ashamed to say it, but Brandon Yu is my older, obviously annoying, brother. Please don't hate me."

"Come again?" Lea probes.

"It's true. He works for Kellan Andrews as his Chief Legal Counsel. He's a lawyer for a billion-dollar empire, so he's my parents' pride and joy, and he can do no wrong. I'm just a lowly wedding planner with a self-made, million-dollar company featured in magazines like *Grapevine, Visage,* and *Bridal Bliss.* Brides wait years to get on my list, but I'm not a doctor or a lawyer, so I'm poor little Fallon. Or worse, 'Brandon's little sister.'"

Allegra clears her throat, holding up her hands. "Okay, so let me get this straight. Beautiful, amazing, badass Fallon Yu and asshole extraordinaire Brandon Yu are siblings? Do we have to back off taking him down?"

Fallon jolts upright.

"Um...maybe you didn't hear me right. I said he's my 'annoying brother' whose perfect shadow I've been living in my entire existence. It's going to be awkward, but he could stand to be knocked down a notch. Do what you need to do and don't tell me about it, so I'm not complicit. Whatever it is, I'll read about it in the papers. *I know nothing.*" She stands and waves her hands. "This never happened."

Lea and Allegra are slack jawed as Fallon pantomimes washing her hands clean and backs away toward the lobby.

Not even ten minutes after Fallon leaves, they get Laura on the phone. To Lea's sheer satisfaction, she agrees to mediation to leave monetary restitution on the table. They spend less than half an hour discussing further documentation before the volume lowers, cutting off my lifeline to the conversation.

I look up just in time to see Lea gesturing for Allegra to close the door.

She's still on the phone, but there's laughing and nodding as she jots something on a piece of paper. Then, through the glass walls of our offices, I catch sight of her watching me just before she ends the call.

What was that about?

A few minutes later, Allegra opens Lea's door, restoring my conversation lifeline as she rounds the corner into her office. Lea wastes no time corresponding with Brandon Yu to coordinate a Monday-morning—not Tuesday—mediation appointment. Lea can take being petty to astronomical levels with the best of them.

I feel her surveying me, so I swivel back toward my computer monitor where, as assigned, I'm still poring over the fine print of ViddyChat's Terms & Conditions. But in my peripheral, I see her set her phone down and walk straight toward my office.

She gives a courtesy knock on the glass and leans into the doorway.

"Don't act like you weren't ear-hustling the entire morning." She waits until I swivel toward her, sporting a guilty smile. "As you know, I talked to Laura."

"Yeah."

"After we discussed the mediation, she asked if we could chat about something on the personal end..."

"To which you said?"

"I'd listen." She shrugs. "Then, I did."

By the pensive, conflicted expression on her face, she's going to make me pry this out of her. I cross my arms over my chest and lean into the bend of my chair as I consider the limited possibilities. What could Laura need to talk to one of my best friends about?

The tightness in my chest is too strong to ignore.

"So, you're standing in my doorway because by 'personal end' Laura means me? She wants to talk to me but did a temperature check with you first before she dives in."

"More or less."

After everything I told Allegra last night, I don't think I fully grasped how much my relationship with the Hammonds has weighed on me and affected the decisions I make regarding relationships and who I allow to get close.

"When?" I ask, finally.

"Sometime this weekend. She mentioned that your—"

"This weekend won't work." I pause for a second, registering this is the first time we've been alone today. "Hey, Le, um...I just want to apologize for being tight-lipped about Laura. Considering the impact my silence could've had on the firm—"

Lea holds up a hand. "We're good. I appreciate the apology just...know that you can tell me anything." Because emotions and mushy moments aren't her thing, she shakes it off with a smile. "Why not this weekend?"

"I really need to smooth things over with Al."

"Ya think?" Lea tilts her head, fixing me with a sarcastic stare. "But you realize you live together, right? You and Al can talk anytime. After all that sighing and saggy body language at dinner the other night, I'm thinking tonight might be as good a time as any." She huffs out an impatient laugh. "Really, don't delay. The sooner, the better...for all of us."

Lea's right.

Allegra and I need to sit down and talk through whatever lingering hurts and hang-ups we're still harboring. We need to get back to the us we planned with the Friendship Contract. We owe each other that much. Once our heads and hearts are clear, then I'll consider meeting Laura for coffee on Saturday.

Except, the workday zips by in a blur of phone calls and combing through copies of contracts and correspondence. I have to process letters and emails and scour timestamps and auto-replies for insight into Brandon Yu's possible arguments and objections to prepare counterarguments. I familiarize myself with the fine print while Lea and Allegra analyze the strengths and exploitable weaknesses of both our case and his.

We've labeled, stapled, and paper clipped a damn good stack of documents to support the case.

By the time we all leave for the day, we're physically and mentally drained. Allegra nods off on the drive, so I tell myself we've got all weekend to talk. In the dim quiet of the loft, we change out of our work clothes and into pajamas. In a routine of orchestrated moves, we brush our teeth then she grabs water for us. A few minutes later, I jerk the remote control toward the television in our bedroom, searching for something mellow to give her the white noise she needs to sleep. Then we slink beneath the covers and drift off with her in my arms.

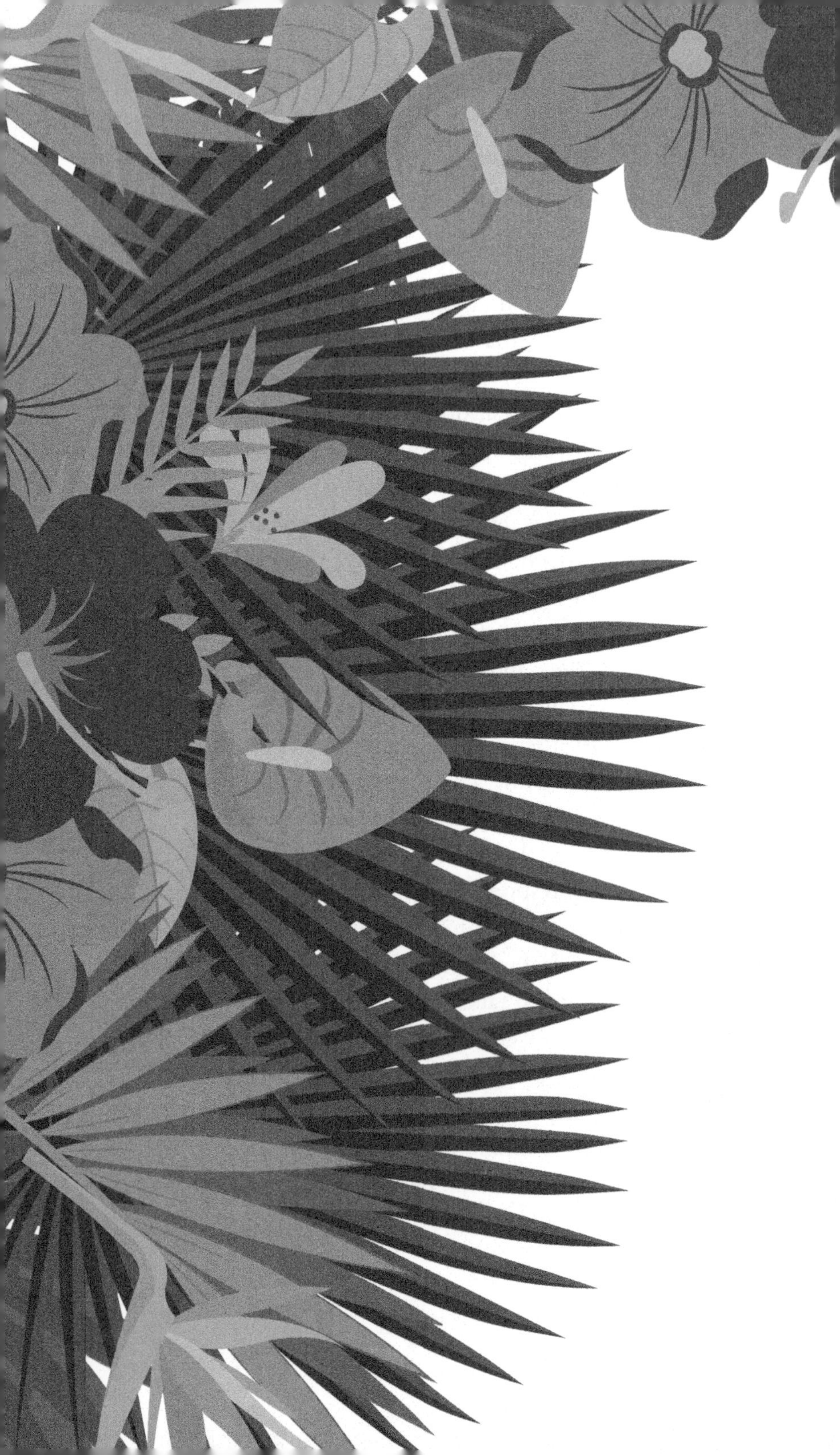

CHAPTER 21
Damon

I awaken sprawled across the cool sheets of an empty bed.

"Al?" I croak, straining to listen for running water in the bathroom or movement in the kitchen, but I'm met with pin-drop silence.

Instinctively, I know she's not here, but I drag myself out of bed and around the mockingly sunny loft, searching for her, anyway. Instead, what I find is a piece of lined paper with the scraggily edge from where she's ripped it from her notebook.

I'm at Mom's for the weekend. I'll see you at work. Go be with your family.

Because I have nothing else to do and hanging around this cold loft filled with reminders of Allegra's absence isn't an option, I text Lea, okaying her to share my cell phone number with Laura. Almost immediately, I receive a text with the address to a cafe close to the loft and a request to meet up at noon. I take twenty minutes to get ready and another ten to type and erase a text to Allegra. Then I sit staring at the screen before I settle on simplicity.

Damon Dawson 11:45 am
I love you.

Lately, that's the only thing I'm sure about.

Fifteen minutes later, I arrive at the café. I spot Laura's blonde curls at a patio table. Well, half of her. It's crowded, and a group of people that are being seated by a server block my view. As I stretch my neck and hold up a hand to grab her attention, the server moves, and I lose my breath.

It's not just Laura.

Seated beside her, I recognize the smiling blue eyes and slightly turned-up nose. Time has hollowed her cheeks a little and there are faint wrinkles twisting the corners of her mouth and eyes, but Jan's face is still the same.

The second she spots me, she covers her mouth with her hands and tears up. A smile lifts the rosy cherries of her cheeks.

It feels like a dream. I've lost all sense of time and space. I don't know if I'm thirty-six or eleven, but as I chew the inside of my cheek and tears singe the corners of my eyes, the little boy inside me wants to run into her arms and never let go.

My throat closes around all the years I both dreamed about and dreaded this moment. As I weave through the crowd entering the restaurant and onto the patio toward Laura and Jan, a weight settles on my heart as I catch sight of the empty fourth chair.

I don't even make it to the table before Jan approaches and pulls me into her arms. She squeezes me so tight, I feel the cracks in my heart melding together. As much as the hurt I suffered warns me to hold back, seeing this woman who I wanted so badly to call Mom and touching her and feeling her tears dampen the fabric of my shirt, I know I'm not the only one who has been hurting.

"Look at you." She pulls back trembling, her lips pursed as

she bites back more tears. "Oh, my goodness, I missed you so much. If Gary were here, he'd..." she trails off, but from the pride-filled expression on her face and the love in her eyes, I hear the rest of the sentence as if she says it aloud.

He'd be so proud of you.
He'd hug and love on you the same way I am.
He'd call you son.

Jan reaches up to swipe the tears from my eyes. "You're such a beautiful man, and I love you more than words can say." Again, she covers her mouth, letting the tears spill freely down her splotchy cheeks.

"We've never stopped loving you, Damon," Laura says. She's crying, too. *Hurting, too.*

"Welcome to the Skyline Cafe. I'm Jo and I'll be taking care of you today..." The server's welcome greeting stalls on her tongue when she notices our tear-strewn faces. Her brows pinch in confusion. "Should I come back? Maybe bring some waters to get you all started?"

Jan waves her off.

"Not at all, honey. This is just me and my kids being emotional, but we're getting ourselves together." *My kids.* "With the sun showing off like this, why don't you start us off with some lemonades while we take a peek at your menu?"

We laugh through our tears, and Jan is still holding my hand across the table as the server returns to take our orders. I think about Allegra as I order the chicken sliders with the ranch on the side. Laura and Jan opt to split a margherita pizza, citing how hard it is for them to eat when their emotions are high.

"Brought you something," Laura says, rummaging in her purse.

Through my tears, I bark out a deep, throaty belly laugh

the instant I spot the neon pink hair. She didn't forget the tiny comb, either.

"I saved it for you in case you needed this in your life. I figured you might, after I saw Allegra's face at the meeting that first day." She winces. "Y'all are together, right?"

"Now, now." Jan flattens her hands on the table, shaking her head. "We can get to love and marriage in a minute. We've got a lot of ground to cover."

My mouth goes dry, and my heart slows to a thud. I set my pony on the table then rub my hands over my pants legs just as the server arrives with our food.

I suddenly understand not being able to eat when emotions run high.

As soon as the server leaves, Jan blindsides me like a hurricane gust of wind with a truth my eleven-year-old self could never have comprehended. The "one minute they're starting the adoption process, and the next Child and Family Services whisked me away" reality I thought I knew is false. She and Gary were proceeding with adoption. They'd already filed the petition-to-adopt forms and were undergoing the home study. During the process, they were asked about their daily routine, education and work history, finances, hobbies, references, and criminal and medical records.

Just before my year mark with the Hammonds, Gary had been diagnosed with stage-two lung cancer. Because his case was localized, his outlook was favorable. So, his doctor removed as much of the cancer as possible. But chemo and radiation were recommended after lingering traces remained in his system.

That's why CFS removed me from the Hammonds. The social worker denied my home study approval because Gary was deemed to have a life-threatening illness. An assessment which, I learn from Jan, turned out to be correct.

Five years after I was gone, he succumbed to the cancer.

"So, I know you harbored anger toward us because you thought we gave you back. But we didn't. You always belonged with us," she says. She says it the same way she always has. "You are part of this family, and we never let go."

The hollow ache behind my heart grows faint until it's nothing more than a faded memory.

"That's why the whole private investigator..." Laura shrugs apologetically. "Sorry to be so dramatic, but we've watched your rise to success from afar for so long. And Dad," she flicks her gaze skyward, biting back another bout of tears, "he made us promise to find you and tell you the truth. We've never stopped loving and wanting you. He wanted to ensure you knew you are our family...his son."

"My son," Jan adds.

"My brother." Then Laura drills it home. "You're *not* alone, Damon. You have us..." Her eyebrows lift slowly as she tosses Jan a mischievous look before turning back to me. "And Allegra, too? Can we talk about the love stuff, now? I don't want to keep crying the entire lunch." She takes a generous bite of pizza.

Jan and I laugh.

"Oh, fine." Jan waves us off, smiling. It's surreal how, after all these years, we still feel playfulness and familiarity. Twenty-five years have passed. Countless homes, Laura's marriage, Gary's death. We still feel like a family.

Like old times, I make Laura go first while I bite into one of my chicken sliders.

Her shoulders sag with disappointment for a moment. She's so eager to hear about Allegra and me, but she beams while telling me about her late husband. I check my phone. It's been over an hour since I texted Allegra and no reply. So, I ignore the hollow ache in my chest as I slip my phone away and settle in for Laura's story about Brian's proposal in front of the Eiffel Tower.

"I can't wait to show you the pictures." Laura beams. "He was adorable. Shaking and trembling the entire time..." She presses her hand over her heart. Then her tears start up again. "Shit, sorry."

Jan hugs her tight. She kisses the crown of her head, soothing her like she's probably done a million times since I last saw them in the flour-covered kitchen island making cupcakes with extra sprinkles.

"I miss him so much." Laura smiles through her tears, still looking at me. "We belonged together. It's the only way to put it."

I'm so engrossed in Laura's stories as she continues telling me about their travels and how they loved to bake and create businesses together. It's everything I want to share with Allegra. I get lost imagining us visiting more islands with tropical gardens and diamond-speckled water. I want to see Paris and Greece and Spain with her hand in mine as we snap photos and absorb little pieces of history together.

"Anyway," Laura's emotion-thick voice tears me from my thoughts. "I told him all about my brother, and I swear up and down you two would've *capital-L* loved each other."

"He sounds like an awesome guy," I say.

"He was. He really *really* was." For a second, she appears to linger in a memory before she shakes her head, as if letting it float away. "Enough about me, though. I need to know if you and Allegra are just dating for fun, or if I just have amazing timing, and we've come back into your life like a good omen right on time for wedding bells..." She dips her chin conspiratorially, waggling her brows.

I'm smiling as I steeple my fingers on the table, but a heaviness settles in my body.

"Let's see... I've loved her for twelve years."

Laura squeals and claps her hands together. "Go on," she says, excitement suffusing her entire being.

"I wasn't going to come today." I wince inwardly. "But she left for her mom's house so I wouldn't have an excuse."

Jan tilts her head in understanding. "I like her already."

"Me, too. I told you, Mom," Laura says.

"She and Lea have also been my best friends for twelve years. So, we're all close. Allegra is beautiful and amazing, fun to be around, and loves movies and traveling." I hesitate for a second as it hits me. *I don't want to waste any more time with Allegra.* "She's it for me."

"Friends to lovers!" Laura squeals again. "It's tricky, but the best relationships are the ones who were friends first. You already know what kind of person you're dealing with, and you love them anyway. It doesn't get better than that."

I flit a glance at these two women who have only ever felt like my family. "I never told her about you or Gary. In my eleven-year-old mind, I thought you gave me back because you didn't want me." I lift my shoulders and let them drop. "My thinking was, why should she love me when no one else did?"

"Oh, sweetheart." Jan reaches her hand across the table to squeeze my arm. "You are worthy of all our love. I'm sure she feels the same way."

Laura straightens. "It'll be hard and lonely but give her some space this weekend. Let her miss you as much as you miss her. Spend some time really thinking about the moments when you felt closest to each other." I get the sense she and Brian may have experienced this at some point. "Make a list if you have to. But come Monday, tell her about everything on it, and you'll know what comes next."

"Okay," I say, but every inch of my heart knows a list won't be enough.

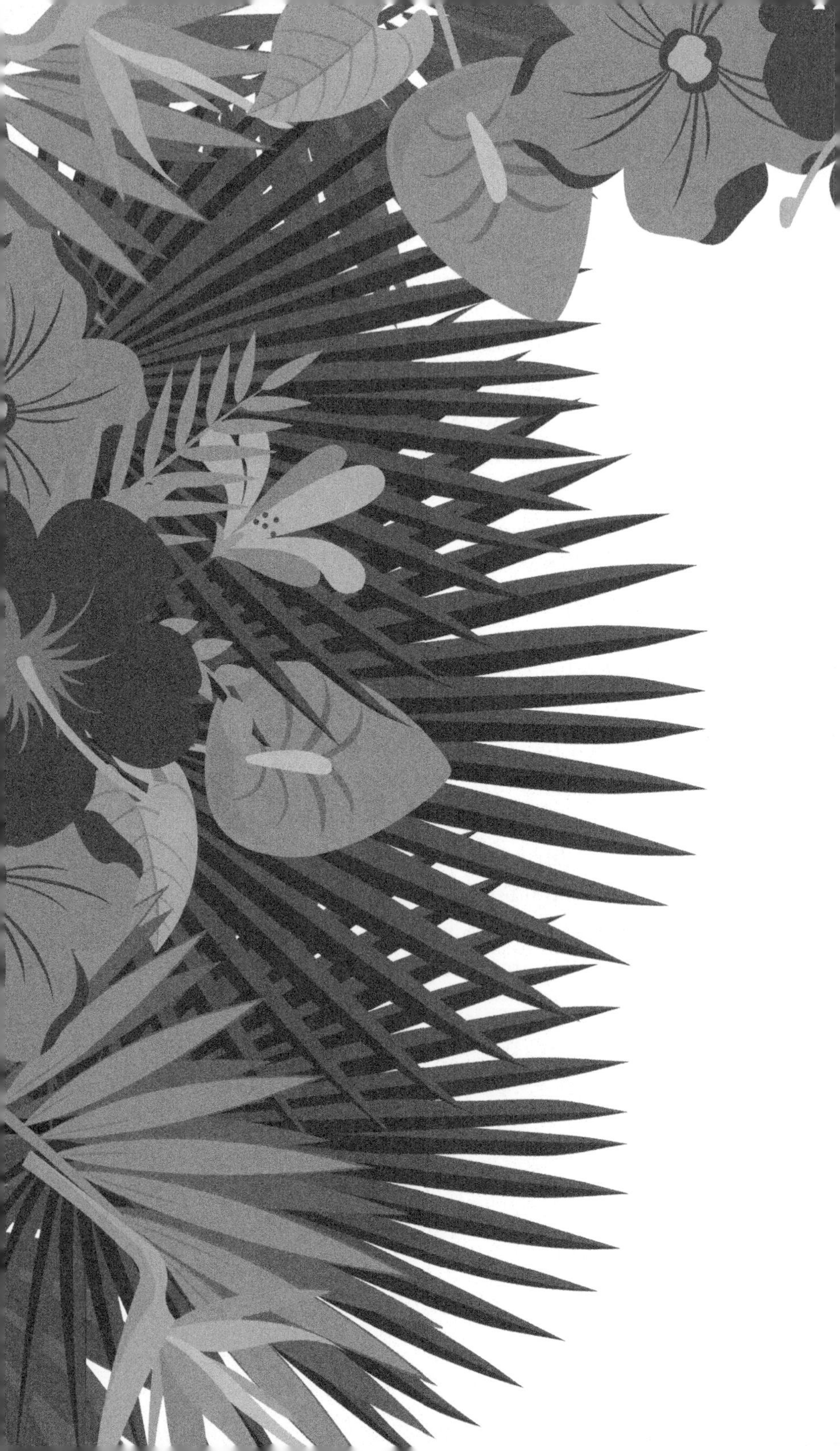

CHAPTER 22
Allegra

"Do me a favor, would you?" Mom asks as I walk toward the hall. She's bent over the oven checking her famous homemade macaroni and cheese. "Text your brother the gate code. It's on the pink Post-it on the corkboard in my office. They changed it last week, but with the wedding and the honeymoon and everything, it slipped my mind to give him the new one."

I catch sight of the corkboard when I round the corner into the office. "Fluorescent or pale pink?" I call back.

Her desk and walls are a windstorm of rainbow Post-its and office supplies mingled in with hair care products in every stage from conception to final packaging. My heart swells when I think about how far she's come from mixing up oils and serums on the stove to managing an entire business while juggling two kids and a day job that was slowly stealing her light.

Warmed with pride, I drag my fingers over the campaign mockups for her new manuka honey nourishing line for natural curls and coils.

"It's the neon one." Mom says. "And hurry. You know how

impatient that child is. He'll be texting me constantly from the gate."

I chuckle, fishing my phone out to text my brother the code, then I head back to the kitchen to set the table. Mom won't let me anywhere near the food, though. She says, this is my home, but it's her kitchen. She won't accept help when she's celebrating finally having both her babies home for a good meal.

Soon, Aaron and Piper come bustling through the front door in matching outfits—a Hawaiian print shirt and a dress with the same bright turquoise and orange floral pattern.

"Aloha!" Piper is glowing as she pulls me into a tight hug, surprised to see me. After she's squeezed me good, she pads down the hall to the kitchen. Aaron and I watch in amusement as she moves on to Mom, banding her fresh-from-vacation glowing arms around her, too. "I love fish, but I'm dying for some of your macaroni, Mama Malone. It smells so amazing."

Aaron and I follow close behind and hang off the island where Mom and Piper are already "taste-testing" the chicken straight off the bone.

I congratulate the newlyweds as I plop down on a barstool.

Aaron gives Mom a big bear hug, lifting her off the ground and swinging her around as she squeals in delight.

When he sets Mom back on her feet, a laugh bubbles inside me.

"Now listen, squirt. You can spare me all the details about the honeymoon, but how is it being a married man?" I ask, amused by the very idea of my little brother who ran from girls on the school playground.

Piper folds her arms across her chest, listening for his hopefully correct response. Happy wife, happy life, right?

Then he turns to me with his shoulders drawn back and his

eyebrows dragged down with suspicion. I sense my question is about to backfire.

"Um, why are you here, Al? And where's my boy, D?"

My cheeks heat as all eyes land on me.

When I got here early this morning and told Mom I was staying the weekend, she about spit out her coffee. Even so, she held her tongue. Leave it to my little brother to skip all the niceties and cut straight through the crap.

"What?" I lean back on the stool and press a hand to my chest in mock offense. "Are you implying I'm here for any reason other than to support my newlywed baby brother and his beautiful wife?"

There are legitimate snickers from Mom and Piper.

Aaron scrubs a hand over his face then fixes me with an incredulous stare. "No implication. That's exactly what I'm saying. Now why are you *really* here?" The impatient tilt of his head as he looks at me over his brow is a warning. *Don't lie to me.*

Not that I ever could lie to my family.

A nervous laugh rumbles through me. I figured the questions would come at some point later today or tomorrow morning, maybe. But I guess now is as good a time as any to clear the thick, interrogational air.

"In that case, yes. I'm here for you all...*and* other reasons." I heave a weighted sigh, then let it all rush out of me. "There's a lot more to it, but Damon is meeting with his foster sister from when he was eleven. She recently reemerged in his life. So, I snuck out of bed before he woke up to give him the space he needs to embrace the relationship he shares with them—without me tainting it."

Aaron surveys me for a second like he's considering the mouthful I just unloaded on him. But then he nods.

"That's cool of you, but 'tainted?'"

Humiliation coils around me.

"Yes. He kept it from me. Our new client...I had to learn from her that she is his foster sister."

"Ouch." Aaron winces.

"Exactly." I jerk up my eyebrows, thankful Aaron gets what's been tormenting me for the past few days.

Mom and Piper say nothing like Aaron is doing a fine job answering their unspoken questions for them. They're happy to take the backseat on this one.

I straighten, plastering on a wide smile. "In the meantime, I get to be here with my family and talk about all the embarrassing—and incriminating—moments that happened during 'wedding weekend.'"

Aaron groans, seemingly happy it's all over, but the crease between his eyebrows lets on that something else is still weighing on his mind.

"All right now, y'all. Come on in here and get some food while it's hot," Mom says. She pivots to pull out serving spoons from the drawer next to the sink, then sticks one in each dish for a makeshift buffet.

Just like when we were kids, Aaron and I line up behind Piper who's already piling steaming greens, cheesy macaroni, and the fall-off-the-bone chicken onto her plate.

Aaron takes two plates and passes one back to me.

I notice his contemplative expression is still in place.

"Penny for your thoughts." I stretch my neck, leaning into his periphery.

"Oh, uh..." He shakes his head and tosses me a quick glance before scooping a generous helping of greens onto his plate. "I was just thinking about the wedding day. In the groom's suite, I talked with Damon. Afterward, he'd seemed off."

"What do you mean?"

"It seemed like nothing. We were laughing and joking. I'd been schooling him about choosing battles in a relationship and complementing each other, you know? He'd joked that it was nothing but a load of bullshit Piper had fed me, so I had to turn the tables on him."

Piper flashes Aaron an appreciative smile.

I tilt my head to either side, ceding Damon's point.

"Anyway, I told him I saw the two of you all lovey dovey and how that part slows after a while. You get comfortable, and hopefully you're left feeling like you belong together—"

"Shit." My throat tightens. I chew the inside of my cheek. "His foster mother always stressed how much he belonged with them." He must've been thinking about his family when I saw him at the ceremony. *I knew something was wrong.* "I mean, we're okay now, but...do you think maybe he was questioning whether we belong together?"

The clink of Aaron's plate on the countertop snags my attention. He sets his hands on my shoulders and squares me to him.

"Listen, I don't know if being in love myself somehow gives me more insight, but what you all have...it doesn't come along every day, Al. Do not throw this away second-guessing yourself or reading into things that may have nothing to do with you." My brother's tone is filled with conviction, like he needs to make sure I'm hearing him.

My phone pings in my pocket, but I don't dare move.

"I know, Aaron. Still, how many guys have I dated and hopelessly fallen for, only to learn I've been completely wrong about them? What if my instincts are just faulty?"

"Oh, here we go," Aaron scoffs. "If this is about Mom and her business way back when, you need to move past that."

"It's all part of what made me who I am."

I know it's killing Mom not to jump in right here to add

her two cents, but she seems resigned to let Aaron handle my hang-ups today.

"But did they break her? Was she too proud to start again and build another business? No. Mom is still killing the game. Sometimes you have to let go of the old stuff to make room for the new, right Mom?"

"Yes, indeed. They only win if you give up," she says. Her voice overflows with pride as she looks on at us.

"I'm serious, Al." Aaron refocuses his attention on me. "Maybe you haven't seen it all these years because you and D have been so close, and you're scared of losing that friendship. I saw the way you were in Hawaii, though. I think we all did." Aaron chuckles.

Mom and Piper hum their agreement.

"Should we talk about how Chelsea was afraid for her life when you shut her down for asking about Damon?" Piper blinks rapidly and purses her lips mischievously.

"Well..." The raised inflection in my voice as I drag out the word tells on me.

Mom dips her chin to look at me over the bridge of her nose. "Mm-hmm. The second you got off that shuttle at the resort, I knew something was going on. Talking 'bout 'it's sort of new' and you all were 'feeling your way around.' Like my own eyes don't work, and I don't know a lover's spat when I see one." She waves me off with a huff of a laugh.

I close my eyes and shake my head. I deserve this from my family, so I'm going to stand here and take it.

"Do you believe my child told me she didn't want to take the *spotlight* off you two?" Mom darts a pursed-lip stare between Aaron and Piper. "Shoot. You and my Damon were practically glowing with love. Anyone would need to have their head stuck under a rock not to see it."

Because I sense the end of this "roast on Allegra" is

nowhere near, I shove my hand in my pocket and pull out my phone to check my texts, and my heart skitters. There's a message from Lea checking in on me, but I can barely focus enough to read it. My attention is fixed on the missed message below it.

Damon Dawson 11:45 am
I love you.

I don't know why, but tears spring to my eyes. All I want to do is go to him. I want to go home. I want to wrap my arms around him and tell him how much I love him and that we can be scared, but he can trust me because we do belong together.

"So, you were saying..." Aaron laughs.

I look up to find the three of them smiling at me as I press my phone to my chest, biting back a laugh...or a cry. I'm not sure which. It's hard to tell with everything I'm feeling.

"It's okay, sweetheart." Mom beams with happiness for me. "Let yourself enjoy this good feeling. He can be your best friend *and* the love of your life."

My stomach feels fluttery and I'm weightless.

When my phone pings again, they all laugh and tell me to go on and answer Damon. But when I draw the phone back and look at the screen, my mouth falls open.

"What did he say?" Piper gasps at the same time I do. "Oh my gosh, please tell me he's not proposing over text. That would be seriously beyond tacky."

My stomach hardens.

"It's Kyle."

The muscles at Aaron's jaw harden and jut out slightly as he walks over to read the message for himself.

Kyle Andrews 11:49 am

I found some of your things. Hopefully, we can meet up today or tomorrow. It'll be good to see you.

"Oh, hell no. Please tell me you're not falling for this weak line." Aaron shakes his head in disbelief.

A warm, fuzzy laugh rumbles through me. "No. I'm just surprised he hasn't reached out sooner." I'm not falling for any of it. They made sure nothing of mine was left behind. He wants to talk before the mediation to save his own ass before daddy steps in. Finally, I see through the haze. Kyle is a manipulative coward who prides himself on always being the smartest person in the room. *Not anymore.*

We're taking this case for Laura, but oh, my goodness, I can't wait to take him down.

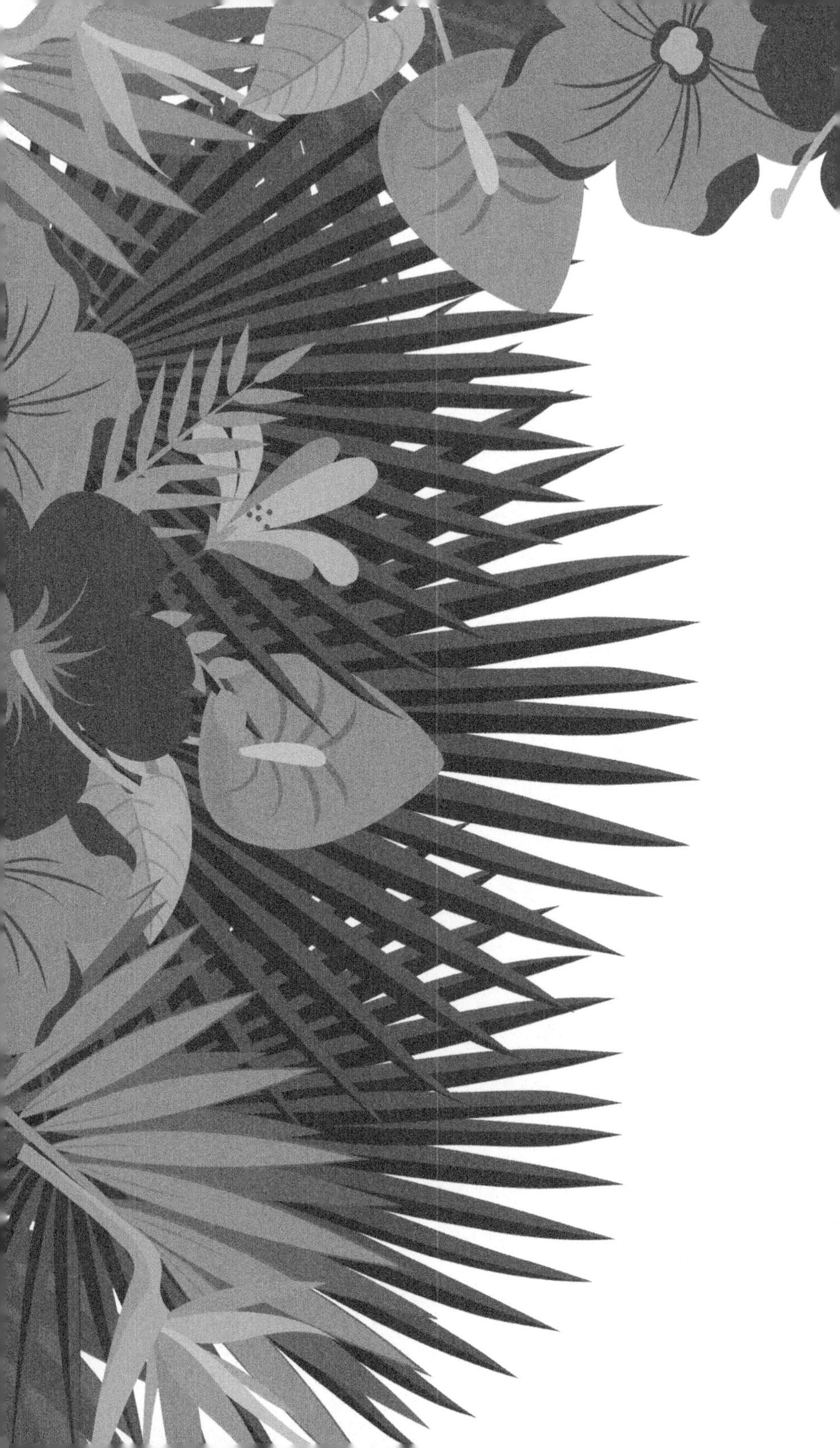

CHAPTER 23
Damon

As planned, Monday morning, Kyle and Brandon Yu enter the Henderson commercial building first. Then Lea, Laura, and I trail a minute behind them. So, the tension in the lobby is nice and thick when the mediator—a big, friendly looking guy I'm assuming is the namesake of Geoffrey Washington Mediation Services—appears in the doorway.

"Right on time," he says, his voice booming off the walls.

Immediately, his happy-go-lucky smile puts me at ease despite his formidable stature. He's got on perfectly tailored and pleated khaki slacks cuffed at the bottom with a white button-down, a red and navy-blue rugby striped tie, and navy suspenders. All he's missing is the cigar to complete the old-money facade.

"I see we're all ready to get down to business. Shall we?" He gives the wall a green-light slap, then turns on his thick-soled heel, indicating for us to follow.

Both parties filter into an air-conditioned conference room with a long mahogany table in the center. There are two chairs on the right closest to the exterior windows, I'm assuming, for Kyle and Brandon. On the left are another four chairs for us.

Per Lea's request, Allegra will get here ten minutes late to avoid a run-in with Kyle. *And, presumably, me.*

Allegra and I haven't seen or talked to each other in days. She never responded to my text, so I don't know where we stand or whether she's spoken to Lea about us.

"I've got water, coffee, tea, pens, notepads..." the mediator lists as he takes the long walk to the far end of the table where a middle-aged woman with short brown hair sits in the corner, ready and waiting at her stenography keyboard. "Let me know if you'll need anything else." He takes the seat at the head of the table and scoots his chair in until his potbelly touches the table.

"Thanks so much for taking us on such short notice. We really appreciate it," Lea shakes the mediator's hand and sits beside him directly across from Brandon Yu.

Which means I get to stare straight ahead at Kyle Andrews. *Lucky me.* I guess it's better me than Laura or Allegra.

"Yes, thanks Geoffrey," Brandon Yu says. He quirks a smile in the mediator's direction, but his focus is trained on the folder in front of him.

Wow.

From the instant he stepped out of his bright red Tesla S Model Plaid sitting in the parking lot, I saw the brother Fallon described in Lea's office. He's a tall, slender guy wearing a tailored navy power suit. In the parking lot, he was still wearing his aviator shades. Everything about him is flashy in a way meant to draw the eye. It seems he's taken the status of his job and converted it to arrogance.

"Well, then..." Mr. Washington's thick salt and pepper eyebrows trench at Brandon Yu's casual informality at using his first-name. He then gives an impatient click of his pen and flits a gaze to the empty chair on our side of the table.

Kyle snorts a self-satisfied laugh, likely assuming Allegra couldn't face him.

Perceptive as ever, Lea presses her lips into a placating smile and meets Kyle's stare as she assures Mr. Washington, "Our associate will be here shortly. I'm the lead attorney, and we've got a lot of ground to cover, so there's no need to wait."

The stenographer's keys click quietly in the corner as we get underway.

After receiving the go-ahead from both parties, the mediator begins his opening statement by thanking us for trusting him to help resolve our clients' conflict. He reassures us we're going to get this done by listening to each other and compromising—a comment, which earns him a not-so-subtle eye-roll from Kyle.

Undeterred, the mediator continues with a few housekeeping tasks to set expectations. Mainly, he's an impartial third party here to assist the disputing parties reach a resolution, and while all participants are encouraged to engage in the discussion, they should do so in turn and in a conciliatory manner.

I'm mentally patting the guy on the back for looking at Kyle as he says that last part when the conference door squeaks open.

"My apologies," Allegra says, flashing a shaky smile as she ducks into the room, interrupting Lea's statement of the problem for ChatVideo.

Every pair of eyes follows her as she slinks into the seat beside Laura. But her gaze centers on me.

Hey, she mouths, nipping the corner of her lower lip. There's a softness to her expression that feels promising.

My heart squeezes hopefully. *Hey* I mouth back.

Underneath the table, Laura gives my knee an encouraging nudge with hers.

"Please continue." Washington nods to Lea.

But she doesn't get a chance.

Not even two minutes after the guy warned us to speak in turn, Kyle huffs out a mirthless laugh, and asks, "Does she really need to be here? Isn't there a conflict of interest if I was in a relationship with the defendant's lawyer when this supposed trademark infringement happened?" He blinks rapidly at Washington, then flits his attention from me to Allegra. "Really, what are the rules about this sort of thing?"

In the corner, the stenographer's fingers move rapid-fire over the keys, amping up the tension in the room.

"Thank you for raising this concern, Mr. Andrews." Mr. Washington smiles. "As a past client relationship with opposing counsel is not relevant to the claims being made, nor a violation of the rules of professional conduct, Ms. Malone may continue to participate in this mediation. And I remind you to refrain from outbursts while the other party is speaking." For the second time, he turns to Lea. "Ms. Cook…"

"Allegra," Kyle bites out, ignoring Mr. Washington. His lips quiver with an insidious indignation as he addresses her, but his glare is fixed on me. "Did you get my text, sweetheart?"

Neither Allegra nor I take the bait.

"Counselor!" Warning sharpens Mr. Washington's tone.

A flush colors Brandon's cheeks as he dips his head in a whisper to Kyle then nods for Washington to proceed.

The mediator's expression hardens as he bites out, "At the risk of sounding like a broken record, please continue, Ms. Cook."

"Yes, as I was saying, under the Lanham Act, the similarity between my client's and the defendant's types of goods, logos, company names, and marketing channels creates commercial confusion for the consuming public. We're asserting that the defendant's initial intent after meeting my client at the Las

Vegas Ones to Watch in Business networking event was to capitalize on ChatVideo's already-growing client—"

Kyle jolts upright.

"You've got to be kidding, right?" His mouth is open, and his eyebrows are raised to his hairline. He's fuming. "This is ridiculous. She's just a bitter woman who's angry because her company hasn't taken off like she thought it would...like mine has. Am I right, Laura? You're mad that I did it better?"

"That's enough." Mr. Washington's voice ricochets off every surface. "Counselor, this will serve as the final reminder. Please speak to your client about the conciliatory nature of this proceeding. We are here to understand both parties and hopefully reach an agreeable resolution." His hand trembles on the table. "We cannot do that if we continue to yell, speak out of turn, and point fingers."

In other words, a tantrum will not make this go away.

Plopping back against the curve of his chair, Kyle scrapes his hands through his hair. The edges of his mouth tighten into a grimace as he pins Brandon Yu with a glare. Once more, Brandon tilts his head close to Kyle's, the tension smoothing his expression and giving away his frustration as he whispers something inaudible.

"It won't happen again," Brandon says to Mr. Washington. "Mr. Andrews is prepared to listen."

Finally, the proceeding gets back on track.

Lea finishes her statement of the problem for ChatVideo under Kyle's heated stare. As expected, Brandon Yu states ViddyChat's problem simply by asserting fair use. Then, both sides present supporting documentation of their key points to the mediator.

After three and a half hours of this, everyone is exhausted.

Even the slow drone of the keys clacking in the corner tapers off. And then the bargaining begins.

"Jesus, in the interest of time, be transparent with me here, Cook," Brandon leans into the bounce of his chair and tosses his pen on the table. "Let's say you've got a magic wand. What does your client want? Best-case scenario." He covers his mouth with his hand, rubbing his finger over his upper lip.

Lea's posture is still ramrod straight with determination, and she lifts her chin slightly. She's rightly confident because she's well prepared.

"My client is seeking an injunction to stop ViddyChat's unauthorized use of her registered trademark, including a change of business logo and slogan, and an immediate stop of the aforementioned television spot," she repeats the same answer verbatim she's given the last three times Brandon rephrased the question. "In addition, monetary reimbursement for losses due to copyright infringement."

Kyle's grip on the arms of his chair tightens until his knuckles whiten.

But Brandon smiles to himself.

He's been holding off, assuming he's worn Lea down. But everyone on this side of the table knows he's been waiting for the part where he solves this pesky problem for his employer and his coward of a son with a check.

"Listen, the slogan, the logo...I agree there are *similarities.*" He flattens his hands on the table. "But the business name is an established, trusted name with a global clientele." He thumbs through the papers in front of him, dragging his finger midway down the page. "We need to be reasonable here. My client is prepared to offer a fair amount in monetary reimbursement, but the name cannot be part of the negotiation."

"This is good," Geoffrey says. "It's important to discuss our non-negotiables as much as the things on which we're willing to bend a little."

Brandon laughs. "And please, let's not confuse trademark with copyright..."

Lea scratches her temple, and I sense she's annoyed by the winding path this mediation has taken. She likes the challenge, but by relying on the money, Brandon has just proven he hasn't done his homework.

"My client is not interested in amounts but a percentage." She turns to Mr. Washington. "I'd like to refer to exhibit H please..."

Because she has the documents memorized, she waits while Mr. Washington and Brandon, with Kyle looking panicked over his shoulder, turn the pages.

A few minutes later, there's a small gasp from Brandon as he closes his eyes.

I'm guessing 'oh shit' is going through his head right about now.

"What?" Kyle whispers. His tone is frantic as he flits a suspicious glance over at Lea, then works his way down to Allegra.

She lifts her head, and if I blinked, I might've missed it, but there's the tiniest smile curving the edges of Allegra's mouth.

The tightness in Brandon's clenched jaw lets on that not only hasn't this cocksure lawyer reviewed the registered copyright for ChatVideo's proprietary software and source code, but he's underestimated the restitution necessary to make the company whole again. Or, as Lea put it, the percentage.

A long silence ensues.

The dynamic change in the room feels almost palpable.

Then Mr. Washington adheres a Post-it note to the page. He lifts his head and scans the faces of our party before focusing on Brandon Yu.

"Given both the registered trademark and software copyright, we've got some great momentum toward settlement," he says, and it's clear he's addressing the room, but he hasn't averted his gaze from Brandon. "You've invested time and money in this mediation, and it feels like we're closer to leaving the building. But it's going to require compromise to close the concessions and resolve this case."

Kyle's nostrils flare slightly as he slouches into the curve of his chair.

Underneath the table, Laura squeezes my hand.

"Please excuse me for a moment," Brandon says, which I'm guessing is code for: I need to give my client the rundown on how his son is at risk of disgracing the Andrews name. Given Brandon was sent to clean up Kyle's mess in the first place, I'm sure this is just the latest in a line of transgressions.

Mr. Washington makes an official break for water, restrooms, and snacks, during which our team huddles outside the building.

* * *

"Wait..." Lea warns as she waits for the building door to close. Her expression is even, but she can't contain the elation from buzzing in her tone. "We've got him right where we want him."

Laura is beaming as she bites her lower lip. "Oh, my goodness, I thought Kyle was going to throw something, he was so mad."

"I'm sure he wanted to." Allegra smiles, tossing me a small glance.

And I'm just as thrilled as the rest of the team, but I can't stop thinking about Allegra and how much I've missed her and how good it feels to have her beside me again. I love her with every fiber of my being.

But I won't jeopardize everything we've worked for today for Laura, ChatVideo, and Malone, Dawson, & Cook.

So, as Laura suggests dinner and drinks tonight to celebrate, and Lea contends the victory will be sweeter when we receive the finalized agreement later this week, I quietly take Allegra's hand in mine.

I swallow and nod along with the conversation while inwardly I'm blindsided by a rush of fire so hot radiating between us, the air feels charged with electricity. The gentle touch is intimate and sexy, almost like foreplay. We both know the gesture means something deeper.

I don't let go as we reconvene in the conference room or when we switch seats to be next to each other, and not even as Kyle pitches a fit when Brandon makes an offer of settlement and Lea counters for fifty-one percent majority share of Viddy-Chat for restitution, retention of copyright control, immediate takedown of the television spot on all platforms, and a change of both logo and slogan.

Since we drove separate cars, it feels like a race back to the loft. Allegra arrives first but I'm already a winner. She's home.

"Bright side?" I glide my hand over the small of her back, guiding her as we enter the elevator and I press the button.

Allegra releases a small laugh. "I'm dying to hear this bright side."

I pivot to face her, cupping my hands to the curves of her cheek. I press a soft, desperate kiss to her lips, savoring the familiar feel. As the elevator ascends, I deepen the kiss with slow drags of my tongue against hers and gentle nips at her lips.

"I missed you so much, Al."

She clasps her hands low and tight around my waist. "I missed you, too. I love you," she mouths into the kiss. "I've always loved you. I just didn't want to tell you in a text. I wanted to feel you and hold you."

The elevator stops, and the door glides open. We pull apart, and I let Allegra exit first.

As she approaches the loft door, she fishes around the bottom of her purse for her keys like she's done so many times before. Then she comes to an abrupt stop.

"I thought about you a lot while you were gone," I say.

She's staring at our new doormat. It's red with "The Dawsons" in our custom white script monogram.

"D, it's perfect—" The rest of her sentence dissolves on her tongue as she turns to me, curiosity lighting her sparkly green eyes.

I suck in a small breath. "You once told me I was your bright side..." I swallow back the emotion rising in my throat. "I spent some time this weekend thinking about the moments when we felt closest to each other. I thought about the day we met in the library so long ago and the fun nights hanging with The Trio, then the drive back from Mots Doux, and our bathroom door confessions." I laugh. "Running in the Honolulu Airport gardens, then the shower..." I bite my lip playfully at the steamy memory.

"The tropical garden at the resort," Allegra adds, fanning herself. Her smile is wide and unwavering.

I nod. "Every second we spent together around that resort was amazing. Plus, both flights..."

Allegra presses her hand to her heart as she blinks back tears.

"Everything keeps coming back to that first night back from Hawaii. By the moonlight, we drew up version 3.0 of The Friendship Contract. Actually, doesn't that seem silly to plan a future relationship with that title?"

She laughs through her tears like she's both overwhelmed and unsure where this is going without a ring in a small velvet box.

"This one's title feels like a better fit for us," I say, shoving my hand inside my jacket to retrieve a single folded paper. As I open it up and flip the marriage license application toward her, a solitaire diamond ring falls from an attached string. "I know things are moving fast. I need to work on being open with you, prove how much I trust you. But my feelings haven't changed, Al. I've never been surer about anything in my life. Marry me, Allegra Marie Malone. Now or later...whenever. I always want to be your bright side."

Tears trail down her cheeks. She swipes her finger beneath her eyes, then smiles. "So, this is like a forever thing, then?"

"I'm thinking more soulmates than roommates." I shrug, savoring her laugh.

She nods a good dozen times, but I remain still, waiting and listening.

Then Allegra steps closer, settles on my knee, and takes my face in both her hands. "I'm in, D. A thousand times yes. I love you, and I want to be your bright side, your home, your family, your best friend...your wife." She presses a sweet, lingering kiss to my lips, and my heart that's felt sluggish these past few days without her—these past twelve years—beats a million times a minute like only Allegra inspires.

I'll never stop loving and wanting her. For the first time in my life, I know exactly where I belong.

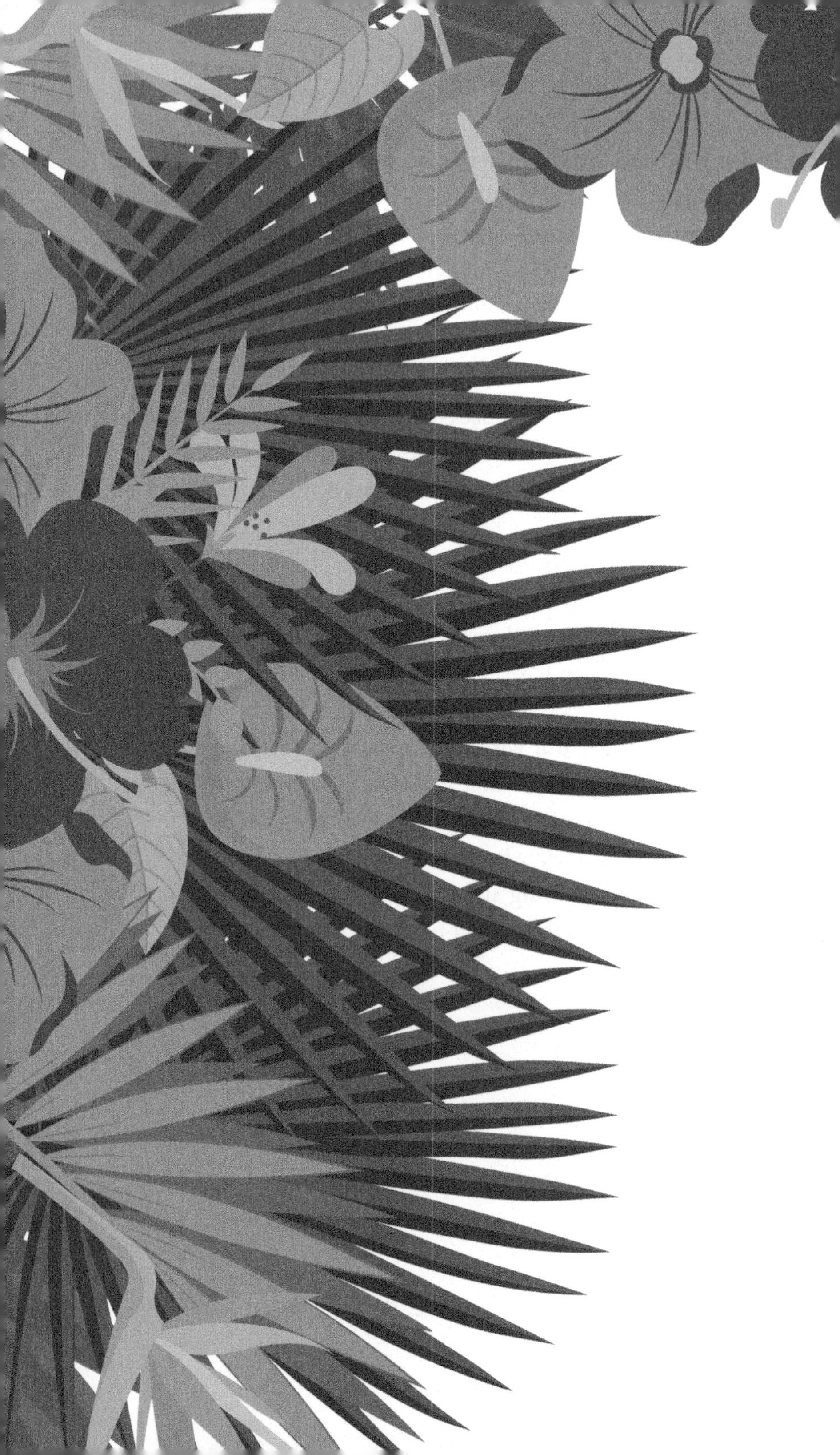

Epilogue
ALLEGRA

All the way from the street, Damon and I hear Earth, Wind, and Fire belting out the soulful, honeyed sounds of "September." It's my cousin Terry's end-of-summer cookout, which means delicious barbecue, good music, dancing, games, and fresh gossip. It's been killing me softly to hold out all week on our engagement news.

"You're sure you want to tell everyone here?" Damon asks as we enter the side gate leading to Terry's backyard.

I raise our clasped hands to my lips and kiss the back of his. "Laura and Jan texted they were already here. As soon as Lea and Fallon arrive, we'll have them all in one spot." I smile. "Work smarter, not harder, right?"

Damon chuckles. "Whatever you say."

As soon as we round the corner into the backyard, we're hit with the smoky, charred aroma of meat on the grill. Music blasts from giant speakers tucked in the corners of the yard, kids run around, family and friends dance, and two folding card tables are set up. I spot some of my cousins playing spades and dominoes.

After we take a lap, laughing and hugging everyone,

including Mom, Aaron and Piper, and Laura and Jan. We settle somewhere in the middle of the joyful chaos.

"Want a wine cooler or a cocktail? A beer?" Damon asks.

"Sure. And if you just happen to find some wings and a bottle of ranch dressing, and, ooh, hot sauce..."

He pecks my lips and backs away, laughing.

My entire heart swells., not just at the sight of so many of my loved ones gathered to celebrate life, but as my brother pulls Damon away to the grill to talk sports with his entire crew of guys. I'm with a man who loves my family as much as I do and who takes every opportunity to show me how much he loves me, too.

I'm still watching him and mouthing how much I love him more when the low buzz of chatter picks up.

"Hey, girl, hey!" Lea coos, entering the yard. She sashays with hands raised high as Fallon trails sheepishly behind her.

"Oh, my goodness, Fallon!" I shriek, tugging them both into a hug. "I'm so glad you made it. There's food, games, and drinks. Fallon stiffens as I release them and gives the yard a tentative once-over like she feels out of place. "Don't you go all quiet on us. Once you're invited to the cookout, you're basically family."

Lea waves at Aaron and Piper, yelling her congratulations before turning back to Fallon to confirm. "It's true. The Malones welcome all strays."

Fallon and I laugh at Lea.

"Okay, but can we just talk about how ViddyChat is all over social media?" Fallon asks.

Lea and I share a meaningful glance.

In some warped attempt to have her man's back, Trish Santos vented about ViddyChat's short end of the deal all over Twitter. After we received the final agreement on Wednesday, we signed a non-disclosure agreement.

Fallon holds up a hand. "Look, I know all about NDAs, so don't worry. Kyle's takedown is all over the internet, and everyone knows Malone, Dawson, & Cook LLP is the firm that took him down." Lea and I hold our tongues, but she's beaming like the Luxor light. "Oh, and my brother... He's officially obsessed with you, Lea. You're the woman who will forever be known for knocking him off my parent's golden pedestal. So, thank you."

"Uh, you're welcome," Lea stifles a grin.

"You've totally made him doubt himself and his entire career. You do not know how much I've been enjoying calling him a loser."

I really try to hold it in, but I burst out laughing. "Oh, my gosh, you are really terrible. I'm so sorry."

"And to show my gratitude, I'm thinking about rebranding with a new logo and marketing campaign for the fall. Wonder if either of you knows any hotshot IP lawyers to further help me piss off my brother?"

"Uh, actually..." I search the yard, spotting Mom. I wave her over, which is as good as a personal invitation to Terry, who's always on standby, fingers ready on her phone to spread the word. "Maybe we can help each other..."

"Ma'am?" Lea blinks a few dozen times, holding her hands up to stop the ball from rolling. "What am I missing here?"

When Terry moves, it's like a bee waggle dance reporting back to the hive about a good source of nectar or pollen she's found in the form of fresh gossip. One by one, people lift their heads or turn, the music is lowered, and gradually, we garner a crowd.

Sensing his presence is needed, Damon walks up behind me, settling his hands on my hips.

Lea covers her heart with her hand. "I am begging you. Do not leave my mind to its own devices, Al."

Damon kisses my neck, and it's all the encouragement I need.

"Well, I'm still not sure if I should be Allegra Marie Malone Dawson, or Allegra Marie Dawson, but—"

The entire yard erupts in hollers and cheers, but Lea screams for an entire minute straight. Just like she did the day we returned to the office after Hawaii, she slaps her thighs and throws her hands up. The holy ghost works its way from the springs in her feet to her fingertips.

"He is almighty. Lord, won't he do it!" Again, she wraps Damon and I in a full-body bear hug so fierce, we feel the love.

"So," I say, turning to Fallon. "Like I was saying, maybe Fallon Events is available to plan our wedding? I hear you've been featured in *Bridal Bliss* and *Grapevine*. What was the other one? *Visage*."

Fallon releases a Lea Cook–worthy scream.

"Allegra, oh my God. Of course!" She throws her arms around me, mumbling about all the ideas already forming in her head.

Soon, someone turns the music up, and Frankie Beverly and Maze blow through the speakers, singing "Before I Let Go." Damon turns me in his arms, and we sing at the top of our lungs. Our bodies move in sync with the melody. I stare into his sparkling eyes, and we sway and dance in the thick of love.

Us, the music, family and friends, food, good times, and love. It's all worth celebrating.

Acknowledgments

Thanks so much for going along on this ride with me. Hopefully, you swooned and blushed, laughed...and maybe cried with me a little. That you chose my book on which to spend your time is my honor.

Thank you to my husband, Daniel Heintzelman, who has allowed me to leap because he's my net, supporting me.

Shout-outs, hoots, and hollers to my writing family, The Wordmakers and my BWP Margo Hendricks for helping me finish books. Thanks to my IG family, Tule sisters, the librarians, bookstagrammers, bloggers, book tubers, booktokkers, reviewers, and my ARC teams! Thank you so much for reading, enjoying, and sharing my stories.

To my editors, Danielle and Danylle, I'm indebted to your polishing skills. Thanks for making my stories shine.

Special thanks to Meka James, Randi Love, A H Cunningham, Toni Wilkerson, and Cat Giraldo for beta reading. Thanks to Fortune Whelan for helping me dig deeper.

Big hugs and smoochie kisses to my family and friends. You are the petals on my flowering tree and the frame holding up my house. You understand and support me even though I'm always with my nose stuck in a book or with my fingers glued to a keyboard spinning tales.

As always, Mommy and Daddy, I love that I'm equally introverted bookworm and (semi-)social butterfly. Thank you for always cheering me on.

My sister, Melissa DeGrazia, let's keep leaping in faith together!

Finally, to my two daughters and my nieces and nephews, I hope my daring pursuit of greatness is inspiration and wind beneath your wings.

About Mia Heintzelman

Mia Heintzelman is a polka-dot-wearing, horror movie lover, who always has a book and a to-do list in her purse. When she isn't busy writing fictional happily-ever-afters, she is likely reading, or playing board games and eating sweets with her husband and two children. She writes fun, unforgettable, more than just laughs romance about strong women and men with enough heart to fall for them.

Website:
miaheintzelman.com

Subscribe to My Newsletter:
miaheintzelman.com/newsletter.html

Join My FB Reader Group:
Facebook.com/groups/2219575585012649/

- facebook.com/miaheintzelmanauthor
- twitter.com/miaheintzelman
- instagram.com/miaheintzelmanauthor
- goodreads.com/miaheintzelman
- bookbub.com/authors/miaheintzelman
- amazon.com/author/miaheintzelman

Also From Mia Heintzelman

THE ALL MIXED UP SERIES
(Each book can be read as a standalone)
Mixed Signals
Mixed Match
Mixed Emotions
All mixed up - the series

STANDALONES
The Friendship Contract

HOLIDAY ROMANCE
Married & Bright
Mingle All The Way
Wrapped up in beau
Cozy Little Christmas

DARK ROMANCE
Devastated: Wastelands Academy Book 1
Ruined: wastelands academy book 2 - releasing Soon

w/a EMMALINE ZANTHI
The Stacks
The Blue Gate

Printed in Great Britain
by Amazon